WIZARD IN A
WITCHY WORLD

JAMIE McFARLANE

Cover Artwork: Silviya Yordanova

CONTENTS

ACKNOWLEDGMENTS

To Diane Greenwood Muir for excellence in editing and fine word-smithery. My wife, Janet, for carefully and kindly pointing out my poor grammatical habits. I cannot imagine working through these projects without you both.

To my beta readers: Carol Greenwood, Kelli Whyte, Robert Long, Nancy Higgins Quist and Linda Baker for wonderful and thoughtful suggestions. It is a joy to work with this intelligent and considerate group of people..

RED

The delicate smell of perfume caught my attention just before a flash of red drew my eye. A pretty young woman opened the door to the bakery, looked my way and gave me an innocent smile before disappearing inside.

For a moment, time froze and my vision became clouded. In my mind's eye, this same girl was being chased by a wolf, calling my name for help. Her desperate cries tore at my soul, spurring my dream self into action. We hadn't ever met, but in the vision, I felt a deep connection to this woman and knew I had to save her. Just as quickly as the vision came upon me, it vanished, leaving my heart racing. I shook my head and looked around, hoping no one witnessed my break with reality.

Picking up my e-reader from the black wire-meshed table where it had fallen, I tried desperately to lose myself in the story again, but my mind continued to wander. I'd only had a few visions in my life and they eventually all came to fruition exactly as I'd seen them. Unfortunately, that's nowhere near as helpful as you might expect. Without a date or some sort of context, I had no idea when or where this event would take place. Replaying the vision over and over, my mind searched for something more, but the dream faded, details slipping through my fingers as dreams are wont to do, leaving only fear, desperation and a hideous sense of foreboding.

It was weird. I'd only been in town a few weeks and my choice of Leotown was purely random, or so I thought, but that was the nature of my life. What I thought was random often turned out to be something entirely different. At least Leotown had an amazing bakery like Wheatfield's, I thought, as I finished the rest of my scone.

With renewed determination to concentrate on someone else's

chaos, I tipped my chair back onto the bakery's brick façade and took a swig of coffee. It wasn't the best in town, but the scones more than made up for the coffee's shortcomings. Geez, get going already, I thought, willing the author to introduce some sort of villainous character. With adrenaline coursing through my veins, reading would be a lost cause unless this guy picked up the pace.

The next thing I knew, a musky scent wafted across my senses. I hadn't even gotten through the next paragraph. My highly sensitive nose is more of a burden than a gift. For the second time in as many minutes, I lifted my head and looked around. A shaggy, heavily-bearded man in rumpled clothing leaned against the brick building adjacent to the bakery. The Old Market District was hardly the place to come if you intended to be picky about smells. Now, where was I again? Damn my A.D.D.

The cheerful ding of bells attached to the bakery door made me sigh. It was the girl in the red jacket, carrying a bag that I was sure contained wonderful baked creations. I sarcastically checked myself. Yup, girl goes into bakery and buys baked goods. Certainly not out of the ordinary or the start of some dangerous journey. Yet a strange urge to take a deep breath and hold it, as if I was about to step forward and peer over the edge of a cliff, overcame me.

My life would have been much simpler if, at that moment, I'd just started reading again. It was irrational to feel protective toward a woman I had yet to meet. Some small part of me wondered if staying away from her would somehow prevent the danger I'd felt in the dream. My instincts, however, were on red alert. Something bothered me about the incongruity of Red and Shaggy. It further disturbed me that once she was past him, his head swiveled, tracking her. When she was a dozen yards away, he pushed away from the wall, looked around to see if anyone was watching and followed after her.

I gave him the same dozen yards. With my reading tablet safely stowed in my shoulder bag, I got up and followed along. They both turned the corner at Tenth Street. Too late, I slowed, nearly running over Shaggy while rounding the corner. He'd pulled up short and was using the shade of the building as camouflage. I'd already committed to the corner, so I walked on past him. Man, did he have a smell.

By the time I overtook her position, Red had slipped into a small gray sedan. I kept on walking, glancing back when I got to the next crosswalk. I paused by the stoplight and watched her drive off to prove to myself that she was safely on her way. I risked a look back at Shaggy and didn't see him anywhere. For once, I was being too sensitive. I crossed the street again and headed back to the coffee shop. If I was fast, my coffee might still be on the table where I'd left it.

As I turned the corner, rough hands grabbed my shirt and pulled me in close. Shaggy had waited for me and we were face to face. His stink assaulted my nose and I placed my hand on his chest and pushed hard. I'm strong for my size - coming from farm country and having had plenty of manual labor in my past - but this guy wasn't moving.

"Are you following me?" he asked gruffly, pulling me in closer.

There was something wrong. Maybe my eyes were watering from the stench, but I had difficulty focusing on his face.

"Back off," I said through clenched teeth.

I grabbed his wrist and released a small amount of energy from my thumb ring. It should have felt like a small taser jolt, which was usually enough to temporarily disable someone. The yelp and relaxed grip I'd expected, but the rest, not so much. For a moment, while the energy discharged into his wrist, Shaggy's face became crystal clear. He transformed into a half-wolf-half-man creature, complete with long fur and pointy fangs, the pupils of his eyes yellow and bloodshot. In short, the worst possible thing I could imagine happening while being confronted on the street. Oh, how I'd look back on that day and wish that's as deep as the rabbit hole went.

His face reverted back to what I would have to call 'Normal Shaggy' from now on, i.e. his human visage. His eyes told me he was not going to be forgiving about being zapped, but he seemed to take a moment to reassess the situation. I guessed he was simply trying to determine what level of violence to respond with. And yes, I was right. I really should have been more prepared as Normal Shaggy swung a fist into my gut. I doubled over and wheezed in pain. He followed up by smashing his other fist into the side of my head.

A shout from down the street warned him that others were taking an interest in our scuffle.

He leaned over and growled, "Don't get involved, Slim, or next time I'll rip off your head."

I felt sure he wasn't speaking figuratively. He pushed, attempting to knock me to the ground, but I still had some pride and resisted. As he walked away, I stood up, using the side of the building to help me.

"Are you okay?" A middle-aged woman approached me with her phone on her ear. "I called the police. They're sending an officer." She held her phone out to me.

I assured the dispatcher I was okay and didn't need medical attention, but he asked me to stick around long enough to talk to the officers. A moment later, a police cruiser pulled up with lights flashing.

A young officer in a dark blue uniform exited the cruiser purposefully, adjusting his belt as he walked toward me. He eased into the conversation by introducing himself as Officer Alan Tuttle, writing my name in his notebook and asking if I needed medical attention. By that time, a second cruiser pulled up. I was pretty sure my situation didn't warrant the extra attention. I've always had a knack for seeing through BS and Tuttle was on the level.

The second officer joined him, standing just behind his shoulder. "Mr. Slade, could you tell us what happened? Start from the top."

"Felix, if you don't mind," I said, allowing my mind a minute to work.

Tuttle just nodded, holding his pen over the small writing pad.

"I was drinking coffee at the bakery. I saw this guy follow a young woman after she left the shop. It seemed sketchy, so I followed them just to make sure she was okay. Long story short, the girl got in a car and took off and the guy figured out I'd been following him."

"Do you know this girl?" Tuttle asked.

"Not at all."

His questions were asked politely enough, but he was trying to establish whether Shaggy and I had any previous relationship. At some point, I either convinced him of the truth or he gave up.

"Very well, Mr. Slade ... Felix. I strongly recommend you avoid this man in the future. If you think of anything else, please give me a call." He handed me a business card and left.

As the cruisers pulled away, I knew I'd be disappointing Officer Tuttle. Shaggy was a werewolf and he was hunting that young woman. Even without my vision, it wasn't the sort of thing I could walk away from. I loped back past the bakery and jumped into my faded blue 1977 Ford pickup. I needed to get to my new lab if I wanted to have any chance of helping her.

I'd rented the top floor of Katherine Willoughby's home. A nicer old girl you've never met, and deaf as they come. The perfect landlady and the perfect setup for keeping a low profile – private apartment with an exterior staircase, alley parking and an empty garage. The apartment had been advertised as having two rooms and a small bathroom. In reality, there was a combined kitchen / den / library and an overflow library that some might otherwise call a bedroom.

I found the book I was looking for in my library and tucked it under my arm. There was wizard's work to be done and limited time to complete it.

My lab was set up in Mrs. Willoughby's garage. She hadn't driven a vehicle in at least a decade and I needed a quiet place to work. The lab was enchanted with a glamour so if someone looked into it, they would see a normal, empty, dusty garage. The doors and windows were locked and I'd even gone to the trouble of enchanting the ground with a 'creepy feeling.' That's not the technical term, of course, but it's more descriptive than the eight syllable Latin phrase that describes the enchantment. Just a few tricks I liked to use to discourage visitors.

The bolt slid back after I waved my hand across the door handle. Kinetic manipulation was a particularly useful ability I'd discovered when I was younger and had become second nature.

Spells to pinpoint Shaggy's location, say, on a map weren't familiar to me, but I did know how to track him. As far as enchantments went, it was pretty straightforward. I placed a copper cauldron over a low flame. Ideally, the cauldron would be silver, but who can afford that? I then pulled out a preserved willow switch I'd collected the week before, bent the narrow end into a circle about the size of a saucer and tied it off with a leather cord.

With the cauldron heated, I added paraffin, mouse toes, moth wings, sulfur and a half dozen other items. The real power of an enchantment comes from the blood of the wizard. Coincidently, it was also the part that sucked the most. I hated slashing my finger - or any other part of my body for that matter - but, it's who I am. With a sharp, ceramic knife, I drew a thin line across my right forefinger. Counting six drops of blood, I mixed and stirred the potion with the straight end of the willow switch, all the while chanting:

Aperi Fenestram Incantatum, Aperi Fenestram Incantatum, Aperi Fenestram Incantatum ...

Energy welled up from the earth beneath my bare feet and transferred through my body, down the switch and into the crimson paste. Instinctively, I knew the spell had activated.

A two-foot square granite slab lay on my enchanter's table and I placed the magnifying-glass-shaped willow switch on its smooth surface. With my bare hands, I lifted the scalding hot cauldron from the flame and poured the contents over the rounded end of the switch, careful to completely fill the circle. Aside from cooling, my enchanted seer's glass was complete. As for my hands... that's an old enchanter's trick, hot and cold had little effect on them when I was working an enchantment.

It was midnight when I got back to the Old Market District. My chances of finding Shaggy's trail seemed good. There was always a lot of helpful natural energy at this time of night anyway, but the boost from uninhibited bar-goers in the surrounding streets would add to it. High levels of energy in the present somehow made tracking remnants of the past a whole lot easier and I would take every advantage I could get.

All was quiet in front of the bakery. The spot where I'd initially observed Shaggy leaning against the brick still reeked of his energy, if not his actual smell.

I pulled the hardened seer's glass from my shoulder satchel and held it as one would hold a magnifying glass, scanning the area a few feet away. Initially, it was just as you would expect. The darkened building shone through the 'glass' portion of the device. The change occurred when I waved my hand from right to left over its surface. Slowly, at first, time through the glass rolled backward, light increasing within the circle until Shaggy appeared. I reversed my hand's direction and swung the glass around to follow the path he took as he turned to walk down the street after Red.

The dimly lit street helped protect me from looking like a complete nutcase as I walked, waving my hand over a wax-covered willow switch. I paused for a moment when the phantom Shaggy took a whack at me. It made me dislike him further if that were possible. I traced his path to a motorcycle parked along the street. I'd need to get my truck if I wanted to keep following. I allowed time to move forward, stopping after Shaggy pulled out into the intersection. It would be easy enough to find him again.

Following the motorcycle out of the busy Old Market was an exercise in multi-tasking I was barely up to. The image in the seer's glass was starkly juxtaposed with my current reality – literally night and day, which was probably the only way I made it through. Traffic lights I was supposed to obey were not in sync with Shaggy's and I found myself waiting almost too long to slam on the breaks at a few reds. More than once, I nearly ran into the back of another vehicle because my brain was focused on the wrong perspective. I also couldn't stop my reflexes from firing when cars in the daylight came at me, even though I knew full-well they weren't really there.

Finally, I turned into an older neighborhood where I watched Shaggy park. In real time, the motorcycle was gone, so this must have been a temporary stop. I parked just behind where he'd been and turned off the engine and headlights.

The ticking of my engine as the metal cooled seemed loud in the still night. I raised the seer's glass and watched Shaggy walk down the sidewalk, only to disappear behind a tree. I'd expected him to cross the street, but he didn't, at least not immediately. I really hoped I wouldn't have to get out of the truck. It wasn't as if it was illegal to skulk around a neighborhood with a magic mirror at one in the morning, but I had to believe it would make some people nervous.

I found Shaggy's visage skulking behind a tree, focused on the run-down, white clapboard single story house directly across the street. Shaggy just stood there, leaning against the tree with his hands in his pockets. His funky smell was faint, but I couldn't determine what it was he found so interesting.

I used the mirror to inspect the house, trying to angle it to where Shaggy's head was pointed. He didn't take his eyes off of the house, but wasn't overly particular about what he was looking at, clearly waiting for someone to come outside.

Rolling the glass forward, I scanned the front of the house, and then I saw it. On the street, in front of the house, was a grey sedan that strongly resembled Red's. It wasn't as if I needed confirmation of who Shaggy was targeting, but a bright flash of red at the front door caused my stomach to drop. She'd opened the door and was hugging an older woman goodbye.

Red left in her car and I expected Shaggy to follow, but instead he crossed the street to the house. Brazenly, he walked into the side yard and jumped the short, chain-link fence. I crossed the street after him. He disappeared through an overgrown hedge running along the side of a dilapidated garage.

It was a terrible idea to follow, but I believed, since his motorcycle was no longer parked on the street, I'd be safe. Pushing my way through the hedge, I got another strong whiff of werewolf. It made sense. The air wasn't moving much back here and the guy had a real stink to him.

His earlier self peered into a window on the side of the house. Ugh, what a creep. With good foliage covering him from anyone on the street, he could stand there unobserved as long as he wanted. Finally, after twenty minutes, he turned and walked out of the yard toward the street.

So... about my thinking no one would have seen Shaggy... never underestimate the nosiness of neighbors. I followed Phantom-Shaggy out of the back yard and for a minute, didn't notice I had company.

"Freeze! Police!" a voice commanded. Crap. I released the spell from the seer's glass and held my hands above my head, dropping the now ineffective willow switch.

TRESPASSING

Once I'd been loaded into the back of the police cruiser with cuffed hands in my lap, Officer Joseph Lozano leaned on the door.

"Would you care to explain what you were doing in Mrs. Barrios' back yard?" he asked.

It wasn't a good time to be evasive, but honesty wasn't an option either. I decided to slice it down the middle.

"It's going to sound nuts," I said.

"Try me. I have some experience with that type of thing," he answered.

Officer Lozano had a forthright aura. He was a man who took his job seriously. I hated lying to him, but there was no chance he'd believe me.

"I was driving on Harney Street, headed home. A large dog ran out in front of me. I thought I'd hit him, so I followed. It looked to me like he'd run into that back yard."

"Care to explain the stick you were holding?" he asked. He didn't believe me.

"I found it on the ground," I said.

"Mr. Slade, have you been drinking tonight?"

"Nothing more than coffee."

"Sit tight. I need to look around and make sure you haven't caused any property damage."

Part of being a wizard - for me - is receiving small glimpses of the future, called portents. It's not like I can see future stock prices or anything. It's more like I can sense likely outcomes of the near future. These perceptions are different than visions... but, I'm getting off track. In this case, I sensed something bad was about to happen to Officer Lozano.

Small flashlight in hand, he approached the house. I'd have felt better if he'd unclipped his pistol, but he clearly wasn't expecting trouble. Methodically, he swept the flashlight's beam back and forth, inspecting the house and nearby grounds. The beam paused momentarily on my willow switch, but quickly continued on.

I had a good view of the officer's path as he approached the back yard, but once he disappeared around the unkempt hedge, I was only able to see occasional sweeps of the flashlight beam.

His startled shout and the light from the flashlight spiraling away into the brush alerted me to something going down. I waved my finger across the lock of the hand-cuffs and repeated the same on the cruiser's door. The lock clunked down and I pushed the squad door open, jumped out, and sprinted into the back yard.

I heard struggling and the growls of an angry canine. "*Lucem*," I commanded. Light burst forward from the wide silver ring on my left hand. The light was blinding initially, but my eyes adjusted in time to see Lozano rolling in the grass, grappling with a large wolf. I didn't know if it was Shaggy, but it was a reasonable guess.

When I'd discharged my thumb ring's energy on Shaggy earlier, I hadn't been overly successful, but then I'd only been trying to get him off of me. Lozano looked to be in real trouble and I needed to act quickly.

The cop was my responsibility, as I'd stumbled into something and dragged him along with me. If I'd thought he could handle a full-sized lycan, I'd have let things play out. Without a gun loaded with silver bullets, Lozano was completely outclassed. Fortunately, I wasn't. Shaggy had crossed a line and he had to deal with me now.

The pair was too entwined for me to do anything long-range, so I ran up on them. The wolf snapped menacingly at Lozano, trying to bury its teeth into his shoulder. Lozano had a good hold of the wolf's neck and was keeping it off, if only for the moment.

I grabbed the back of the wolf with my hands and pulled hard. This was two hundred pounds of mean that had no intention of being dislodged. I was fine with that. I'm a wizard who'd worked most of his teenage years throwing bales of hay and mucking out stalls. Brute force was my first choice, but I had better options if he wanted to play it that way.

"*Adoleret*." The command activated the ruby on my right hand. A gout of fire burst forth and I directed it across the back of the wolf, brushing his fur and directing the flame toward its head. The blast only lasted a few seconds, but it was enough. The wolf jumped forward, yipping in pain, forgetting all about Lozano. Tail between its legs, the wolf made a mad dash out of the yard.

"Are you hurt?" I asked Lozano, who'd rolled to his feet, gun in hand.

"On your face, drop your weapon," he commanded, his gun leveled on me.

I sighed. I could only imagine what was floating through this poor man's head. I complied, sinking to my knees and lacing my fingers behind my head. He walked behind me, pulled my right wrist behind my back, paused for a moment, then pulled my other arm back, locking them both into nylon zip-cuffs.

"I'm going to stand you up," Lozano directed, grabbing the back of my arm. He counted me down and steadied me as I stood.

"Thanks," I said, turning around.

"How'd you get out of the cuffs and my cruiser?" he asked.

"You didn't get the door fully closed," I said. "And I think your cuffs are faulty."

He wasn't buying it. "Where's your weapon?"

"Look," I said. "I know you won't believe me, but I don't have a weapon. That dog left because I kicked him. And before you ask, I got out of the cruiser because it sounded like you needed help."

He raised an eyebrow and a calm, cold power of judgement passed over me. It wasn't a spell, at least not in the traditional sense, but he was directing a small amount of power to get a read on me. More than likely, it was involuntary on his part, but the capability to accurately assess people was probably why he'd chosen to be a police officer in the first place.

"You're right. I don't believe you," he said. "Tell me again. Why you were in Mrs. Barrios' backyard?" He'd led me to his cruiser and leaned me up against the front quarter panel.

"Looking for the dog that attacked you," I said. "I saw it out on

Harney and thought it ran into her back yard. I don't know Mrs. Barrios." It was a truer version than I'd told earlier. For now, I'd avoid lying.

In the wan light my eyes picked up on a dark, growing stain on his shoulder. That was a problem. If he'd been bitten by the wolf, his life was about to change dramatically, and not for the better.

"Something's off about your story, Mr. Slade," he said. "But, I don't have time to dig into it tonight. I'm going to run you for outstanding warrants. If you turn up clean, you'll be on your way."

With the door open, Lozano sat in his cruiser and typed on the computer's keyboard. A second cruiser pulled up and another officer got out and approached. They talked for a few minutes before Lozano came back over to me.

"Turn around, Mr. Slade," he said.

I pushed off from his vehicle and turned so my back was to him. He snipped the zip-cuffs and I rubbed my wrists to return the circulation.

"You're free to go," he said as I turned around to look at him. The wound on his shoulder bothered me. I wasn't an expert on Lycanthrope, but I was afraid he'd been infected.

"Lozano," the other officer said, with urgency in his voice.

We both turned to see the other officer's gun raised and flashlight pointed at the front door of Mrs. Barrios' home. Lozano instantly responded by pulling his own gun.

"Slade, get in the back of the cruiser," Lozano said, without looking at me.

Through the full glass panel of Mrs. Barrio's front door, the mangled form of what was likely the old woman was eerily illuminated by the officer's light. She lay resting against the glass, a thick smear of blood marking her slide down to the floor.

I considered running, but something supernatural was at work here and I needed more information. Not to mention, running would put me at the top of the suspect list - if I wasn't there already. So I obeyed and climbed into the back seat.

The cruiser's radio popped to life as dispatch acknowledged

Lozano's new report and informed them that additional units and emergency vehicles were enroute. The two officers approached the front of the house cautiously, clearly not willing to wait for the cavalry.

With the body lying against the front door, they had a decision to make. They could force the door open, but it would move the body. Lozano didn't pause long and extended a telescoping baton. He smashed a large window on the porch, cleared the glass and stepped inside, with gun drawn. He'd produced a second flashlight and the beam bounced around the inside of the house as he carefully made his way to the front door and the body. Once he came into view, the other officer followed him inside through the broken window.

Lozano reached down and placed a hand on the body. A minute later, he looked up, shaking his head. It didn't take a cop to figure out that whoever lay there was dead. With a corpse behind them, they worked through the small house, clearing rooms as they went.

The quiet of the night was shattered by the arrival of the first in a series of police cruisers and emergency vehicles. I watched with some interest as they secured the scene and eventually packed the body of the victim into a black bag.

An hour later, a dark brown four-door sedan pulled up and a thickset, middle-aged woman climbed out from behind the wheel. Her curly hair was pulled back into a hastily formed pony tail. No doubt, she'd been pulled from bed. A badge hung from a chain around her neck. The first officer she approached pointed to Lozano, who acknowledged her presence with a nod and walked toward her.

The two of them talked, looking in my direction several times. I had the capability to eavesdrop on them, but decided to forgo it for the time being. Werewolf kills were sloppy and Shaggy, if that's who'd done it, would have left plenty of physical evidence, none of which would point to me.

When they finished talking, Lozano approached the cruiser and opened my door. As I exited the vehicle, I held out the handcuffs I'd retrieved from the backseat, which earned me a raised eyebrow.

"The detective would like a word with you," he said, accepting the handcuffs.

I nodded and followed him over to where she was talking with another uniformed officer. Lozano stood a respectful ten feet from her position and waited. She waved him over as soon as she was done.

"Mr. Slade, I'm Detective Dukats," she said, holding out her hand.

I tried to hide my sigh of relief. If I were on her suspect list, she certainly wouldn't be introducing herself. I shook her hand and appreciated that she returned a firm grip. Having spent my earliest years in the Midwest, I subscribed to the belief that a weak handshake was an indicator of weak character.

"Am I in trouble here?" I asked.

"Should you be?" she asked. It was just the type of leading question I'd come to expect from investigators.

"No. But I've been locked in the back of a squad car for the better part of two hours," I replied.

"I see," she said. "No, it looks like the same animal that attacked Detective Lozano also attacked the woman who lived here."

"Is he going to be okay?" I asked.

"Barely broke the skin," she said. "He'll be fine. Tell me, Mr. Slade, do you own any pets?"

I shook my head. "No, Detective. And that thing that attacked Officer Lozano wasn't anyone's pet."

"Why do you say that?"

"I'm just guessing, but it seemed wild to me. I don't think we're talking about a dog. I'd say it was a wolf," I said.

"You think there's a wolf running around town?"

"First, I'm sure there are wolves running around." I nodded toward the north. "I grew up on a farm not sixty miles from here and we ran into wolves from time to time. It's a certainty they've been in the city."

"Tell me why you're here," she said.

"As I told Officer Lozano, I was driving along Harney and thought I hit a dog. I followed it back here and got out of my truck to see if I'd hurt it," I said.

"And, you think it killed Mrs. Barrios while you were talking with Officer Lozano?" she asked.

"I have no idea," I said. "I was sitting in the squad when he was attacked. I didn't know there was a problem inside the house until the other officer shone his light on the front door."

"We've got you on misdemeanor trespassing, but I'm inclined to believe your story for now," she said. "I'd like to send Officer Lozano to accompany you home. If he doesn't see any evidence of large dogs at your residence, we'll drop the issue entirely."

This had to stop before it gained momentum. "I'm not consenting to a search of my premises."

"We could take you down town for questioning," she said. "And I could probably get a warrant." Her aura shifted slightly. She wasn't sure about the warrant.

"What if I agreed to allow Lozano a walk-through - not touch anything and not take any pictures unless he finds evidence of a dog?" I said.

"Sure. Lozano, could I could I speak with you?" she called, moving off to instruct the officer.

I walked down to my truck and was glad that it fired right up. I was pointed the wrong direction and had to perform a three-point turn in front of Lozano. He'd already rolled his cruiser down to where I was and stayed close behind me as I headed home. It was four o'clock in the morning when I pulled into the gravel drive that led to Mrs. Willoughby's old garage. Lozano parked directly behind the truck, blocking me in.

"What's in the garage?" he asked when he got out of his cruiser.

"Nothing. I park in there sometimes. You can see the entire thing if you look through the window on the side." I had no intention of opening the door for him. He could get a warrant if it came to that.

He walked up to the side door and shined his flashlight into the space. As expected, it showed a dusty, but relatively clear garage without anything required to keep a dog. He stepped back and directed his flashlight around the yard, looking for evidence of a kennel or dog run.

"So do you have a lot of nights like tonight?" I asked as we walked up the steps to my apartment.

"Enough," he grunted.

I fumbled with the keys and opened the door to my apartment, making a show for him. I couldn't remember what shape I'd left the apartment in and was disappointed as I scanned the interior. The place was a wreck, but it was just as I'd left it.

If he was off-put by the mess, he didn't say anything.

"Satisfied?" I asked.

He stumbled and grabbed his shoulder. I caught him and guided his body into one of my two kitchen chairs.

His voice wavered. "Thanks."

I poured a glass of water and placed it on the table in front of him. "You mind if I take a quick look at your shoulder? I probably have something that'd make it feel better."

"You have a lot of books on the occult," he observed. "Are you some sort of shaman?"

His question caught me off guard. I felt like I'd underestimated his skills of observation. "Something like that. You mind?"

He looked skeptical, but the beads of sweat on his brow gave away the pain he was feeling. "Sure, but nothing weird, okay?"

"All natural. Nothing to be worried about," I said.

I grabbed a couple of clean towels and a salve I kept on hand for cuts and abrasions. It certainly wouldn't ward off a lycan infection, but he'd feel better for a few hours. Most of all, I wanted to get a good sample of Shaggy's spit, and if I were really lucky, blood. So, sue me. I wasn't just being nice.

He gingerly pulled the shirt off his shoulder. The wound wasn't deep. He'd held the wolf off heroically, but as far as I knew, there were no small werewolf bites. After cleaning the skin, I liberally applied the white, greasy paste and covered it with a large gauze pad.

"That feels a lot better. Bueno," he said. "You remind me of Mi

Abuela."

"Is your grandmother a shaman?" I asked.

"She's Virarica."

I'd have to look that up later, so I just nodded. I'd been able to save blood and grime from the front of his shirt, so it was time to work on getting Lozano out of my apartment. He was entirely too familiar with my universe and I didn't need him getting curious about where I fit in.

"I hate to make this all about me, but are you satisfied that I don't have any dogs?" I asked.

"You're good, Mr. Slade," he said. "You mind if I ask what you do for a living?"

"Odd jobs, mostly," I said.

He made a move to stand and sat back heavily as if his legs didn't agree with his desire to leave. I didn't know much about lycan bites, but what I did know told me he was in for a rough ride the next few days. His body would initially fight the infection, but there were only two ways it could go. He would either be dead or he'd recover and turn into a wolf every full moon for the rest of his life.

"Can I help you down to your cruiser?"

"No," he said, finally standing and walking to the door. "I'll be fine."

WHYTE WOOD COVEN

I picked up the towel I'd used to clean Lozano and clipped off pieces that contained good samples of his blood, dropping them into a glass specimen jar. It was possible the scraps contained evidence of Shaggy, but I'd have to deal with that later. I sealed the jar with a cork and wrote on the glass with a grease pen using a runic alphabet I'd developed. The words glowed as I etched them into the fabric of the bottle and disappeared once I placed the container onto the nearly empty shelf.

Needing to preserve the samples I'd gathered, I rooted around and finally found the right spell book. It was a reliable tome given to me by my first mentor, Judy Babcock, an ordinary looking witch who resembled a housewife more than a mid-level earth witch. She'd discovered me when I was fourteen and had just burned down my high school's gymnasium. Apparently, the spell I'd stumbled onto couldn't be extinguished without a counter curse. Fortunately, her coven set things right and she'd taken on the task of overseeing the emergence of a new wizard.

I missed hanging out with Judy and 'the girls,' as she called them. My recent departure from home in North Carolina was still fresh in my mind. I hadn't even known I was headed to Leotown until I arrived and decided it was where I should be. It made a certain amount of sense. Visiting my old foster family was at the back of my mind, but so far, I hadn't made the effort.

The components of the spell were a mix of things I had in stock and others I needed to gather: nail clippings from a raccoon, caraway seeds, ash from garlic stalks and five more things I didn't have. I wrote out the list and stuffed the piece of paper into my pocket, pausing to look up at a staccato tapping on the kitchen window. A large raven was perched on the sill, looking in.

"Maggie. Hold on, I'm coming." I closed the spell book, slid the window to the side and pulled the screen off.

"Cawwk." She greeted me as she fluttered through the window and landed on a pile of books.

She and I both looked around the room for her perch. Maggie was generally good about not doing her business in the house, but it wasn't a hundred percent type of thing. It took a few minutes to unearth the stand and clear a spot on the floor. As I'd learned a few times, a little effort upfront would pay off in the end. Maggie and I were still working on our communication. I could only understand a few things she said, but I didn't need to be a wizard to know she was hungry. She was always hungry.

"Good to see you, dear," I said, setting the perch next to the table. She fluttered gracefully to it and grabbed on firmly.

Maggie had been with me since before I'd known I was a wizard. Originally, she'd just followed me, always watching from nearby trees. I'd been freaked out by her behavior at first. Of course, I didn't realize the big black birds I started to see everywhere I went were all the same raven. It had been Judy Babcock who'd suggested Maggie might be a positive character in my life and that ravens were not some evil omen.

The last time I'd seen Maggie was in North Carolina. The poor girl had to be hungry after that long trip, but I was prepared. I'd been saving a thick strip of funky smelling beef and tied it to the perch. She bobbed her head half a dozen times in appreciation. I didn't even wonder anymore how she'd found me. It was just the nature of our bond.

"What do you think of the new place?" I asked. She understood me, although she ordinarily ignored idle chit-chat. "Thinking about doing a reagents hike early tomorrow. Want to go along?"

Finding wild sage, sumac, ginger, goldenrod and a dozen other native plants was a good way to fill my cupboards without going broke. I had fond memories of running around the woods with half a dozen semi-clothed, middle-aged women in Judy's coven in search of usable plants. It was one of the few activities I could participate in and I'd enjoyed it immensely.

As expected, Maggie focused on her strip of meat.

It had been a crazy night and I was exhausted. I lay back on the couch, picked up my e-reader and tried to remember where I was in the story.

I awoke to the sound of pounding on my door.

"Hang on," I growled, trying to focus on the wall clock in the kitchen. One o'clock. I'd only been asleep for a few hours.

The pounding started again.

"I said, hang on!"

I yanked the door open, prepared to give some asshole salesman a good piece of my mind.

"What... do you want?" I asked. My bluster evaporated as I recognized the woman standing in front of me. It was Red. In person.

"Mister Felix?" she asked. It sounded more like mee-stir. Cool. I'd always had a thing for accents, but maybe I paid too much attention to that sort of thing.

"What are you doing here?"

"I need to talk to you. May I come in?" she asked.

Water splashed from the hood of her cloak and it dawned on me that it was raining. The weather explained why I'd slept so deeply. As a wizard, my strength was tied to the natural forces around me and rain was a powerful regenerator.

A hint of her perfume caught me and something else ... a wisp of evergreen and clay.

At this point, I need to admit that I'm not always the sharpest knife in the drawer, especially when it comes to attractive young women with accents.

"Sure," I said, stepping aside.

She smiled demurely and reached up. The gesture seemed natural and harmless - that is, until the point when her hand touched my chest. Fire coursed through my body as she lifted, tossed me over a chair, and then jerked me back onto the couch.

"Shit! What the hell?" I groaned. This girl had a serious attitude problem.

Red jumped over the chair and placed her knee on my chest, right where her hand had burned me. She shoved her finger in my face.

"Quiet, Felix. I'm going to ask you some questions and I need you to be truthful with me." Her innocent, doe-eyed persona had completely evaporated - not to mention her accent.

"Damn it, I was letting you in, wasn't I?" I asked.

"What were you doing outside Victoria Barrios' house last night?"

"What's it to you?"

My chest hurt where her knee pressed on me and there was only so much humiliation I was willing to take, even from a beautiful young witch. I shifted my position and tried to sit up.

She murmured an incantation and touched my collar bone. Her finger felt like a blowtorch.

"Knock that shit off!" I snapped. "Or I'm going to start taking it personal."

"Tell me." She wagged her finger menacingly.

The magic she was using was as familiar to me as my own. She was obviously part of a local coven, as no witch would be dumb enough to use this much magic outside her own territory. The pine and clay told me they were earth witches, just like Judy's coven. I concentrated and felt three additional souls supporting her. They were standing with shoes off, toes dug into the soil and hands joined. They had to be close by. Why the hell were they focused on me?

I grabbed her hand and twisted hard. The look of surprise on her face gave me a feeling of smug satisfaction. I bet she hadn't expected *that* when she'd come into my house and tossed me around. Who was she to start this crap? Dark feelings turned into their own power and I pushed her back, sending her sprawling on her butt against the overturned chair.

"Is that how you want to play it?"

She raised her hands defensively.

"Cawwk." A dark shape flitted through the open kitchen window and into the living room. Maggie landed between us on Red's knees, spreading her wings protectively.

"Crap." I backed up and dropped to the couch.

I closed my eyes, trying to center myself. It had been a long time since I'd come that close to losing it. I pushed away the darkness and breathed out the way Judy taught me. My heart rate slowed and my breath shuddered.

I heard Red get up and knew she was trying to slip past me to the still-open front door. I flicked a wave of power, slamming the door shut.

"Sit, if you know what's good for you," I growled, still not completely in control.

She returned to the couch and sat quietly.

After a few minutes, I opened my eyes. Red sat rigidly, a look of fear on her face, her original confidence shattered. Maggie was back on Red's knees.

"Who are you?" she whispered.

"You already know my name." It wasn't the answer she was looking for, but it was the only one she was going to get until I had some answers.

"Felix Slade is all I know."

"Don't you mean we?" I asked.

Her eyes grew wider.

"Call your coven and have them join us."

"What are you going to do?" she asked. "I'd rather die than give them to you."

"I'm not going to do anything to you or your coven. Don't turn this on me. You're the ones who barged in here," I said.

"So you say. Can you get this bird off me?"

"That bird saved you, so I'd show some respect," I said. "And her name is Maggie."

Maggie bobbed her head in agreement. She expressed her desire to get back outside, so I stood up and offered my arm. Flying indoors was hard for her, given the broad wingspan, but she knew I'd help and she jumped onto my arm. I walked her into the kitchen and lifted my arm to the window sill.

"Cawwk," she chided and dove out the window.

"She's your familiar?"

"More like a friend," I'd always been uncomfortable with the other term. It didn't fit my relationship with Maggie.

"Why were you at Victoria's house last night?" Red pulled the willow switch I'd used to form the seer's glass from her purse and threw it on the coffee table.

"Where'd you get that?" I asked.

"So, you *were* there," she said.

No use denying it. "Yes. I was there."

She started chanting an incantation. I didn't recognize the words, but power rolled off her in waves. At the same time, my attention was caught by the sound of bare feet slapping up the stairs to my apartment.

I sprang to action, grabbing the grease pen from the counter. In the middle of the kitchen floor, I crouched and drew a large circle, finishing just as my front door exploded inward.

"*Sphaera*." A translucent bubble popped up around me, binding to my hastily drawn circle.

The storm outside intensified. Through the splintered door frame, a violent wind whipped rain against the house.

The first person through the door was an older woman, mid-fifties if I were guessing right. A dark green dress thrashed around her matronly figure and long black and gray hair blew wildly around her face. She stepped across the rubble of my door, looked once toward Red and then bee-lined for me, gnarled staff in hand. She was followed by two others, progressively younger, but similarly dressed.

Red joined them as they formed a circle around my ring of protection, joining hands and chanting. With my shield in place, I heard their words, but felt none of the magical energy they generated. Sparks bounced off the circle from all directions, but nothing penetrated.

As they continued, the chants grew louder, rain and wind poured into the apartment, and lightning intensified. I wasn't sure how much of a beating my hastily drawn circle could take, but so far, it was holding.

As interesting and exciting as it might seem to be surrounded by four women bent on your destruction, there's only so much it can do to hold your attention. After ten minutes, I'd become bored. Sparks, chants, gouts of flame, icicles… whatever. I had the same problem with Independence Day fireworks celebrations. Five minutes in and I'd seen everything I needed to. Way too repetitive after that.

I sat on the floor, pulled out a small pocket knife and peeled dirt from under my fingernails. If there was something I couldn't abide, it was dirt under my nails. I blame Judy. She had a huge herb garden and didn't mind putting me to work in it. I really wished I'd taken the time to bring a chair in with me. I'd have to remember that next time.

After another ten minutes, the storm outside began to pass and the magical attacks slowed. I suspected the coven's energy was dissipating. The older woman's face was drawn and her arms were shaking. Red had opened her eyes and was looking around their circle, worry on her face. I had to admit, at this point, I didn't much care. They'd barged into my house and made a mess of things.

"What in the hell is your problem, Red?" I growled.

"You will be vanquished," she declared bravely.

"Vanquished? Who talks like that? The way I see it, your coven is about to run out of gas and I haven't even started swinging yet. Tell the sisters of mirth here to drop this bullshit and we can talk it out. Otherwise, we can turn this into a real pissing contest."

The older woman opened her eyes and looked at Red. She attempted to project an aura of strength but I saw the fatigue in her face. Wordlessly, the four of them dropped their hands and the magical buffeting abated.

"Are you going to behave?" I asked the older woman.

She swayed slightly and locked eyes with me. I felt like a child caught telling a lie. With the circle up, I knew her attack wasn't magical, but man, she really had that stare down. I fidgeted uncomfortably.

"Why did you murder Victoria?" she asked.

"Mrs. Barrios?" I asked, furrowing my brow. "I didn't."

"You were there. You admit to using your evil enchantment at her home. Do not lie to me. Who was your accomplice?"

"What evil enchantment?"

"This," Red said thrusting forward the willow switch I'd used as a seer's glass.

"No good deed," I muttered under my breath.

"What is that?" The old woman snapped.

"Knock it off," I said. "Here's how we're going to do this. When I drop my circle, you get to make a choice. You can keep coming at me and we'll see what's at the end of that road or we can sit down and talk like rational people."

"*Finis*." As with most of the incantations I knew, Latin was the primary language. The power didn't come from the words, but from my ability to channel the correct magic. Using a second language was simply a helpful focusing mechanism.

The older witch's face showed her internal struggle as the spell circle dropped. If someone were going to make a move, it would be her, so I prepared for a new round of hostilities. In the end, however, she relaxed and the other women followed her lead.

I sighed. "It feels like we're off to a bad start. Perhaps we should try again." I held my hand out to the matriarch.

She paused and then reached out her hand, slipping it past mine to grab my wrist. It was an intimate gesture that allowed her to read my blood – but it also allowed me the same access.

"Tell me, Felix Slade. Did you participate in killing Victoria Barrios?" she asked, not letting go.

"No."

"Why were you at her house when she died?" She was probing for more than the truth and I suddenly felt naked.

"Really? A lie detector test?"

"Tell me."

The old girl had some bite to her words. Her magic pushed at me, but wasn't enough to compel my answer. I stayed relaxed. I had no reason to fight her questioning.

"I was tracking a werewolf that followed Red to Mrs. Barrios' house earlier that evening."

"He tells the truth," she said.

"And…" I said.

She looked at me confused. "And what?"

"This is where you apologize for busting up my house and assaulting me," I said.

"You are right, Mr. Slade," she said, dropping my hand. "On behalf of the sisters of Whyte Wood Coven, I humbly ask your forgiveness."

"I'm going to need a new door," I said.

"Kelli?" she asked.

"I'll call Andy," a red-haired witch in her early thirties offered.

"Mr. Slade, how do you know it was a werewolf following Gabriella?"

"Gabriella, is it?" I asked, lifting my eyebrows at Red.

"The werewolf, Mr. Slade," the older witch pushed.

"Trust me. Shaggy is a werewolf. Now, you tell me why he was tracking Red there and why he would murder your High Priestess?"

One of the other witches gasped with a sharp intake of air.

"How do you know Victoria Barrios was our High Priestess?"

"I didn't, until you confirmed it. And now, you aren't answering my questions. Why was that werewolf tracking Red?"

"My name is Gabriella," Red said.

"Stay out of this, Mr. Slade. There are things at work here beyond your understanding," the older witch said. She turned and walked over the broken front door and out into the storm. Wordlessly, the other witches turned and followed her.

"Yeah. That's not creepy," I said as Gabriella, last in line, disappeared through the doorway.

Half a second later, she stuck her head back in the opening. "Owe you coffee?"

"Uh, sure. Anytime."

"Tomorrow morning? Howling Hounds?"

"Can we make it eleven o'clock? I've errands," I said.

"Sure. I don't get up most days until then, anyway." With that, she ducked back out into the rain.

MUD ON MY FACE

My first order of business was to stop the rain and everyone else from coming into my tiny apartment. The witches had really done a number on the front door, making me wonder what kind of stuff they ran into to have developed so much offensive capability. My experience with Judy and the girls had been completely different. They'd been all love and light, a lot more likely to drop their clothes and run naked through a moonlit forest than bust down a wizard's front door.

The rain was lessening and it was still early in the afternoon. I grabbed my wallet, walked down the stairs and hurried out to the truck. Even if I had the spell components, I still couldn't cast a protection enchantment without a door to cast it on. My gathering trip had been planned for tomorrow morning and that would be my first chance to gather the components I needed. Securing the apartment for the next twenty-four hours would require a more mundane approach. That decided, it was time for a trip to the hardware store.

Thirty dollars later, with a new hammer, staples and thick plastic sheeting in hand, I was ready to at least cover my front entrance. The rain had stopped and I rolled down the windows of my old pickup. I loved how the air smelled after a rain.

The sound of a motorcycle echoing against the buildings caught my attention and I swung my head around, looking for its source. Ordinarily, it wouldn't be cause for alarm, but my sixth sense screeched a warning, so I turned down a side street. It wasn't until I'd taken the next turn that I caught a glimpse of a biker. While she bore a certain resemblance to Shaggy, her gender was a dead giveaway that I was just being jumpy. I looped back around and headed home.

As soon as I pulled into the gravel drive and turned off the truck, I saw Mrs. Willoughby sitting on her small back porch. I walked up to the house, plastic wrap under my arm, and prepared for the worst.

"Problems, dear?" she asked.

"Yes, sorry, Mrs. Willoughby. I broke the door, but I'll fix it," I spoke just short of yelling so she'd hear me.

"You're handy, just like my Carl. I know you'll fix it. You're a responsible young man. No, you had a visitor while you were out. She told me to give you this." She held out an envelope.

"What did she look like?"

"Tall for a woman," she said. "Not very friendly. But I'm afraid my eyes aren't very good."

"I'm sorry you had to deal with that. If she comes by again, just stay inside." I placed the envelope in my front pocket.

Mrs. Willoughby gave me her best motherly smile. "You be careful, Felix. She felt dangerous."

"I will, Mrs. Willoughby, and thank you," I said and excused myself.

Forty minutes into hanging the plastic sheeting, a workman's pickup truck drove in and a middle-aged man hopped out. He had bright red hair and a good start on a potbelly.

"Felix Slade?" he asked when he reached the bottom of the stairs.

"I am," I said walking down to him.

"My wife, Kelli, asked me to take a look at your door. Said you'd had trouble with the storm."

"Right. Sure did. I wasn't expecting you so soon," I said.

"Things are slow today and she wanted me to come over right away," he said. "That it?" He nodded up the stairs.

"Sure is." I wanted to look around to see if there was another empty doorway, but I thought that might be rude.

"I'm assuming you want it done right? By that, I mean you want to match the style of the rest of the house?" he asked as he followed me back up the stairs.

"Aren't all doors pretty much the same?"

"Nah, these old houses have a style all to themselves. I might be able to fix the old door, though," he said.

"I don't think so. It was pretty damaged." I held the plastic sheeting aside so he could get in.

It only took one glance on his part. "What in the world? Did you take a lightning strike or something?"

"Something like that," I said.

"Crazy storm. I'll just need to take some measurements. Looks like I'll be able to fix the jamb alright, though. It'll be an easy repair," he said.

"When do you think you can get a new door?"

"There are a few places close by that collect and sell old doors. I'll head over there right now. If I get lucky, I'll find one and be back in an hour. So … you know Kelli from the store, then?"

It's not like I'm much of a mind reader, but I do get feelings from people. Some are more closed off than others. Andy, not so much. He was insecure and wanted to make sure I wasn't a threat to his marriage.

"Bookstore. We share the same interests." I gestured to my stacks of books. It was an easy guess that a witch would have piles of books. "Not sure how it came up, but I mentioned the storm damage and she thought of you. She never mentioned her store, though. Where'd you say she works?" I applied a small amount of mental pressure, not wanting him to become distracted.

"Twisted Tallow. She's the day manager," Andy said. "It's one of those … you know … specialty stores."

I smiled. I did know what he was talking about, but I'd had a hard day and couldn't let the opportunity pass. I whispered back, "Sex toys?"

"Nooo," Andy answered, scandalized. "Witchcraft, Voodoo, that sort of thing."

"Ohhh," I said, feigning sudden understanding. "That must be interesting."

"Bunch of hocus pocus if you ask me," he said. "Anyway, I've got what I need. I'll find a door, even if I have to cut one down a bit."

"Sounds good, Andy. Feel free to finish it up even if I'm not here." I watched his retreat down the stairs.

Back in the apartment, I pulled a beer from the refrigerator. It fizzed up and I had to hold it over the sink. After wiping it down, I sat on the couch, fully intending to close my eyes. The sound of the forgotten envelope folding in my pocket reminded me of its presence and I pulled it out.

Dear Mr. Slade,

Please let this letter serve as notification to you that you are hereby required to register with the Greater Leotown Witches' Council within sixty days of your arrival in Leotown, or by the end of the second lunar cycle, whichever comes later. You may complete your registration by dropping by our offices at 1100 Jackson Street between the hours of 12:00pm and 4:00pm weekdays.

Sincerely,

Magister Liise Straightrod, Esq.

As soon as my eyes finished reading her name, the paper turned to ash in my hands. It was a good thing I had a strong memory.

Well crap. I'd been in Leotown for forty-five days. We were two days from a full moon, which gave me roughly two weeks to the end of my second lunar cycle. I shook my head. I wasn't ready to deal with a Witches' Council and really didn't have the first clue as to what sort of power they might have in the region.

My initial instinct was to pack my stuff into the back of my truck and move on. In less than two days, I'd been attacked by a lycan and a coven of witches, been at the scene of a murder and held by the police, had my apartment inspected and my door blown in and now a Witches' Council wanted to know all about me. It wasn't a great start to my new life. I just knew I was going to look back to this moment and kick myself for passing up the smart choice. The thing was, I'd seen the future and Red needed my help.

***

I pulled to a stop in the parking lot of the recreation area that ran for several miles along the river. To the west was Leotown and to the east was miles of undeveloped forest that eventually gave way to a farmer's fields.

Perhaps the most valuable skill Judy Babcock taught me was how to harvest spell components. The simple enchantment, *lutum ubertatis*, caused significant plants and wildlife to become illuminated in the moon's wan light. As a rule, Judy and crew avoided the actual full moon, not because it was a bad time to harvest, but because of the off-chance of an encounter with lycan. They also preferred to gather in the nude, but I'd found I could successfully skip that part.

Clipping the truck keys into the pocket of my favorite leather backpack, I swung it over my shoulder while loping through the thick grass. The only reagent I needed for the harvesting spell was good old-fashion mud, the stickier the better. I'd found the best results occurred when I gathered it from a moving natural water source.

At the tree-line next to the parking lot, I waited for my eyes to adjust to the dark. It was a new forest for me and I listened with interest, immersing myself in its particular chorus. The cicadas had quieted down, but the frogs were in full voice. I even heard a few hoots from a friendly owl. I stood motionless for longer than was necessary, caught up in the enjoyment of being wrapped in nature's embrace. I hated to break the rhythm by moving.

Finally, I set out. I had a basic idea where the river was and carefully made my way toward it. There was probably a path from the parking lot that would lead to the river's edge, but I preferred to engage nature on her terms and allowed the forest to guide me. So sue me, I'm a tree hugger.

The sound of the river was unmistakable as I joined with a small game trail. Stealth wasn't my strong suit and I knew I'd already scared off all of the animals which would ordinarily use the trail. The moon's reflection on the river's surface filtering through the thinning trees was my first strong indication that I'd arrived. I pulled off my shoes and socks and set them down on the bank next to my pack. I hated wet socks, but didn't mind mud between my toes.

I slipped and slid down the bank, grabbing exposed roots and digging my toes into the cold mud. At the bottom, I turned and looked across the river to the blinking lights of Leotown. What a great night.

I reached into the water and drug my closed fingers through the loose mud, shaking out excess water. I calmed my mind and closed my eyes, swirling mud from brow to chin on both sides, chanting *lutum ubertatis* over and over again. I pulled a pocket knife from my belt and sliced into my finger, drawing blood and mixing it with the mud on my face. As the enchantment activated, power surged through the muddy bank, tingling as it traveled through my body, finally exiting through my eyes.

The river bank lit up in a display of spectacular colors; the trees glowing with a blue hue, their leaves a lighter shade, each different plant species a slightly different color. This forest was as rich an environment as I'd ever seen, I wished Judy was here to share it with me. A mother raccoon and her babies had slipped down to the water's edge and were quietly sifting through the washed-up debris.

"Hello, Mrs. Raccoon," I said. She looked up, startled to see me so close to her family. While under the effect of the *lutum ubertatis*, I gained a small amount of dominion over lesser beasts. Since I needed nail clippings, it felt like a perfect opportunity. "Would you mind if I trimmed your nails? I promise to go easy on you, with no harm to your kits."

She had little choice, but I hoped my words would comfort her, if only by my tone of voice. As she lay down next to me on the bank, her children regarded me, no doubt their mother's behavior confusing. I'd harvested plenty of nails from small animals and went to work, quickly clipping the ends of her nails into a small plastic pouch. Once gathered, I reached up to the top of the bank and pulled an apple from my pack, cutting slices from it and leaving them next to her. Judy had been insistent that to take something created a moral imbalance unless we left something of greater value. Personally, I just liked the idea that her kits would eat well because we'd crossed paths.

I clambered up the bank, dropped the bag of nail clippings into my pack and pulled my socks and shoes on, smiling. Only twenty minutes in and I'd already found a raccoon. Roots, herbs and vines all glowed in front of me on the game trail. By bringing to mind the items I needed, the visual clutter faded away.

It was after four thirty in the morning when I finally finished, the sun still hours from making its presence known. My pack was full and I'd even partially filled the emergency pillow case I'd brought along. I was whistling when I exited the trees on the north side of the parking lot. The *lutum ubertatis* was fading as I stepped onto the mown grass.

My first indication of another presence was the ticking of a cooling engine. I'd been parked for too long for it to be my Ford and was able to just make out the top of another vehicle on the far side of my truck. I was a difficult person to spook, but this was trouble.

I decided on the direct approach. I didn't want to make more out of the situation than necessary, quickly stepping over the chain that hung between low posts, separating gravel from grass. Before I could jump in the passenger side and leave, a large, human form rounded the front of my truck. With ten feet separating us, I pulled up short, the darkness still obscuring details. The air hung heavily with a musty scent.

"I'll have you move away from my truck. I've no quarrel with you," I said.

The form grew in front of me, cloth ripping. It was female - definitely female - of a species I didn't recognize. I knew this because she had taken several steps forward, pulled a ruined shirt from her torso and discarded it on the ground. Seven feet tall, heavily muscled and strange gray skin. Her brow was heavy and her ears were long and pointed. She was both terrifying and beautiful. "This area is claimed. You have no right to these woods," she growled at me.

I'd be dishonest if I didn't mention that I was very aware of the fact that she stood naked from the waist up. I'd witnessed plenty of nudity, but for some reason it never got old and she was fascinating.

"Shit, you're amazing. What are you?" I asked.

She looked back at me with a small tilt of her head. I could almost see the wheels turning in her head as she tried to figure out if I was messing with her.

"You're trespassing," she said. The word trespassing coming out something more like 'threshepashing.' The small tusks inside her mouth made it difficult for her to form words.

"These woods are the public lands of Chamber's County recreation area," I said. "What's your claim?"

"Not my claim. You just have no right," she said.

"I feel like we've gotten off on the wrong foot here. I'm Felix Slade and I'm new to the area. I intended no offense," I said.

"I know you, Slade," she said derisively. "You've offended."

"How's this going to go?" I asked.

"I'm going to kick your ass. I'll not break anything. Don't resist or it goes worse," she said, definitely struggling to talk.

"Yeah, so that's not going to work for me," was what I was going to say, but I got out 'Yeah, so...' and she was on me. Man, was she quick on the draw. I only had time to swing my pillowcase into her face and try to twist away. Not my most elegant moment, as she batted the case out of the way with one hand and with the other she made hard contact with the side of my face.

Her first hit dropped me to my knees, which she expected, because she quickly followed up with a knee to the chest, flipping me over.

"*Scutum*," I roared, lying on my back. An invisible shield popped up between us and she flailed as she came in contact with it, lunging to finish me off while I was on my back. The unexpected barrier confused her sufficiently to cause her to stumble and trip.

I pulled my feet beneath me and stood up at about the same time she rolled back to her own feet.

"If I have to go offensive, you won't like it," I said.

She growled. "You have no idea the shit you've stepped in."

"I'm not afraid of you and I'm certainly not going to stand here while you hand me a beating," I said.

"Not me you need to be afraid of," she said, taking another swing in my direction. I redirected the shield to deflect her.

"Deep shit," she said. "Take your beating."

I crouched down, keeping my shield at the ready and pulled a length of a blackberry bramble vine from the pillowcase. There was maybe a minute left on my shield spell and I needed to do something to avoid getting overly aggressive with her. I fumbled with the vine, allowing the thorns to puncture my skin, and dropped it on the ground.

"You should stop this," I said, standing up. She'd pulled a long knife out and it was taking more and more of my concentration to keep the shield between me and her attacks.

"*Rhamno*," I incanted.

The power channeling through me from the ground responded. I'd made a connection with this land and it recognized my call. I dropped the shield and twisted my hand, directing the sprouting blackberry bramble to wrap itself around the creature's legs.

Her immediate response was escape, which was both expected and the worst thing she could do. The magic of the bramble spell used her struggling to establish an even stronger hold.

I grabbed my pillowcase from the ground and turned toward the truck.

"It will only get worse if you run," she said, her lisp made more pronounced by her struggles.

She'd just summed up most of my relationships with women.

The bramble spell wouldn't hold her long, so I hurried. My high from a great night of gathering was completely ruined by the encounter. Before leaving, I looked on the other side of the truck and found an older, albeit well-maintained Jeep. I memorized the license plate, although the vehicle was fairly unique looking with its tall antennae and camo-patterned paint.

Witches... lycan... and now I strongly suspected I'd just been attacked by a troll. I was starting to wonder if it was just me or if Leotown was simply lousy with supernaturals. The bottom line was, I needed more protection on my apartment.

For a wizard, protection spells come in a variety of flavors. Today, I needed physical protection. Turns out that's not too difficult. It's basically the same enchantment as the shield spell I'd released from my pinky ring. It requires some modification to allow friendlies to pass, but I could lay one down in forty-five minutes or so.

I rolled to a stop in front of the garage and pushed my way into the lab. The sun was just coming up and I laid my treasures out on the table. As much as I wanted to get the protection spell in place, I needed to protect my plants first. If I didn't cast a freshness spell on the herbs, tubers and mushrooms, they wouldn't last more than a week. I spread everything out in thin layers, taking up all of the open counter and table space. It had been a fantastic haul.

Under the granite counter was a book filled with my common lab spells and first was the freshness spell. Lavender, salt, magnesium silicate (talcum powder) and a few more components were dropped into my copper cauldron and gently warmed. A drop of blood when thoroughly mixed and the magic word, *conservare*, chanted until the potion turned transparent, was all it took. I poured the contents of my cauldron into a plastic household sprayer and spritzed everything.

The next task was to work on the physical protection enchantment. Nettles, thorns and poison oak were the hero components for this enchantment. Paraffin or clay was used as a binder, but that was about it. I mixed an extra big batch and set it with several drops of blood. If I haven't recently mentioned it, I'd like to reiterate how much I am *not* a fan of that part of the enchantment process.

Five hours after I left the woods, I finally finished painting the enchanted paraffin on the last opening of my apartment. Andy had been as good as his word and found a door to replace my sheeting. If he hadn't been so quick with the repair, I would have had to get much more creative in protecting the entrance. I glanced at the clock. My timing couldn't be better. There was just enough time to get a shower and clean my cauldron before meeting Gabriella for coffee.

METRIC CRAP TON

I wasn't sure what to expect from a place named Howling Hounds, but was pleasantly surprised to discover a clean, upscale coffee shop. I was fifteen minutes early, so I ordered coffee and a piece of pumpkin bread. It was then I discovered they had a shortage of open tables.

If I hadn't been meeting Red, I would have left. I was stuck needing that table, so I did what any self-respecting wizard would. I looked around, found my target and planted a suggestion that perhaps they'd left their windows down and it was about to rain. If it had been a sunny day outside, I'd have picked something else, but with the recent rain and cloudy sky it worked flawlessly. The older woman interrupted her daughter mid-sentence and hastily escorting her out of the shop.

"That wasn't very nice," Red said from behind me as I set my pumpkin bread on the table.

I was taken aback by Red's appearance. I'd known she was attractive when I'd first seen her at the bakery, but today she was dressed in a narrow black skirt and blood-red blouse. Her long black hair was pulled back in a tight bun. In short, she had transformed from witch to business woman and she was gorgeous.

"Uh, right," I said. "Did you get your coffee?"

She smiled. She might have had some idea of her effect on men.

"I'll be right back." When she went to the counter, I did my best not to watch her walk away.

I overheard her talking to a barista. Apparently, she was a regular here. They had her coffee ready and she had cash in hand.

"Thanks, Mike," she said over her shoulder as she walked back to the table.

"So. What? Are you a lawyer or something?" I asked.

She grinned. "You have a problem with that?"

"No. I just haven't known that many witches who have professional day-jobs," I said.

"Shh," she said, looking around to see if anyone heard us.

I whispered, just for the effect. "Spelled the table. No one can hear us."

She raised her eyebrows. "You can do that?"

I wasn't in the habit of talking about the spells I knew and immediately regretted saying anything.

"What was yesterday all about?" It was time to change the subject and I took a bite of the pumpkin bread.

"Felicia doesn't want me saying anything to strangers," she said.

"After our tussle on the couch, we're hardly strangers."

"About that. Are you feeling okay? I've never had to attack someone and I feel terrible," she said. "What about your chest?" She reached toward me and instinctively I backed away.

"I'm tender, but nothing I won't get over," I said. "You were channeling a crap ton of energy. How's that hand?"

She turned her hand over so I could see it. The skin had blistered on the palm and her fingers were bright red.

"Looks painful." I held her hand gently while I inspected it. "I have something at the house that would make it feel better."

She pulled her hand back. "It'll be fine."

"Is Whyte Wood Coven normally that aggressive? I pegged you for Wiccans, but I've never seen a Wiccan go after someone like that," I said.

She laughed. "Know a lot of witches, do you?"

Memories flooded my mind. "My foster mom is a witch."

"Who?"

"She's not from around here." It was mostly the truth. I'd moved in with Judy when we both lived in a small town not far from here before moving to North Carolina.

Her next question went directly to her purpose. "What are you doing in Leotown, Felix?"

"So much for the social call," I said. "You answer my questions,

I'll answer yours."

"It's not like that," she said.

"How is it?"

She stared at me for a solid minute before replying. "You scared Felicia," she said. "She felt something when she read your blood. I felt it too when we were on the couch, like you were barely keeping a lid on things."

I tried to squeeze out a laugh. "Isn't that true with everyone?"

"No. It's not."

"What do you want to know?" I asked, then huffed a laugh. "Right. What I'm doing here. That's easy. I had to get out of North Carolina and I picked Leotown."

"Why Leotown?"

"I grew up on a farm about sixty miles from here and I've always liked the city," I said.

"Who brought you here?"

"No one. Your turn," I said. "Why'd you attack me?"

"We got a tip you were involved in the attack on Victoria."

"A tip with my name and address? That's a heck of a tip."

Red recognized it wasn't a question and nodded her head in agreement. "What were you doing at Victoria's house?"

"Tracking a lycan that was tracking you," I said.

"Me?" That sent her eyebrows up.

"Remember when you went to Wheatfield's last Sunday?"

"The bakery? How do you know about that?" she asked.

"You picked up a tail when you were there," I said.

"A lycan followed me from the bakery?"

"That's right," I said.

She frowned at me. "Were you following me too?"

"No." I put my hands up defensively. "I was the guy reading a book trying to mind my own business. When Shaggy followed you, I thought you might be in trouble. You know… back before I found out you were a bad-ass witch and all."

Her smile at my characterization was distracting.

"So you followed me to Victoria's?" she continued.

"I followed Shaggy, who followed you over to Mrs. Barrios'.

Only I didn't follow until later that night, when the attack occurred," I said. "Shaggy waited for you to leave the house and then must have let himself in."

Red's eyes went flat. "You were watching me?"

"No. Sort of. It's complicated. I used a spell." I hoped she wouldn't push me. I wasn't about to explain how I'd made the seer's glass.

She nodded, knowing better than to try to pin me down any further. "After I left, what happened?"

"Shaggy went into Mrs. Barrios' back yard and as far as I knew, didn't come out. About midnight, I followed his tracks and that's when the police nabbed me," I said.

"What was this Shaggy doing in her back yard?"

"Looking in her window."

"Shit. You think he did it?" she asked.

"It seems likely, doesn't it?"

"So, you didn't see the attack?" Red asked.

"No, but I saw the result. Mrs. Barrios was definitely mauled by an animal. It was gruesome," I said.

Tears formed in her eyes and I reached over to place my hand on top of hers, mentally kicking myself for being insensitive. We sat quietly until she pulled in a big breath and let it out in an uneven sigh.

"We don't know why she was attacked. Victoria was a powerful witch, but her mind was slipping. I doubt she could have defended herself," Red said.

"What can you tell me about Leotown Witches' Council?" I asked.

"What do you mean?"

"I got a nasty-gram, asking me to register."

"The five covens of Greater Leotown have formed a council," she said. "The most powerful, Illuminaire, runs the council, although each coven has a seat."

"So, you've registered?" I asked.

"Yes."

"Why?"

"It's how we keep the peace. The council draws territory lines and resolves disputes between covens," she said.

"Like deciding who can gather reagents from Chamber's County Recreation?" I asked.

"You didn't."

"I did. I ran into a rather unfriendly troll for my trouble," I said.

"That territory is claimed by Illuminaire," she said.

"It's public property. They can't claim a recreation area."

"Not sure what world you're living in, but they've laid that claim," she said.

"How powerful is Illuminaire?" I asked.

"Forty witches."

"Straightrod in charge?" I asked. "She signed that letter they sent."

"Pishh. Hardly." Red practically spat the words. "No. Straightrod is a minor witch who happens to also be a lawyer. She's a major pain in the ass though, so stay out of her way."

"So why coffee? Don't get me wrong, I'm all about being seen in public with beautiful women and all..." I let the words trail off.

She looked down at the table and then back up, smiling. "I'm offended. Can't a woman ask a man out for coffee?"

"Depends on what else you're after, because I had to buy my own coffee." I tried to keep a straight face.

She rolled her eyes and pushed away from the table. "I have to get back to work, but next time, dinner's on me."

I stood up and grabbed her arm before she could go. "Look. Whatever you're into with Shaggy, you need to be careful."

"Whatever I'm into, Whyte Wood will handle. We've been handling our own business for a very long time," she said peevishly. I recognized the defensive posture and realized she felt I was denigrating her coven.

"Don't be like that," I said. "I'm just concerned. I saw what that lycan was capable of and I'd hate to see anyone else get hurt. And, if anyone knows what you can do with your hands, it's me." I gave her my best smile.

It took her a moment to finally respond. "You're incorrigible," she said and walked out, with just a trace of a smile.

I turned back and grabbed my last crumb of pumpkin bread, washed it down with the cooled coffee and followed her out the door.

I'd hoped to learn more about the Leotown Witches' Council from Red. The idea of registering went against everything I knew. Wizards, and most witches for that matter, didn't write their names down on a list for anyone. It was a matter of history that our kind tended to get barbequed when those types of lists got into the hands of the wrong people. That said, I wasn't against talking to Liise Straightrod.

Howling Hounds was only six blocks from the address Straightrod had provided for the Witches' Council building, so I decided to walk. The day had warmed up nicely and my legs had gotten a bit stiff while sitting with Red. Most likely, the muscles hadn't recovered from my gathering trip the night before.

Turns out that 1100 Jackson isn't a real address. I realized this when I arrived at the corner of Eleventh and Jackson and discovered 1102 was the first address to the west of eleventh street. Initially, I was just going to walk away, but curiosity got the better of me.

"*Altum Visu,*" I said, waving my hand across my field of vision, revealing the energies of the mystical plane.

To the best of my understanding the mystical plane is an alternate dimension that shows all types of energies. Magical energies are brightest and mundane energy, like that which is required to hold one brick on top of another, are more muted.

A hidden doorway appeared in the brick wall of the building in front of me. The ornately carved double doors sat beneath glowing words that hung in the air - Greater Leotown Witch Council.

I drew in a big breath, sighed, and then grabbed the shiny, bronze handle on the right and pushed it inward. A spark of energy erupted at my touch and a force tried to probe my being. I wasn't prepared for the assault and it almost got past my defenses. Fortunately, constantly maintaining a strong defense was something Judy had drilled me on.

Initially, I was incapable of letting go of the door's handle as the probe's energy intensified. I ratcheted up my own defenses and the pain intensified. I was going to have to go on the offense, since I sure as hell wasn't going to let some random force violate me.

"*Scutum*," I said.

The shield was the least provocative spell I knew and worked like I'd hoped, creating a barrier between my hand and the offensive door handle. I pulled back and let go of the shield spell.

A voice in the back of my mind urged me to turn and walk away. Unfortunately, I almost never listened to that voice. I knew it was a bad idea to go forward, but I've always been curious. Someone had constructed a door, of all things, to breach my psyche. I certainly didn't know how to do that.

The narrow hallway was lined on both sides with dark wooden paneling. There was gray slate flooring underfoot and a golden chandelier that glowed like the sun. A stairway was set back a few feet and led to the second level. On the left side, in the back, was an unmarked door.

The entryway smelled of pine cleanser, smoke, and just a hint of blood. There was either a practicing enchanter nearby or something bad had recently happened in the foyer. I suspected the latter. The entire foyer was bright with magic and it was giving me a headache. It was probably not necessary to see the mystical plane anymore, so I dismissed my spell with a wave and the word, "*Finis.*"

I blinked a few times, allowing my eyes to adjust to the natural sunlight shining from large skylights in the ceiling above. The natural light was a dead giveaway that witches were in charge.

"Mr. Slade, I presume."

The voice belonged to a narrow woman dressed in a gray wool business suit, her straight, muddy blond hair pulled into a tight bun. She'd appeared at the top of the stairway and looked over the railing as she slowly descended. A veritable mountain of a man followed behind, dressed in slacks and a short-sleeved dress shirt complete with a dark-red tie. To say he looked uncomfortable in his outfit was an understatement.

"I am," I said.

She continued down the stairs and for a few moments it was just plain awkward. Neither of us said anything until she arrived at the bottom.

"Magister Liise Straightrod," she said, holding her hand out.

I wasn't sure if I was supposed to shake it or kiss the oversized ring on her finger. The only reasonable option was to shake it. Her hand tried to snake forward and I knew she was going for my wrist so I released her, allowing my arms to drop to my sides.

"You sent a letter?" I said. It was a statement that I caused to sound more like a question.

She looked at me appraisingly, with lips pursed. The goon behind her tensed up. I should have been more worried, but I was still annoyed by the trap at the door.

"Yes, of course. We have many things to discuss. This way, please," she said.

I felt like I was being led to the principal's office as I followed her down the hallway. Her still unnamed thug waited for me to follow before he fell in line. Apparently, I was going to have to name him myself. I decided on Caboose, given his position in line and the red tie.

Straightrod pushed open the only other door in the foyer and I followed her through. This hallway had a few doors, all on the right side. She opened the second door she came to and gestured for me to go in, without entering it herself.

"Aren't you joining me?" I asked, pulling up short.

"I'll be along shortly. You didn't provide any notice that you'd be visiting today, so it will take me a moment," she said.

Caboose was breathing down my neck and for a moment I wondered what would happen if I refused to go into the room. But I wasn't ready to get into it with him, so I complied. The only furniture was an old, rectangular wooden table with a single chair on each side. Given the interrogation room layout, I was disappointed not to see mirrored glass on one of the walls. But then, I was dealing with witches and glass would be too obvious.

I'd been up for much of the night and was tired, so I sat in one of the chairs. Caboose shut the door from the outside. I slid the chair back, balanced it just right and leaned against the wall. It was about as comfortable as I was going to get, so I closed my eyes and tried not to wonder what I'd gotten myself into.

Apparently, I dozed off since the next thing I remembered was the sound of a door slamming and my chair abruptly falling forward.

"Please, Mr. Slade. You're marking up the walls," Straightrod snapped.

I was so distracted by the fact that she'd used a wand that I forgot to be annoyed by her abrupt entry.

"Mind if I take a look at that?" I asked.

"At what, Mr. Slade?" She looked at me like I'd asked her to square-dance.

"Never mind," I said.

"Quite."

She placed a thin manila folder on the table between us as she sat across from me.

"What do you need to know?" I was bored.

"Fill this out, please," she said, pushing a piece of paper and a pen over to me.

The top part of the form was ordinary: name, city, state, zip type of stuff. I filled it in, figuring it was information they already knew. If it had stopped there, I'd have been fine. As it was, the questions became progressively more intimate: asking about my lineage, coven affiliation history and a number of other things I wasn't about to answer. I pushed it back to her.

"You are required to complete the form," she said and the paper made its way back to my side of the table.

"I'm not a witch and therefore have no coven affiliation. As for lineage, I don't know. I was raised in foster homes," I said. It was a shading of the truth. I had memories of my parents, but I wasn't about to share the few details I had.

Straightrod glared at me. "You're lying."

"Not really. I'm not a witch and you're not getting my lineage," I said. I looked at the paper in front of me, grinned and pushed it back again.

"Are you refusing to register?" she asked.

"No, I'm refusing to share my lineage." I let out a breath. This was getting old. "Fact is, I don't know anything about my parents and it's going to stay that way."

Involuntarily, she glanced over her shoulder, giving away that she was in communication with someone else.

"I see. You have not filled in information about your disciplines." She tapped the paper and made as if to push it back my way.

"Maybe you're not getting it. I'm not a witch. I don't do things like you do."

"You're claiming to be a wizard then?"

"If you need a name for it, sure, I'm a wizard," I said.

She sucked in a breath. Apparently, she wasn't expecting me to admit that. I wondered if I'd made a mistake.

"You're trespassing, wizard. Leotown is claimed," she said.

"Hold on there." I put my hands up defensively. "I'm not looking to step on anyone's toes. I was raised by witches and know for a fact we can get along."

The woman practically snarled at me. "Impossible! No witch would raise a wizard."

"Are we done here?" I asked.

"No. There's another matter. You assaulted Amak, one of our employees," she said.

"Did not. I don't even know anyone named Amak."

"She was sent to discipline a thief on our claimed lands next to the river," she said.

"Oh right," I said, nodding. "That *was* me. I was unaware of your claim and, in her words, she was going to hand me a beating."

"As she'd been instructed."

"Look," I said. "I'm sure you're all pretty busy around here and I'd be willing to cede your coven's claim to part of the river if you want to provide a map. Look at it from my perspective, though. It's a public space and you didn't clearly mark it."

"Ignorance of a law isn't a valid excuse for breaking it," she said.

"Do you punish regular people for picking flowers in the recreational space? Do you send Amak Angry-Pants after them too?" I asked.

"Mundanes. We call them mundanes. And no, we don't consider their activities to be stealing," she said.

"Because they're not witches." I shook my head. "Well, guess what, I'm not a witch either. What does your law say about that? I think you just told me that your employee attacked me out of ignorance and owes me an apology."

"Don't try to turn this on us," she said.

"Are you saying your laws are just convenient for you to get what you want?"

"That's enough, Mr. Slade."

"I couldn't agree more. I'll see myself out." I stood up.

"You don't want us as your enemy," she said.

I stepped away from the table and stared at her. "You're right, I don't. You're not leaving me another choice. You and your employees have done nothing but threaten, assault and ask questions that no self-respecting wizard would ever answer. I came here out of respect and you've shown me none. I'm a simple guy and I can see where this is going. We might as well get right to it."

She stood to block my way and I brushed past her, grabbing the handle of the door to the room.

The last thing I heard was 'Don't...' as the knob transferred a metric crap-ton of energy into my hand.

ULTIMATUM

I woke up in the dark on a cold, hard surface. It was impossible to tell what time it was or how long I'd been out. The first thing I noticed, aside from a pounding headache, was that all of my jewelry had been removed. The smell of urine, sweat and mold permeated the room and a stream of water was running nearby.

"*Silici Scintillam Excudit,*" I said, holding my right hand away from my body.

A glowing ball of flame hovered over my palm, illuminating the room. The space was small, roughly six by eight feet. The walls were made of granite blocks and the only exit was a heavy wooden door with a small window blocked by iron bars. I'd been tossed in a real, live dungeon.

I ran my hand across the cot, checking the mattress. It wasn't good. Whoever'd tossed me on the ground might have done me a favor. Nope. After sitting on the cold, stone floor for the last few minutes, I realized even a dirty mattress would be more comfortable.

To extinguish the light, all I needed to do was close my hand. My eyes adjusted to the pitch black cell, but and I looked out through the iron bars on the door. A small amount of light glinted off free flowing water that ran along a stream bed only a few feet from my cell.

"*Altum Visu.*" I waved my hand in front of my vision, pulling up my view of the mystic plane. The door showed almost no energy and I got a strong sense of iron. It was good composition for us magical types. Iron was an energy sink and while it didn't cause direct problems, I had very little in my arsenal that would do much to an iron core door. That said, it also wasn't booby-trapped and I didn't have to worry about getting laid out by it.

I reignited my small flaming ball and tried to send it through the iron bars. I hadn't expected it to be wildly successful, but was disappointed when it extinguished before making it through. Such was the nature of iron.

Apparently, I'd caught someone's attention and heavy footfalls of something big approached. Out of a sense of self preservation, I backed away from the door. A face appeared through the bars. It was the troll woman from the forest in full form.

"Heya, hot stuff," I said.

The sound of a heavy club hitting the door reverberated through the cell and she spoke to me in her gravelly voice. While the phonemes didn't line up with any words I recognized, the message was clear - I was to stay away from the door.

"What a lovely singing voice you must have," I said, quoting one of my favorite movies. "Now, listen up Drusilla or whatever your name is. You better get someone down here who can talk to me before I start tearing this cell apart."

She hit the door again with her club, growled something unintelligible, and stalked off.

With my view of the mystic plane, I determined that only the door and its hinges were made of iron. The rest of the walls were granite stone block. In that my primary competence as a wizard was earth magic, there were some things I could do. A stone cell wouldn't hold me forever. That said, I wasn't interested in tipping my hand just yet.

About an hour later, after I'd done my best to clean off the filthy mattress, I heard a door open at what I estimated to be forty yards away. The dungeon had otherwise been quiet and as far as I could tell, I was its only inhabitant.

I hadn't released my view of the mystic plane, mostly because it was otherwise entirely pitch black and I didn't feel like holding the little flame ball forever. As it was, I was able to - sort of - see through the walls. My view was far from perfect, but two people were coming my way. One figure lit up like a Christmas tree and the other, not nearly as bright. The second figure was a woman and her power signature felt familiar, although I wasn't sure why.

Keys jangled as they were inserted into the door.

"Finis," I whispered, dropping my planar view.

The door swung open and the bright light of an electric lantern illuminated the cell. The woman entered first, but her face was in shadow and all I could make out was a dark cloak. I held up my hand to shield my face and blinked my eyes rapidly, trying to adjust to the brightness.

"I can't leave you alone for even a minute."

The woman's voice belonged to Gabriella and my heart did a little leap of joy. I wanted to say something snarky, but all I felt was relief that it was someone I knew.

"Oh, hey. Were we doing dinner tonight?" I asked.

She pulled the hood of her cloak back, revealing her smiling face.

"You're such a smart ass," she said. "You want to get out of here?"

"I was just trying to decide if I was going to have to tear this place down or not," I said, only half joking.

Her face turned serious and she looked around, but Amak had hooked the lantern on the door and disappeared. "Don't even joke about that. You've freaked out enough people for one day."

"How so? They're the ones who booby-trapped the doors," I said.

"Would you like legal representation?" she asked.

I looked quizzically at her. "Do I need it?"

"How much are you enjoying the dungeon?"

"I'd sure like a lawyer," I said, nodding enthusiastically.

"I thought you might," she said. "Amak, Mr. Slade and I will be meeting with Camille and Felicia."

The troll woman stepped into view as if she'd been listening from the hallway. She had transformed back into her more human-looking form. "Very well, Ms. Valverde," she said, glowering at me.

Amak turned away from the cell and disappeared. This time I could hear her shuffling off. I exited the cell behind Gabriella and we walked along a rough passage cut from the rock cavern we were in. A small stream trickled along, paralleling our path. But after a few steps, the stream turned back toward the path and disappeared under a wooden bridge.

"Are we still at 1100 Jackson?" I asked.

We were walking single file and Gabriella looked over her shoulder as she spoke. "No. We're offsite at the council's headquarters."

"How long was I out?" I asked.

"No idea, but you and I had coffee yesterday," she said.

I suddenly became concerned about how I might look. Surely, I'd had to use the restroom at least once in that period of time. I sniffed the air and the only thing I could pick up on was the musky dungeon smell and the pleasant scent of Gabriella's perfume. I surreptitiously used my hands to try to discover if bad things had happened and was relieved not to find anything.

We exited the dungeon into a more modern looking room. It, at least, had bright white paint on the walls and an elevator opposite the heavy wooden and iron door we'd just passed through. The brighter light gave me my first clear view of my rescuer. Her cloak was deep crimson and I laughed softly to myself. I'd yet to see her not wearing something red. The laugh earned me a questioning look from Gabriella as the elevator moved upward unsteadily.

Gabriella and I followed Amak out of the elevator and down the hall until she walked through a set of glass doors on the right. She stopped and held the door, clearly wanting us to walk through. As I passed her, Amak growled a quiet warning. "I've got your number, witch."

I turned back to her, not willing to let it slide. "Fee-fi-fo-fum to you, too."

She glared at me as the door shut between us.

"What was that about?" Gabriella asked.

"We have history," I said.

She shook her head as she led me through the hallway of a beautifully maintained, Victorian mansion.

"I've requested a meeting with Camille Parasyn. She's the leader of the Witches' Council as well as the Illuminaire coven. She's a very powerful witch. I'd recommend not trying to piss her off," Gabriella said.

"It'd be nice if I were afforded the same consideration. So far, I've been treated more like a piñata by Leotown," I said.

"Yes, you have, Mr. Slade. On behalf of Leotown, I apologize for the rough treatment you've received while in our care."

We'd just entered an office where three women were seated. I recognized Straightrod and Gabriella's coven leader, Felicia, as I entered. The third woman I assumed was Camille Parasyn. For such a powerful witch, she was diminutive in size, probably weighing no more than ninety pounds and well under five feet tall.

As she crossed the office, power radiated from her. It was a neat trick, one that I hoped was intentionally created and not because she had so much power that it just rolled off. She extended her hand and since I wasn't the type to hold grudges, I accepted. Her grip was firm but nothing excessive. I appreciated that she made no attempt to read my blood and I relaxed … slightly.

"It is nice to meet you," I said politely.

"You as well, Mr. Slade. Not to sound indelicate, but I'm going to release a minor spell that was cast on you and you'll have an immediate desire to find a restroom. It is directly behind you and to your left," she said, pointing.

I raised an eyebrow and as I did, she incanted, "*Finis.*"

I was impressed. Spells like that were more my forte, not typically used by any witch I'd ever known. My stream of thought, at that moment, was interrupted with the worst possible I-have-to-do-the-needful feeling I'd ever had. I turned abruptly and did my best not to duck-walk my way to the restroom Camille had thoughtfully located for me.

A few minutes later, I exited the restroom and heard laughter from the office where I'd left Gabriella and the other witches. I could only imagine what they were talking about, but I would do my best to maintain my dignity.

"Very well. Mr. Slade, please join us." Camille pointed to a chair next to the table where she sat with the other witches. She poured a glass of water and slid it and a manila envelope in front of me.

"Thank you," I said, opening the envelope and discovering my jewelry. As I pulled them from the envelope, I could feel they'd been drained.

"The big question we've been tossing around is just who is Felix Slade and why is he in Leotown?" Camille said. "Would you care to shed any light on that?"

"First question is a lot harder than the second," I replied. "I'm in Leotown because I needed a new home and it's familiar. I grew up not far from here, moved away and now I'm back. As for who I am ..." Gabriella laid her hand on my arm causing me to pause and look at her.

"As legal counsel, I need to let you know that you are under no compulsion to reveal your lineage," she said.

I watched for Felicia's reaction. As far as I could tell, Gabriella had just stepped between me and the ruling elite of Leotown. For her part, Felicia was nonplussed.

"That's not what Straightrod said," I said, looking directly at the woman.

"I merely asked about your lineage. It was up to you to answer," she retorted.

"Not necessarily our finest moment," Camille said. "Liise may be a bit zealous, but she does a great job at keeping us all in line."

I was annoyed at how easily Camille dismissed Straightrod's abusive approach and it must have shown on my face.

"Now, now, Mr. Slade. Look at it from Liise's side. She had been asked to register an unknown witch. It wasn't until later that she discovered you were no witch at all. It's a delicate situation to say the least," Camille said. "You seem a bottom-line kind of man, so I'll cut to the chase. We need to know if you're going to be a problem."

It wasn't a question, so I just looked back at her. It started to become uncomfortable after a few minutes had passed. Gabriella prodded. "Felix?"

"I didn't hear a question. More accurately, I don't know how to answer because I don't know what you define as a problem," I said. "If by being a problem, you mean following strange men who are tracking women without their knowledge, then the answer would be yes. Or if you mean picking herbs on public lands, again, there's a good chance of it. Otherwise, I'm not sure what you mean. I can tell you that I don't have a dungeon where I'll throw people who I find annoying." I looked at Straightrod pointedly when I finished the statement. "Can you enlighten me as to what you mean by being a problem?" I asked, switching my gaze back to Camille.

She didn't flinch. "I'll make it simple. We'd like you to register as an unclassified supernatural. And with that, you will agree to submit to the authority of the Greater Leotown Witches' Council in matters involving the supernatural within Leotown."

"If I don't?" I asked.

"We'll ask you to leave in the politest manner which achieves that objective," she said.

"If I understand this correctly, you're asking me to submit to the authority of your council. A council at which I have no representation. You do remember how the United States came into being, right?" I asked.

"See what I told you?" Straightrod said, uncontrollably. "He is impossible."

"No, Liise. That's a legitimate point and I'm surprised it hasn't been brought up before," Camille said. "Unfortunately, it's not the type of thing we can solve while we're sitting here and it doesn't resolve our problem."

"I have no idea what I'd be submitting to," I said.

The phone on Camille's desk rang. She looked at it with an uncharacteristically concerned look.

"I believe you have retained counsel who is intimately familiar with our laws and could explain this to you. But, for sake of clarification, I can hit some of the highlights. First, as an unclassified super, you have no right to a territory," she said.

"You want me to move?" I asked.

"No. As an unclassified you have no residential restrictions.

Territory for witches is mostly a responsibility for defending that territory from spiritual and mystical attack. It also delineates the boundaries of recruiting. If I understand wizards correctly, you care little for recruiting," she said.

"True enough," I said. "What about Chamber's County Recreation Area?"

"That is my coven's territory and you will need to get my permission to be there," Camille said.

"And?" I asked.

"That's hardly the purpose of this meeting," she said.

"I disagree. You want to know if I'm going to be a problem. Seems like you have the power to eliminate a source of conflict," I said.

"Are you threatening me?" she asked.

"Think of it as me asking for your permission," I said.

She closed her eyes and sighed. "Fine, Mr. Slade. You are allowed to utilize the Chamber's County Recreation Area," she finally said. "Anything else?"

"I'd like a chance to read through your agreement," I said.

"You've a week."

"Ma'am." I only half recognized the troll woman. This was the first time I'd seen her in decent lighting. I didn't fully understand trolls, apparently, as she seemed to have two forms. Astonishingly, the 'small' form she presently assumed was just under six feet tall, but with her face and ears smoothed, she fit within human norms. Gone was the odd grey skin, tusks and pointy ears.

"Yes, Amak? What is it?"

"It's...." The tall woman looked at me pointedly.

"We're all friends here. Right, Mr. Slade?" Camille asked.

"We're well on our way," I said.

"It's just... There's been another murder," she said.

"Who?"

Felicia reached out to Gabriella, her face ashen. She already knew something. `

"Benita," she said.

Tears streamed down Gabriella's face. She clearly knew the woman.

"Where? How?" Felicia asked.

"Her apartment. And, it was another mauling... just like Victoria Barrios," Amak replied. "Her daughter, Clarita, is missing. Police think it might be an abduction."

MIRANDA

"Mr. Slade, this is an internal matter. Amak will drop you in town," Camille said.

I stood and laid my hand on Gabriella's arm. "I'm sorry, Gabriella."

My heart broke at the depth of pain in her face. This wasn't my place, so I walked toward the door where Amak stood waiting.

Felicia hurried past me with Gabriella one step behind. Amak was blocking our way out, still looking uncomfortably at Camille.

"Move!" Felicia placed her hand on Amak's chest.

There was a weird moment when the six-foot-tall troll looked down her nose at Felicia, who couldn't have been more than five foot three inches - and that was with heels. Felicia's physical contact was a challenge and Amak looked like she might reciprocate. Then a small amount of energy welled up and discharged from Felicia. Amak's eyes glazed over and she passively took a step away from the door. I would love to have known what in the world Felicia cast to make that happen, but it was neither the time nor the place for inquiry.

"You're with me, pretty boy," Amak said, her eyes clearing as she shook her head.

I followed her through the brightly lit mansion into a wide hallway that joined with the front entryway. The leaded glass doors in front of us soared to fifteen feet. Amak walked fast and I did my best to keep up with her as she pushed her way through the doors and jogged down wide stone steps two at a time. We arrived just in time to see Gabriella's sedan exit the bricked, circular drive.

Amak wasn't wasting any time and headed directly to a small parking lot where her Jeep was parked. I hustled after her, although I was pretty sure she couldn't leave without me.

"Are we okay?" I asked. Amak had removed the Jeep's soft top and I used the roll bar to help me swing into the seat next to her.

"I still owe you a beating, but it's nothing personal," she said, placing her hand on my thigh. "I could probably come up with something we could do to work off your debt, though."

"Oh?" I asked and then it hit me what she was suggesting. "Oh… Uh… let's put a pin in that. Okay?"

She spun the Jeep's wheels in the loose sand on top of the brick pavers and I hurriedly pulled the seatbelt across my chest, struggling to click it in place.

"Just keep it in mind," she said and patted my leg.

We rode in silence down a long, asphalt lane that wove through a field of uncut grasses. It was late enough in the fall that the grasses had turned amber and red instead of the green hues of summer. A pheasant ran across the road in front of us and Amak veered in an attempt to run it down, cackling as she did.

The fields gave way to a pine forest, which we drove through for about half a mile before reaching the main gate. Once through the gates, we turned onto a rural two-lane highway and headed toward Leotown.

I finally got my bearings as we crested a hill and the skyline of Leotown rose in the distance. We were a solid thirty-five minutes from downtown, coming in from the north.

Amak turned on a heavy-metal station and seemed to be enjoying herself. Between the music and the wind buffeting us through the open cab of her Jeep, there was no potential for conversation. That suited my mood just fine. I leaned my head back and stared out at the corn fields. Rows and rows of stalks whizzed by, my eyes trying, in a millisecond, to follow each row to the horizon before being forced to move on to the next.

She turned the music down when we finally made it into the downtown area.

"Going to your house?" she asked.

"No. Howling Hounds."

"Copy that," she said.

When we arrived at the coffee shop, I was annoyed to find that my truck was no longer parked where I'd left it.

"Damn it! I must have been towed," I said.

Without warning, Amak turned hard, executing a U-turn in the middle of the street, bouncing over the curbs of the center divider.

"What in the hell?" I complained.

"Impound yard isn't that far. Been there a few times," she said. "Witches are always losing their cars."

Fifteen minutes later, we pulled into an industrial area under an elevated section of one of Leotown's main thoroughfares. The impound lot was surrounded by a twelve-foot-tall chain-link fence, complete with circular razor wire on top.

I hopped out of Amak's Jeep as she drove up to a break in the fence where a guard shack had been set up.

"Thanks for the ride," I said.

"Stay out of trouble," she said and pulled away, throwing gravel from her vehicle's heavily knobbed tires.

I chuckled to myself at how our relationship had changed within the last thirty-six hours.

The interior of the guard shack was empty and the lights were off. I did a quick, mental check and realized it was Saturday. Sure enough, the sign inside the window announced they were closed for the weekend. Remind me again, why I liked this town? I considered calling a cab, but it was mid-afternoon and a nice day. I could afford to walk, even though I was five miles from home.

An hour and a half later, I rounded the corner at the bottom of the hill two blocks from Mrs. Willoughby's house and my apartment. My heart sank as I saw a veritable host of police cruisers parked on the street and in the driveway leading to my lab. Whatever was going on, wasn't good.

The door to my lab was destroyed and two people were rummaging through my stuff. The brand new door to my apartment had received the same treatment and even more people were inside.

I caught the eye of a uniformed officer as I stepped toward the dirt path leading to the house.

"Hold on there," she said, stepping between me and the stairs.

"What's going on?" I asked.

"Who are you?"

I frowned. "Felix Slade. I live here."

She took a step back and pulled her gun from its holster. "On the ground, Mr. Slade," she demanded.

"What's going on? What's this about?" I asked.

"ON THE GROUND," she repeated. This time she attracted the attention of the officers tearing apart my lab.

I sank to my knees and placed my hands behind my head. Rough hands grabbed my wrists and twisted them one at a time behind my back, locking cuffs on as they did.

"Stand up, Slade." I recognized Officer Lozano's voice. He pulled on my arm as I complied.

"What's going on?" I asked, turning toward him.

Any doubt as to whether or not Lozano had been infected by lycan was gone. He looked like crap. His eyelids were red and puffy and his eyes extremely bloodshot. It looked like he hadn't shaved in weeks.

"We're taking you downtown for questioning," he said.

"Am I under arrest?" I asked.

"What? Are you Clarence Darrow or something?" The female officer asked.

"Yeah, something like that," I said.

Lozano stepped in. "Lieu wants you to come downtown for a conversation. That going to be a problem?"

"Are you asking or telling? I haven't heard my rights, so it sounds like you're asking. But then, you're trashing my place and I'm in cuffs, so imagine my confusion."

"Let's say Lt. Dukats is giving us a lot of room on this one. She tends to do that when children are missing," he said.

"I'll go with you, but if I'm not under arrest, you're taking the cuffs off," I said.

"We'll take 'em off when we get to the station," Lozano said as his partner patted me down, pulling my wallet and cell phone out as she did.

She pushed my cell phone and wallet into my front pockets.

"He's clean."

"Let's go." Lozano pushed me in the direction of the street where several cruisers sat.

"I'll catch up with you at the station, Joe," the female officer said.

"Yup."

"Tell me you have a search warrant for my apartment," I said.

"We do," he said opening a door for me. "Hold on." He uncuffed my right hand and re-cuffed me so they were in front and then helped me into the back seat.

Ten minutes later, he pulled into the parking garage beneath the station and opened the door to the cruiser.

"Cuffs?" I asked, holding them out to him.

"Don't push it, asshole," he said.

There have been times in my life when I've regretted the lack of a filter between my brain and my mouth. This turned out to be one of them.

"Rough night?" I asked. It had been the full moon and he looked like hell. It wasn't much of a bet that he'd turned into a wolf last night and awakened this morning naked and in a strange place.

I didn't see it coming when he grabbed and pushed me back into the cruiser. He brought his elbow around and cracked me on the side of the face.

"Keep your mouth shut." His breath stunk and I got a whiff of musty dog.

"Problem, officer?" A woman's voice asked from behind us.

"No, Mr. Slade here stumbled. Just helping him back up," he said and pulled me off the trunk of the cruiser.

"That right?" The uniformed woman looked at me questioningly.

"Yeah, caught my foot in the seatbelt on the way out," I said.

She nodded and walked off.

"You talk to anyone about it yet? Like your Grandma?" I asked.

He looked at me angrily, but didn't toss me again. "My Grandma? What the fuck are you talking about?" He pushed me toward the doors of the basement entry.

"You said she's Virarica," I said. "She'll know what's going on with you."

"She's not in the picture and how do you know something's going on?" he asked and pushed me through an automatic door.

"How's this sound? You blacked out last night and woke up in a strange place."

He spun me around and got in my face again.

"What aren't you telling me?" he asked. "What do you have to do with this?"

I wasn't going to be his mentor on this. "I've already said too much. You need to talk to your grandmother."

"She's involved?"

"No. There's no freaking conspiracy," I said. "You're sick, she's a shaman. You need her help."

"I don't believe in that crap," he said.

I shook my head. "You're about to."

"Shut up."

He grabbed my arm and led me to an elevator. We rode in silence and got off at the third floor where he locked me in an interrogation room. Once he was gone, I slid my hands beneath the table and released the locks on the cuffs.

Twenty minutes later the door opened and Lt. Dukats walked in.

"Thank you for coming down, Mr. Slade," Dukats said.

"Like I had a choice."

She looked at the cuffs I'd set on the table.

"We're looking for a missing girl," she said. "We think you know something about it."

"Clarita Barrios?" I asked.

"So you do know something. Where is she, Felix? It will go a lot better for you if you tell us now."

I mentally face-palmed. I shouldn't have acknowledged anything. "No. I was with friends when they received a call that Clarita was missing."

"Where were you last night around ten o'clock?" she asked.

"Spent the night in the country - same friends," I said.

"Who? Anyone corroborate this?"

"Camille Parasyn," I said. I had no idea if she would vouch for me, but I doubted she would want me to expose that the Council had locked me up in their dungeon last night.

"Phone number?"

"I don't have her phone number, but it shouldn't be that hard to find," I said. "You tossed my apartment. Do you like me for a murder or a child kidnapping?"

"Two murders of women who, upon investigation, appear to be heavily involved in the occult. And, when we *tossed* your apartment, we found a significant number of books and paraphernalia related to the occult," she said, enunciating the word tossed strangely.

"What's wrong with the word 'tossed'?" I asked.

"Makes you sound like a bad T.V. show. We don't talk like that," she said.

"Am I under arrest?"

"Should you be?"

"No. I think you've asked to talk to me because you didn't find anything. If you thought I was good for this, I'd be under arrest," I said.

"You're involved in this, Mr. Slade. I can feel it," she said.

I could feel it too, but hell if I knew how. All I really knew was that a wolf was after Gabriella and that Joe Lozano needed a friend in the worst way.

"We found bloody scraps of cloth in a glass jar when we searched your things. Do you want to tell me about that?"

"No," I said. I didn't know if they would be able to match it back to Lozano or not. It might be hard to explain why I had a swatch of towel with Lozano's blood, but I didn't think it would be a big problem.

"We're having them analyzed. I've got to be honest, they seem like trophies," she said.

"Were they covered by your search warrant?" I asked.

She pulled a paper from beneath her notepad and handed it to me. It was the search warrant that covered my apartment, the garage and my truck. I didn't understand much of the legalese, but it seemed broadly defined.

"Judges are pretty lax when it comes to murdered mothers and their missing children," she said.

"Do you have any other questions for me?" I asked.

"What were you doing in the country with your friends last night?"

"Sorry, not without a lawyer," I said.

"Don't you want to help us find this missing girl?"

"If I could help you, I would. You have to have some reason why you think I'm part of this and it has to be something more than my reading habits," I said.

"We received an anonymous tip that you grabbed the girl," she said.

"That's convenient."

"You're not being very helpful," she said.

"That's because I don't know anything. Can I leave?"

"No. Felix Slade, you're being held for questioning related to the kidnapping of Clarita Barrios…"

TINY FOOTPRINTS

For the second day in a row, I found myself in a cell. Leotown is a city of half a million, twice that if you include the outlying areas. As a small city, it saw its fair share of crime, although on a Saturday night most of what the lockup processed were the drunk and disorderly. To say it wasn't conducive to sleep was an understatement. Although by five o'clock Sunday morning, we'd stopped adding to the population and I was able to cat-nap while resting my head against the wall behind me.

"Slade."

The sound of my name woke me from a fitful sleep. A uniformed officer stood by the door to the cell. He'd placed the keys into the lock and was looking directly at me. I stood up, gently pushing Gorby, my late night sleeping companion back to a fully upright position. Gorby stirred, snorted and resumed his blissful sleep.

"What's up?" I asked as I approached.

"You're being released," he said.

I looked at the clock on the wall across from the cell. It was eleven o'clock. I walked through the door, waited for him to relock it and followed him down a hallway to a desk where he directed me to sit. Once I'd complied, he handed me a clipboard that had the inventory of the items they'd taken when I'd been booked. He placed a basket on the edge of the desk containing my belt, wallet, keys, phone and jewelry. I quickly slid the jewelry on and signed the paper acknowledging receipt.

The officer stood up and escorted me to a steel door. He pressed a button on an intercom and said what I assumed was his name. A moment later, a buzzer sounded. He pushed the door open.

"There you go," he said.

I didn't hesitate and walked into a reception area where a number of people were seated, all eyes on me. Whoever they expected, it wasn't me and as a group, they all looked away.

"Felix."

I turned toward the voice and saw Gabriella, standing at the edge of the room. As usual, she was gorgeous, dressed in tight, blood-red leather pants and a loose beige sweater.

When I walked in her direction, she held her arms out as if to hug me. My face undoubtedly showed horror and my hands went up in protest. I was a mess and knew I stunk of last night's cellmates.

"Did you bail me out?" I asked.

"Give me a hug. And don't be silly. You haven't been charged with anything. There's no bail," she said.

I gave her a hug and released her as she stiffened.

"Ripe, right?" I asked.

"It's horrible. Is that all you?" she asked.

"Close quarters in the drunk tank. I may have to burn my clothes," I said.

"Don't take this the wrong way, but I'm putting a sheet on my car seat before you get in," she said as she led me out of the building.

"What are you doing here? How'd you know I was locked up?" I asked.

"I got a call from Camille. She was visited by Lieutenant Dukats who wanted to know where you'd spent Friday night."

"How'd that go?" I asked.

"She vouched for you, although she didn't appreciate being dragged into it," Gabriella said.

"Tough shit," I said, half under my breath, which earned me a raised eyebrow from Gabriella.

I followed her to her gray Civic. She opened the trunk, pulled a tarp out and handed it to me. It was lightly misting, but had rained significantly the night before. I was surprised that I hadn't picked up on the rain, even while I was in the cell.

"Is that why you're here? Did Camille tell you to come down?"

I asked.

That stopped her.

"You think I came down here - on a Sunday morning - because Camille barked at me?"

I knew I'd stepped in it, but wasn't sure what I'd said wrong. It was the story of my life.

"I've no idea why you came down here," I said. "I had a bad night. So far, every turn I take in Leotown, someone's either trying to pound me, lock me up, or both."

"Get in," she said. Her words were clipped. and I could tell I hadn't made things any better.

I opened the passenger door, unfolded the tarp and laid it on the seat.

"Do you want breakfast?" she asked. She wasn't looking at me, which was not a good sign.

"Thank you for coming, Gabriella."

"Tell me right now, Felix. Are you involved in this in any way?" She turned to me, her gaze fierce.

I held my hand out to her - wrist facing up. "Read me. I won't hold back."

"You shouldn't do that. You trust too quickly," she said.

"You may be right. But trust is earned and every time I wake up in a cell, you're right there."

She slid her hand over mine and rested her middle and index fingers on my wrist, closing her eyes. I reciprocated and stretched my fingers over her wrist as well. Involuntarily, she gasped at the intimacy of our touch, her panic communicated through the tips of my fingers.

I sensed a swirl of emotion: distrust that seemed related to the missing girl Clarita, fear, compassion, anger and a deep sadness for the loss of her coven sisters.

"Oh Gabriella, I'm so sorry."

Fresh tears rolled down her face as she shared her pain.

"Tell me Felix, what are you?"

"What do you mean?"

"I can read your emotions and your aura, but your magic is

inaccessible."

"I'm a wizard," I said.

"How is that different than being a witch?"

"I don't really know. I just know that when I tried to join Judy's - my foster mom's – circle, it didn't work very well," I said. "It's one of the reasons I left North Carolina."

A dark shape flew through my peripheral vision. I tracked it to a tree and saw Maggie take a high perch. She acknowledged my gaze by bobbing her head up and down.

"Is that Maggie?" Gabriella asked, following my eyes up to the tree.

I'd forgotten Gabriella still had hold of my wrist and must have felt my reaction to the raven.

"Yes. Maggie worries about me," I said.

"You're fond of her, aren't you?"

"Hard to explain, but she and Judy are the only family I remember with any clarity."

"I can't imagine growing up without my family." Gabriella released my hand and cut off the transmission of a fresh wave of grief. She pulled away from the curb. "About that breakfast?"

"Are you sure you want to be seen with me? I haven't showered in at least two days," I said.

She wrinkled her nose. "Drop by your apartment for a shower first?"

"I'd go for that."

We drove in silence for the few minutes it took to get to my apartment.

"What happened here?" she asked as she pulled onto the gravel drive that led to my lab. The entry door to the garage had been covered with plywood.

"I figured you already knew. They got a search warrant on my place," I said.

"On what grounds?" she asked, jumping out of the car.

"Apparently, there was an anonymous tip that I'd taken Clarita," I said.

"That's ridiculous," she said. "You were locked up."

"You know that and I know that, but the cops didn't," I said.

Gabriella followed me up the stairs to my apartment. The door was also replaced by a wide sheet of plywood.

"I hope you have renter's insurance?" Gabriella asked. "The city won't pay for this."

"Even if they didn't have a good reason for knocking it down?"

"A warrant is all the reason they need," she said.

I lifted the edge of the plywood and it pulled back easily. Someone had already removed the panel and just laid it back in place. The damage to the door was considerable, like a power saw had been used to cut the frame out.

"What a mess," I said, pushing the plywood sheet to the side.

"What happened?" Gabriella asked.

"Protection spell on the door," I said.

"They couldn't just break it down?" Gabriella asked.

"No. That enchantment would require magic to undo it. For the record, I was just trying to prevent fricking Shaggy and the neighborhood witch patrol from breaking my door down. I never figured on the cops," I said.

"All this damage looks like it will be expensive to fix," she said.

"Yeah. And no, I don't have renter's insurance," I said. "I've been meaning to, but no time."

I flipped the lights on to find my apartment had been thoroughly trashed. Books were strewn about, chairs and couch turned upside down and stuffing literally ripped from the cushions.

I sighed and set about righting the furniture so we'd have somewhere to sit. I found the kitchen table, flipped it upright and slid two chairs in place. All I could do with the couch was push the stuffing back inside and flip the cushions over to hide the tears.

"Rain ticket on breakfast?" Gabriella asked.

"No I'm in. I can clean this up later. I've hardly eaten for the last two days," I said.

"Where's your truck?"

"City impound. When Straightrod abducted me, it got towed," I said.

"Straightrod said you attacked her and that's why she had to put you in the dungeon."

"That's crap. I tried to walk out of her interview and the door was booby-trapped," I said.

"What do you think that's about?" Gabriella asked.

"The conversation went south when I admitted to being a wizard and wouldn't divulge my lineage," I said.

"Magic is inherited and Straightrod is fastidious about tracing family trees. If she could figure out your lineage, she'd know your strengths," she said.

"And weaknesses."

Fifteen minutes after taking refuge in my bathroom, I emerged clean and shaved. Gabriella had used the time to clear a pathway through the room and had most of my books stacked against the wall, out of the way. She was standing by the piles, browsing through one of the books. She looked up and shut it with a snap, setting it back on the stack with an embarrassed look on her face.

"Sorry. Just curious," she said, looking guilty.

"Did you find anything interesting?"

"The book? I couldn't even read it, but the pictures were interesting," she said.

I stepped around the chair and was surprised when she flinched as I picked up the book.

"Hey, seriously, no big deal. I invited you into my house. It's natural you'd find these books interesting," I said.

She sat on the edge of the cushioned recliner and I reopened the book - one of several taxonomies of mythical creatures from the middle-ages.

"It's a beautiful tome," Gabriella said. "How did you find it?"

"My family, I guess," I said. "The only thing I have from them are these books."

"There are so many," she said.

"Thirty-six," I said. "I should know, because Judy made me cast preservation spells on every one of them every year."

"You can read this?" she asked as I flipped to a page I'd been wanting to look at since I'd met Amak. The picture of a female troll had been drawn by a Benedictine Monk, its similarity to Amak clear.

"It's Latin, so it's not bad. Aramaic and Greek I struggle with," I said. "Although I only have one book of each of those."

I handed her the book. "If you take me to breakfast, we can bring it along."

Her raised eyebrows conveyed surprise. "What do you feel like eating?"

"I'm starving, but I'm not picky," I said.

"I've got a place," she said and stood, accepting the book. I followed her down to her Civic and jumped in the passenger side.

Twenty minutes later, curiosity finally got the better of me. "Where are we going?"

"Chatty Katty's," she said.

"Ask a stupid question," I said.

Gabriella smiled but didn't respond. Another fifteen minutes passed before we pulled into a parking lot next to a large, old house. Aside from a wooden sign hanging from an iron post, I wouldn't have known it wasn't a residence.

She led me up the steps onto a wide porch and through the front door. My stomach growled at the smells that greeted us. The first floor of the grand old house had been converted into seating areas; tables and booths tucked haphazardly into every nook and cranny. The décor was every bit as eclectic, ranging from candles and garland to strings of lights and copper lanterns.

A woman dressed in a long, dark green dress and an apron approached wearing a wide smile. My best guess put her in her mid-forties, maybe early fifties. When Gabriella turned toward her, the older woman tipped her head sideways with a sorrowful look. "Gabby, come here, dear," she said, pulling Gabriella into what I could only describe as a motherly hug. "I heard about Victoria and Benita. I'm so sorry."

"It's horrible," Gabriella said, still held in the woman's embrace. "We don't know where Clarita is."

"I know, dear." She patted Gabriella's back and allowed her

gaze to settle on me. She snapped her head back and blinked her eyes.

"Who is this?" she asked, pushing Gabriella away and reaching her hand into her apron. I could just make out the shape of a wand pushing against the fabric of the deep pocket.

I held my hands up defensively.

Gabriella placed her hand gently on the woman's forearm. "Mari, I'd like to introduce you to my friend, Felix."

Mari made no attempt to greet me and stood her ground. "We'll serve no Left Hand here," she said. To the right, I felt a presence descend the stairs. At the same time, a third woman pushed through saloon styled doors at the back of the house, her face orienting on me as she emerged.

Many of the restaurant's patrons turned to look at us, drawn by the attention.

"Felix is not Left Hand," Gabriella replied, in a hoarse whisper.

"Time out. No need to get hostile," I said. "I'll leave quietly."

"No, Felix." Gabriella put her hand out to stop me. "This is a misunderstanding."

I dared a look up the stairs and found myself looking at a woman similar in age to Mari with her wand already drawn.

"Step out the door and bother us no more," Mari said. Her simple incantation pushed me toward the door. I wasn't about to cause a fuss, so I allowed the inertia of her spell to propel me.

"His aura is shrouded, but I sense darkness." This from the woman who'd exited the kitchen.

"He is not a witch! Stop it," Gabriella said.

"What do you mean?" Mari asked. "I see his mystical energy as clearly as I see your face."

"Felicia will back me on this. She has read him, as have I," Gabriella said.

The mention of Felicia seemed to sway Mari and she lowered her hand. As she did, the urge to walk out the door diminished, although honestly, I hadn't felt overly compelled.

"What are you then? You are no warlock," The shapely woman from the stairs pushed her way past Mari. Of the three of them, she was the youngest and most dressed up.

"I should get business cards that read 'Felix Slade – Wizard' and right beneath that, 'I don't know my lineage, so don't ask!'" I retorted.

"So you claim. There hasn't been a wizard around here in decades." Mari elbowed her way back to the front of the group.

"So I claim!" Gabriella declared, taking a step forward.

"Girls. If Gabriella vouches for him, then that's good enough for me to make him breakfast. Mr. Slade, do you promise to behave while you're here?" the older of the three asked.

"Depends on the service, I suppose," I quipped.

She held my gaze for longer than was comfortable, then laughed a short bark, "Fair enough. Big plate of huevos rancheros, in that case. You've already met my sister Marigold, the ironically named Willow is my other sister and I'm Bluebelle, although most people call me Belle."

I held my hand out to Willow, who eyed me like I was trying to pass her a rattlesnake. I pulled my hand back, holding it up in defense. "Fair enough. Nice to meet you all," I said.

"Back to your breakfasts," Mari announced to the handful of people still watching us. "How about a nice private booth in the back?"

"Thank you, Mari. If I'd thought there was going to be a problem, I would have called first," Gabriella apologized.

"Your boy here reads like a police blotter," she said.

"I know, right?" Gabriella slid into a booth that looked over a large garden within a greenhouse. The restaurant separated from it by a glass wall.

Mari allowed me to pass and I slid into the other side. "I'm right here, you know," I said.

Mari patted the top of my hand. "You sure are, sweetie. Gabriella, would you like your usual?"

"Yes, please."

"I'll be back with drinks," she said and turned away.

I watched her leave with a look of surprise on my face.

"How does she know what I want?"

"Belle already offered to make you huevos. It would be insulting if you asked for something different," Gabriella said, pulling the leather book we'd brought along. "What's the title of this?"

"Taxonomy of Extraordinary Creatures," I translated. "Or that's pretty close."

She leafed through the pages to a section on werewolves. "These pictures are amazing."

I tapped an ornate heading with my finger. "You need to learn Latin."

Mari returned and placed empty cups, a silver pot, and a tin in front of Gabriella. Before I could say anything, she poured delicious smelling coffee into my cup.

"You didn't even ask if I wanted cream," I said, catching Mari's eye.

"Certainly. Would you like cream with that?" she asked and walked away without waiting for a response.

I stared after her retreating form.

"Do you take cream with your coffee?" Gabriella asked.

"No."

"She's a witch, Felix. This is her life - think about it. She doesn't have to ask," she said.

I nodded in understanding. "Right. Good point," I sat back in the booth. It was the most comfortable I'd been in several days.

"You look tired," Gabriella observed.

Her eyelids looked as puffy as mine felt. "I am, but I'll get over it. How are you doing with all this? You have to be under a lot of stress."

"I'm scared for Clarita. Killing Victoria was one thing, she was a powerful witch who had enemies. I could almost understand the past catching up with her. But Benita? No way. She wasn't even a particularly powerful witch. The only reason she was allowed in the coven was because she was Victoria's daughter," she said.

"What about Clarita. Is she a witch?" I asked.

Before she could answer, we were interrupted.

"Hope you're hungry. Belle packed your plate about as deep as

I've seen it," Mari said, sliding a platter filled with diced fried potatoes, green peppers, onions and four eggs over easy, all slathered with a pile of white gravy. "Belle nixed the ranchero sauce. Apparently, you're more of a cream gravy guy."

I nodded my head in appreciation. She was right about that.

The plate she placed in front of Gabriella contained a single pancake and a side of strawberries.

"Thank you, Mari," Gabriella said.

"You bet. And the hot sauce is behind the napkins," she said and bustled off.

I reached behind the napkins, pulled out my favorite wooden-topped, glass bottle of hot sauce and sprinkled on a liberal dose. The food smelled so wonderful, I forgot about Gabriella for a few minutes.

I finally paused long enough to take a big drink of coffee. Gabriella hadn't eaten a bite of her pancake yet and was staring at me, horrified.

"What?"

"Do you always eat this much?" she asked.

"There's bacon in these potatoes. Do you want to try some?" I asked, ignoring her question.

"Vegetarian." She picked up her knife and sliced a small hunk from her pancake.

"No syrup?" I asked.

"I hope you were just guessing about Clarita," she said.

"Guessing what? That she's a witch? That's not much of a guess. Magic follows blood lines," I said.

"Not always for witches," she said. "But Clarita is a very special little girl. She will possibly be the most powerful witch of her time, certainly within Leotown."

"You can tell this already?"

"Yes."

"How many people know?"

"It's a well-guarded secret. Which means just about every witch in Leotown knows. Victoria was proud of her grand-daughter. It was like she felt like she'd failed with Benita, but Clarita redeemed her."

"That's a lot to lay on a little girl. How old is Clarita?"

"Six years."

"Ugh. I was six when I was abandoned," I said. "I don't remember my parents, other than some feelings."

I sat back and put my fork down. I couldn't believe I'd actually told her that. Besides Judy, I'd never shared it with anyone.

"I'm sorry, Felix. This must bring back some bad feelings," she said.

"Was Clarita home when her mom was killed?" I asked.

"Yes. The police have evidence that suggests that."

"Like what?"

"Her bare footprints were in the blood."

I gritted my teeth. The callousness made my blood boil. "That's heinous."

"Will you help us find her, Felix?"

"I'm not exactly a favorite with you witchy types. How does Felicia feel about my involvement?"

"She doesn't like it, but I'd make a deal with the devil if it'd get Clarita back."

I nodded. She might just be doing that.

BLOOD TRAIL

"We should get going," Gabriella said. "I love the sisters, but they're unrepentant gossips."

"Place has a nice feel," I said. "Judy would like it."

"Going so soon?" Mari asked, appearing at our table. "Was something wrong? You've hardly touched your plates."

"It was delicious," I said. I'd eaten well over half of the food on my plate.

"Tell Belle we're sorry, but events of the last week have made eating hard," Gabriella said.

Mari placed her hand on Gabriella's arm. "Be careful, child, you're in a precarious position and are making decisions that will endanger many." Mari's speech wouldn't have been particularly creepy if her eyes hadn't fogged over as she warned Gabriella.

Gabriella didn't even bat an eye, however, and patted the older woman's hand. "Thank you, Mari. I'm afraid we can't turn back. A girl's life is at stake."

Mari's eyes turned back to normal. "Quite so, Gabby. My visions are not clear, only the danger to you and those around you. I cannot help but feel that Felix Slade is fuel to this fire," she said, looking pointedly at me.

"What do we owe you?" I asked, trying to get Mari onto a different subject.

"Belle won't accept payment. She says I was rude."

"Not at all," I said. "You're protective of your friends. Hardly a fault."

"Aren't you the charmer." A smile crossed her face.

As subtly as I could manage, I dropped a ten-dollar bill on the table and followed Gabriella out of the home, turned restaurant. I wondered how many of the other patrons were witches and how many were just here for the atmosphere.

"Sorry about that," Gabriella said once we were driving out of the parking lot. "I hadn't expected such a bad reaction from Mari. They're generally so nice."

"Tell me about the attack on Benita," I said. "Amak said it was lycan."

"The police blocked access to her apartment," Gabriella said. "We tried to go over, but there's police tape all over the place."

"No ransom note for Clarita? A call or anything?"

"Who would they call? Victoria was Benita's only family and now they are both dead," she said.

"First things first, then. I take it your coven doesn't have a good way to locate Clarita?"

"Do you?" she asked.

"Not without her blood, but I have an idea. We need to go to my lab," I said.

Mrs. Willoughby was out back when we arrived.

"Is that trouble?" Gabriella asked.

"Could be. Most landlords don't like it when cops destroy property because of a tenant," I said. "I'll talk to her."

I walked up to the stoop where she sat in a padded vinyl kitchen chair.

"Hi, Mrs. Willoughby," I said when I got close enough for her to hear.

"Felix. We need to talk," she said.

"I understand," I said. "I'm sorry about the police breaking down the door."

"Second time in as many weeks. I know my home doesn't look like much, but it's all I have. I can't have it destroyed, no matter how much I like you."

"I'll set things right, Mrs. Willoughby. The police let me go because I didn't do anything wrong. They shouldn't have broken in like they did," I said.

"I don't know what you're mixed up in and I probably don't want to." She looked up at me with something akin to pity. "I need you to move out, Felix."

"One more chance, Mrs. Willoughby? I'll get the doors

replaced. The apartment and garage will look better than they did before," I said.

"I don't know, Felix." She was wavering and I felt horrible putting her in this position.

"One month. If I don't have it fixed to your satisfaction, I'll leave," I said.

Mrs. Willoughby dropped her head and thought. "I suppose I can live with one month. But if you bring any more trouble here, I'll be forced to ask you to leave."

"Fair enough," I said.

I walked back to where Gabriella was leaning against her Civic. "How'd it go?"

"I've a month to fix everything and clean up my act," I said.

Gabriella nodded. "She's scared. You can't blame her."

"Agreed." I pulled open the overhead garage door. I ordinarily used the side door, but at the moment, it consisted of a sheet of plywood nailed to the siding. The police had sawed through the frame when my protection spell prevented them from breaking the door down.

"A nice job of rearranging, courtesy of Leotown's finest," Gabriella said.

"I'm looking for glass jars with snippets of black cloth in them. When I was being questioned by the police, Lt. Dukats told me they'd found them. I hope they missed at least one," I said.

Gabriella helped clean up the mess as we searched. "You picked all this from Chamber's County Rec area?" she asked while shelving the last of the tubers.

"I'd have had a lot more if I'd brought a bigger bag. I don't think anyone is harvesting there. Just look at these Cortinarius mushrooms. I've never seem 'em so big," I said.

She furrowed her brow at me. "I don't even know what you'd do with a Cortinarius."

"Maybe I'll show you someday." I placed large chunks of broken glass into a box. "They really did a number on this place."

"Maybe you left them in your apartment?"

"We can look. But I know I brought them down here to

preserve them," I said.

"Then the police probably took them. If they even suspected blood, they'd take them all in for testing," Gabriella said as we exited the garage and ran up to the apartment.

I pulled the plywood back so Gabriella could enter and flipped on the lights. I sighed, the apartment was still pretty hopeless. Fortunately, my everyday filing system wasn't all that exacting, so I had that working for me. The two of us picked up most of the mess, searching as we went. I found my stash of empty specimen bottles, but none contained Lozano's blood.

"What I can't wrap my head around is why your coven is being attacked by lycan. Do you really think it's all about Clarita?" I asked.

"I don't know. We're down to three witches in Whyte Wood coven and that's not enough for us to hold our territory," Gabriella said. "Kelli has a family and she's scared. I'd be surprised if she doesn't move to another coven."

"She can do that?" I asked.

"Of course. Felicia would hate it, but you can't blame Kelli. If this is a territory grab, she'd be safer in a larger coven. Whyte Wood weakened as Victoria got older. I loved her like my grandmother, but she drove younger witches away," she said.

"I didn't even know witches had problems like this. Judy's coven was so warm and friendly," I said.

"But, they made you leave," Gabriella said. "Every coven has its warts, Felix."

I'd struck a nerve and in response she'd punched back.

"You don't know anything about it," I said. "No one in Judy's coven was committing murder."

"You can be an ass. You know that?"

"Me?" I asked. "Your coven starts a war with god knows who and now you want me to help bail you out."

"Fine. We'll solve this by ourselves. Felicia didn't want me talking to you anyway" Gabriella shook her head in disgust and stood.

I stood up with her. "Wait. Don't go. I want to help find

Clarita," I said, grabbing her elbow.

She pulled her elbow free from my grasp. "You've got a dumb way of showing it."

"I'm just saying…"

"You're just saying everyone needs the help of the mighty wizard," she said.

"Shit. Why does everything get so damn complicated with you? I want to help because there's a little girl who saw her mother get killed. I'm just pissed that everyone in this damn town is using me as their punching bag," I said.

She turned back to me, but I could still feel a wave of hurt and rejection rolling off of her. I stepped forward, placed my hands on her waist and pulled her to me. She resisted for a moment and our eyes locked. I wondered if I'd misread the situation. A smirk played across her face and she wrapped her arms around my neck as we kissed.

"You really can be an ass," she said, her warm breath caressing my face.

I was star-struck by the moment we were sharing and wouldn't have cared if she had called me a hippopotamus. I sighed and leaned into her again, not wanting to lose the moment.

Twenty minutes later, we'd moved to the couch and she finally pushed me away.

"What would Felicia say about that?" I asked.

"Moons of the equinox," she said with a deliberate eye-roll. "You suck at being romantic."

"Sorry. Right. I should just keep my mouth shut."

She placed a finger on my lips. "That's probably for the best."

I playfully grabbed her hand, then stopped, distracted by her painted fingernails. "What do you know about Benita?" I asked.

"We've been friends a long time, she was a lot better than Victoria gave her credit for," she said.

I held her hand up so that she was looking at it as well. "She'd fight back, wouldn't she? If anyone were trying to hurt her and Clarita, she'd fight back, right?"

"Of yeah. She was hot-tempered. She'd have gone down

fighting," Gabriella said.

"She'd have her attacker's blood under her nails."

"Probably."

"If I could get enough material, I might be able to track them. That's why I took Lozano's blood. I was hoping I'd get some of Shaggy's spit too, but the cops took care of that," I said.

"Her body has to be in the morgue."

I stood up and held my hand out to her. "Road trip."

"They won't let us in."

"It's Sunday. How many people could there be?"

"Seriously?"

"What's the worst that could happen?" I asked.

"We get arrested and put in jail," she said.

"It's where I started the day. And do you think they'd really lock us up for visiting a friend who's passed?"

She looked at me like I was nuts, but took my hand all the same.

As I pushed open the plywood, she stopped for a second, looking at the jagged opening.

"You might consider a lock next time," she said.

"Didn't stop your sisters. So if you think about it, this is your fault," I said as I hid a smile.

"Don't push it."

"Seriously, any chance you'd call Kelli and see if she'd ask Andy to come back? I told Mrs. Willoughby I'd fix the doors," I said as we walked down the stairs.

She pulled out her cell phone and pinched it between her shoulder and chin as she unlocked the Civic. The woman's driving terrified me. She backed the vehicle out at high speed, caught the phone in her hand, switched to drive, and sped down the hill.

"Andy will come by tomorrow after work. He has a line on a matching door, whatever that means," she said and tossed the phone into her purse. A few minutes later she pulled into on-street parking.

"How do you know where the morgue is?" I asked.

"Started out in the district attorney's office," she said.

"Started out?"

"Job didn't fit my personality," she said.

"That sounds like a story."

"You'd have the same problem. I can read people and wasn't willing to prosecute the innocent. Turns out that's not how the system works." She pointed to a ramp that led to a lower level of the building we'd parked next to.

"In the basement?"

"Service entrance. No cameras down there," she said. "Hope the door's unlocked. Sometimes they leave it open if they've had intake."

"How many people will be on staff?"

"No idea. Skeleton crew on Sunday night, though," she said.

A chill wind passed through me and I became intimately aware of the fact that we were approaching a morgue. I'd never seen a ghost before, but I also knew better than to look into the mystic plane next to a place where so many dead bodies had been.

The basement doors looked much like the entry to an emergency room. Wide sliding glass doors stood closed and the lights were turned down.

"Doesn't look too busy," I said and walked up to a steel door ten feet from the glass ones.

"Where are you going?" Gabriella whispered loudly.

"Why are you whispering?"

"I don't know," she whispered back.

I pulled on the door. It was locked. I waved my hand across the deadbolt lockset and pulled the door open.

"After you," I said, gesturing at the opening with a smug grin on my face.

The hallway we entered was well-lit and we followed it to the end. We stood next to the only other door and listened to make sure the coast was clear. Opening the door, we entered another, wider hallway.

"This way," Gabriella said, turning to the right.

"Hey, what are you doing down here?" It was a man's voice

from behind us.

"I've got this," Gabriella whispered and turned around.

"We're here for an I.D.," she said. "Got a call."

"How'd I miss you?" the man in scrubs asked.

"Didn't see you at the desk," Gabriella said. "We thought you might be back in the bunks. Didn't find you back there and... I didn't catch your name."

"Jeffery. Who'd you say you were here to I.D.?"

"Benita Barrios," she said.

He shrugged and walked past. "Thought she'd been identified."

"Some sort of screw-up. Police rolled me out of my nephew's birthday party for this crap," Gabriella said.

"Justice never rests," he said. "Are you new? I haven't seen you down here before."

"Yeah. Who else would they send on Sunday?"

"I read you. Ask me, weekends are the best. Stiffs don't talk and the coroner is always in a hurry." He led us into a room with three stainless steel, person-sized tables and a bank of square doors along the back wall.

He walked up to a computer terminal. "You say Barrios?"

"Yes." Gabriella said, breathing deeply. I hoped she'd be able to keep it together.

"Can you hand me your badge? I need to log it," he said.

"Hang on," she said and reached into her purse. "Oh no, I left it at home."

"You know your number?"

"One-nine-six-... Crap! No, I can't remember it. Don't make me go back. It took me forever to get down here," she said.

"No problem. Give me your last name and I'll look it up," he said.

"Trujillo," she said.

The screen in front of him displayed the picture of an ebony-skinned woman. She was attractive, but nothing like Gabriella.

"What is this?" he asked. Before he could finish, I placed my hand on his shoulder.

"Don't turn around. This doesn't need to go poorly. We just

need to I.D. Barrios."

"Hey, look," he said, raising his hands. "You want to look at a D.B., no skin off my back. Slap me a C-note and I'll forget you were ever here."

I only had sixty-three bucks in my wallet. I held three twenties up so Gabriella could see I was short. She rummaged through her purse and handed me two more.

"Which drawer?" I asked, setting the bills on the keyboard in front of the morgue assistant.

"B-3," he said and started to turn.

"Don't do it," I said. "The less you know, the safer you'll be."

"Not my safety you should be worried about," he said.

"Felix, someone's in the hall," Gabriella said. It was unnecessary as a wave of wet dog smell had arrived just before she spoke.

"Lycan," I said. "Multiple."

The door burst open and Shaggy walked through with a red-haired man and a dirty-blonde haired woman right behind him.

"Thought I told you I was going to rip your head off if you got in my way again," he said.

"Where's Clarita Barrios, Shaggy?" I asked.

"I think I'll leave this to you all," Jeffery said, slinking toward the door.

"You said no witnesses," the woman growled as she pulled her shirt off. I was proud of myself for not finding the action distracting for once. Her motion was followed by the sound of cracking and popping of bones and ligaments as she changed, howling in agony.

A gray wolf sprang from her pants and attacked. From the corner of my eye, I saw the red-haired man begin his transformation.

"*Scutum*," I said, stepping between the lycan and Gabriella. The wolf deflected off the shield, yelping in pain as she struck it. "I can't hold this forever." In truth, I could possibly hold it for two minutes. "Stay behind me."

"Shaggy, we don't need to do this. Just return the girl," I said.

He hadn't transformed, but barked commands. The grey had recovered and moved with the red, trying to flank us. I moved in response, trying to keep Gabriella between me and the steel table behind us. I couldn't hold my shield much longer so I released it.

The red wolf to my left rushed us, growling and snapping as he closed in.

"*Adoleret*," I said at the last moment, releasing the small amount of energy that had charged into my ruby ring. A cone of flame seared the wolf, causing it to instinctively pull off, screeching in pain. The cone extinguished and the ring was drained.

The red wolf's attack had been a gambit to draw my attention. I'd only had a few options and hopefully that one reduced my attackers. Unfortunately, the female gray had recovered and was attacking from the side.

"Wolf's bane brings great pain." Gabriella flicked her hand out of her purse. A flash of light and a cloud of smoke popped next to the gray causing her to howl and stumble, her attack aborted.

"Crap, you're pathetic! We'll just do this old-school. Especially since I've never had the pleasure of kicking a wizard's ass," Shaggy said. "At least they won't have to take your body far." He pulled a pistol from the back of his pants and leveled it at me.

"You're this big, scary lycan and you're just going to shoot me?" I asked. "What kind of chicken shit is that?"

"Dead is dead. Dumbass," he said.

"So you're not going to rip my head off then? I'm disappointed. All bark, no bite?"

"You really want to do this? Fine." He placed his pistol on the table next to him before unbuttoning his shirt.

I smiled and twisted my wrist, causing the barrel of the pistol to orient on Shaggy. The red wolf barked a warning and Shaggy turned, but it was too late. I flicked my thumb and pinched my finger, firing the revolver. There was a deafening bang and the gun spun wildly across the room.

Shaggy crumpled to the ground as his pack members turned toward me, growling defensively.

I pointed at the body. "You'd better get him to the hospital."

Shaggy howled in pain, writhing on the floor.

"Felix, he's shifting," Gabriella warned.

"Damn, we've gotta get out of here," I said.

I took a step toward Shaggy, which earned me a growl from his red companion.

"*Scutum.*" I pushed my faltering shield into the two wolves. The touch of the invisible shield startled them and I used their confusion to kick Shaggy in the abdomen where he'd been shot.

"Felix, what are you doing?" Gabriella asked.

"Go," I said and sidled toward the door. My shield was sputtering and I was glad the wolves couldn't see it failing. I took a chance and pushed at them, which earned me further growling and barring of teeth.

Gabriella and I ran through the door. The last thing I saw was the black wolf that had attacked Lozano trying to gain traction on the tile floor. I pulled the door closed a second before a heavy body crashed into it.

"Help me with this," I said.

Gabriella grabbed the U-shaped handle. I waved my hand across the lock and felt a satisfying thunk as the bolt was thrown.

"That won't hold them for long," Gabriella said as the door bowed outward in response to another heavy body slamming against it. She grabbed my hand and we sprinted down the hallway, sliding around the corner and ducking into the corridor that led to the service entrance.

The sound of breaking glass and the screech of metal hinges alerted us to the fact that the wolves had breached the morgue's door.

"We can't outrun them," I said.

"Can you lock the doors?" Gabriella asked as we burst through the exterior metal door.

"No," I said. I didn't have time to explain that it was an emergency exit door.

We raced up the garage's ramp to the wan light of the late fall afternoon with sounds of pursuit close behind. We reached Gabriella's car and I spun around, knowing we wouldn't have time to unlock the doors.

"Close your eyes!" Gabriella said.

Too late, I saw her drop her purse, a can of something in her hand. A stream of liquid shot past me and hit the closest of our pursuers. The smaller gray wolf skidded to a halt, yowling in pain.

The wind picked up a good portion of the pepper spray mist and blew it back in my face. I stumbled and turned to the Civic, running my hand across the lock on the passenger's side, pulling the door open.

"Get in!" I said.

Gabriella didn't require any prompting and jumped in, scrabbling over to the driver's seat. With tears streaming down my face, I followed behind her, closing the door just before the much larger Shaggy slammed into the vehicle. The window splintered on impact.

Time slowed as Gabriella fumbled with the keys. Shaggy's giant head swept the rest of the glass from the broken window and I pushed away from him, crowding into Gabriella to avoid his snapping maw.

"*Lucem*," I said, holding my hand forward. It was a lame spell for the situation, but the only thing I could think of. My silver ring blazed brilliantly for a moment and immediately extinguished. Shaggy recoiled up and away, slamming his head into the car's door's frame.

The Civic lurched forward and Shaggy snapped his jaw ineffectively, losing his balance. Gabriella swerved into a parking meter peeling Shaggy from the side of the vehicle.

"Are you hurt?" Gabriella asked as she gained speed.

I looked out the back window. The wolves appeared to be gaining on us, but Gabriella wasn't messing around and they soon fell behind.

HOMBRE LOCO

"Damn, woman, you were brilliant," I said, laughing due to the excess adrenaline.

"Three lycan! I can't believe we got out of there alive." She was panting in her excitement. "How weird is it that the big guy's name is Shaggy? How did Jeffery know to call them?"

I grinned but didn't set her straight. I was pretty sure the guy's name wasn't really Shaggy.

"We were only there for five minutes before the dogs showed up. That wasn't enough time for Jeffery to call. They were following us," I said. "I hope he got out of there okay."

"Drop you at your apartment?" she asked.

She didn't get it. "You think this is over?" I asked. "Gabriella, they'll find you. We barely escaped with our lives."

"I have an appointment. I'll be safe," she said.

"An appointment? It's Sunday, what kind of…" Then it hit me. "No. You've got to be kidding."

"I'm really sorry, Felix. What happened in your apartment was a mistake. I shouldn't have let it go that far," she said.

"Boyfriend?"

She nodded.

"Shit, Gabriella. That's cold," I said.

I got another of those pitying looks. "It's not like that. I messed up. I just really need your help finding Clarita."

"Which is it? You messed up or you need help finding Clarita? From where I'm sitting, it feels like you're using me."

"What do you want me to say? They're killing my family," she said.

"This guy, is he going to keep you safe from lycan?"

"I'll be fine. He lives in a high security building. I'm really sorry. I didn't mean for things to go like this," she said as she turned into the gravel drive in front of Mrs. Willoughby's garage.

I opened the door and swung my legs out, brushing broken glass from my lap. "Screw off, Red." I slammed the door behind me. It didn't exactly have the effect I was looking for as the window was missing, so she still had the ability to talk at me as I stalked up to the garage.

"I'm sorry, Felix," she called.

I pulled the overhead door up and slipped under it, allowing it to slide down behind me. "Whatever."

I knew it'd been too good to be true. Gorgeous women like Gabriella – strike that – Red, didn't ordinarily pay attention to loner types like me. I sighed, annoyed with my hubris. I shook my head and switched gears. A little girl was missing and if I could do anything about it, I would.

The first order of business was to recharge my jewelry. If Shaggy pulled up right now, things could get ugly. I was surprised that Gabriella - Red - was treating the attack so cavalierly. There was no reason to think the werewolf was tailing me and every reason to think he was after her. Yet, there she was, running off to the symphony with Mr. Perfect. I hated the bastard already. I needed to let go of my anger, but I was struggling.

I breathed in deeply and released slowly, closing my eyes in an attempt to focus. I pulled out a gnarled walking stick I sometimes used when hiking in the Appalachians and with its foot, drew a wide circle in the dirt of my lab. I took my jewelry off, laying it to one side of the circle.

From my shelves, I pulled a can of gypsum and spread the white powder liberally in the trench I'd drawn with the staff. Gypsum, most commonly found in drywall, was a great catalyst for my spell circle. Its fine powder bonded well with the ground.

"*Sphaera*," I said, after stepping over the white border. The translucent barrier popped up around me as I sat, crossing my legs and assuming a classic lotus position. For me, meditation was a critical recovery tool and sitting in the middle of a spell circle was a great way to guarantee I wouldn't be interrupted.

My thoughts flicked back to Gabriella and I pushed them

away. The attack at the morgue took another forceful push, but my mind refused to quiet. Images of Victoria Barrios slumped at her front door and thoughts of Clarita being kidnapped jumped to the forefront. I pushed away the distractions and dropped into a deeper meditation. Finally, my spirit relaxed and my connection with the earth strengthened. An hour later, I opened my eyes, recharged.

"*Finis.*" I dropped the circle and stood, stretching stiff legs.

The trip to the morgue hadn't been a complete waste. My current theory was that Shaggy was either holding Clarita or worked for whoever was. Either way, he knew where she was. I slipped my jeans off and laid them out on the granite slab, inspecting the right leg where I'd kicked Shaggy. The dark blood stain stood out on the worn fabric. I'd like to say I'd kicked him when he was down just to collect the blood, but that would have only been partially true.

I folded the fabric of the jeans, laid them across my copper pot and looked beneath the counter. The chemist's wash bottle was right where I'd left it, next to my griffin beakers. The police had either missed these or dismissed them as uninteresting. Not having ready access to running water in the lab was one of my only complaints about the space. I'd solved the problem by stocking glass jugs of spring water, one of which I pulled out, partially filling the wash bottle.

A spray of water across the bloody crease in my jeans yielded a satisfying pink stream into my cauldron and I adjusted the jeans to collect as much blood as possible. In the end, I collected half a cup of the pink-tinged spring water. I separated the fluid into three specimen jars, complete with runic inscriptions and a preservation enchantment on two of them. The third I'd be using more immediately.

The next problem I needed to solve, however, was that of storage. The last batch of Lozano's blood and what I'd hoped was Shaggy's had been lost to an ill-timed search warrant. The niggling question in the back of my head was whether the missing samples had been the real reason for the search. Other items in the lab had been broken or destroyed, but not much else had been taken. I was going to do my best to make sure these samples were around when I needed them. The protection enchantment I wanted to use on the extra jars required a chameleon's tail, something I didn't have. For now, I placed one of the jars on my shelf and hid the other in the garage's open attic, atop a piece of well-weathered plywood.

I placed my spell book next to the cauldron. I remembered most of the steps for the locater enchantment, but I'd ruin my blood sample if I missed a step so I set about scraping, cutting and powdering the components I needed. I was missing two ingredients and as I worked I considered how I might get them. The answer was as close as Mrs. Willoughby.

Leaving the burner on low heat, I ducked beneath the garage's overhead door. It was only five thirty, so I wasn't worried that she might be asleep as I knocked on her back door. The smell of fresh baked bread and the sound of a loud T.V. reassured me of her presence. It took several tries before she finally answered the back door.

"Felix. I wasn't expecting any company tonight," she said. "Come in, come in." She stepped back into her kitchen and looked up at me expectantly.

"Hi, Mrs. Willoughby. I'm sorry to bother you, but I have a splinter and was hoping you would have a needle I could use to remove it," I lied.

"Oh, dear. I'm afraid my eyes aren't as good as they used to be, but I can try," she said.

"No, no. I can do it, but it's in there good. I just don't have a needle."

She walked to the kitchen counter and pulled open a stubborn drawer. "Yes, I've one right here. Are you sure you don't want me to give it a try?" She held out a needle in her shaky hand. I noticed she had an abrasion on the back side of her hand as I accepted.

"What happened there?" I asked.

"Oh that? Clumsy me. I touched the side of the oven," she said.

"It looks painful."

"It will heal," she said. "When you get as old as me, you learn to accept life's small setbacks."

Her statement made me feel guilty for being one of her life setbacks.

"I've a cream that would make that feel better. Would you mind if I got it for you?" I asked.

"I put butter on it, but all that does is get the attention of Chelsea," she said. As if on cue, a gorgeous black cat nimbly jumped onto the counter and stared at me through green eyes.

I frowned. Old wives' tales were rarely helpful. "I don't think butter is the right thing. Hold on, I'll be right back."

"Door will be open, dear. Just come on in," she said, sitting down at her kitchen table.

I pushed the needle into my shirt like I was pinning on a flower and ran up to my apartment. Mrs. Willoughby was a frail old woman and it made me sad to think she didn't have anyone looking after her. I scraped a few applications of the salve Judy taught me to make into a container with a clean wooden tongue depressor. Growing up with a big-hearted witch had impressed upon me the value of helping others. The kid in me wished that somehow Judy would know I was helping Mrs. Willoughby.

I knocked on Mrs. Willoughby's door and pushed it open.

"Hello. I'm back," I said loudly. She'd invited me, but I felt a little weird walking into her house, unannounced.

Mrs. Willoughby was petting Chelsea, who was sitting comfortably in her lap at the kitchen table.

"Have you had dinner, Felix?" she asked.

"Not yet, Mrs. Willoughby," I said, sitting down at the kitchen table next to her. "I'll probably have something simple in my apartment."

"Nonsense, I just made fresh bread. It's cheating, really. I used my bread maker. It's not as good as I used to make, but it's close," she said.

"Could I see your hand?" I asked.

"You needn't bother, Felix," she said.

"That wasn't how I was raised and you really shouldn't put

butter on a burn," I reprimanded lightly.

She nudged Chelsea from her lap and laid her hand on the table between us. Her thin skin made the burn appear worse than it was.

"I'm going to put a bandage over this, we shouldn't let Chelsea lick it. I don't think the salve would be harmful to her, but you never know," I said.

I placed the small container on the table, dipped my finger into the greenish mixture, dabbed it onto the open sore and covered it with the bandage.

"You've a healer's touch," she said.

I smiled. "I'll leave this with you. Apply it every morning," I said as Chelsea jumped into my lap and thrust her face toward me. I'd been around enough cats to know she was inviting me to give her jaws a good scratching, so I obliged.

"At least take a few cookies with you?" she asked.

My stomach growled loudly in response. I didn't think she'd heard it, but the cookies sounded good.

"That sounds good," I said.

"There's a bag in the freezer, take the whole thing. I'll make more in the morning."

"Are you sure?"

"They're just cookies, Felix. Of course I am," she said.

I wasn't turning down cookies twice, so I opened the freezer door and grabbed the bag, pulling a cookie out and offering it to her.

"Not before dinner for me," she said.

"Thank you, Mrs. Willoughby," I said.

"Call me Katherine."

"I'll check on you tomorrow to make sure that salve is working. Okay?" I asked.

"As you wish," she said.

By the time I'd walked the twenty feet to the garage, I'd already polished off two cookies. The bump in blood sugar was very welcome.

Back in the lab, I pushed the needle through a wine cork I'd retrieved from my apartment. I picked several of Chelsea's black hairs from my shirt, dropped them into the cauldron and then poked my finger with the corked needle, spreading a few drops of blood on the end.

I incanted *"Inveniet"* as I dropped the cork and bloody needle into the mixture. A puff of white smoke slowly escaped the cauldron. After pouring the enchanted liquid back into the specimen jar, I set it on the granite counter. As the contents settled, the cork rose to the top and the needle spun in a circle, finally coming to a rest. I'd become the proud owner of a one-of-a-kind Shaggy compass.

The crunch of tires on gravel and the flash of headlights breaking through the small cracks of the overhead door alerted me to the arrival of a visitor. I quickly pulled my jewelry on and checked the Shaggy compass, which pointed northeast, and more importantly away from the driveway.

Banging on the plywood preceded the sound of Joe Lozano's voice. "Slade. Open up, I know you're in there, I see your lights," he called out.

"Just a minute."

I turned off the burner, pushed my spell book under the counter, jammed a stopper into the jar containing the Shaggy compass, and stashed it in my pocket. I looked around for anything incriminating and didn't find it.

At his insistent banging, I lifted the overhead door, ducked under and lowered it before Lozano could figure out I wasn't moving the plywood on the side door. I didn't want to give him a chance to enter the lab if I could help it.

Lozano looked even worse than he had the day before. He stunk of booze, his eyes were bloodshot and he looked like he hadn't shaved for a week.

"What's happening to me?" he asked, grabbing the lapel of the light coat I was wearing.

"Joe. Stop. We can't talk out here," I said.

"What?"

"Have you talked to your grandmother?"

"She's just a crazy old woman." The smell of alcohol wafted freshly across my nose.

"Get in," I said, pushing him toward the passenger side of his black, four-door pickup.

"You're not driving my rig," he said.

"What? Things aren't bad enough? You want a D.U.I. on your record?"

He grumbled something, but complied, opening the passenger side door. I climbed into the driver's seat and adjusted the seat back. He picked up a bottle of cheap whiskey from the center console and took a swig. "Want to get caught up?" he asked.

I shook my head, started the truck, put it into reverse and turned around to look out the back window. A lump formed in my throat at the sight of two kid's car seats.

"Where does she live?" I asked, heading toward downtown.

"You're going in the right direction," he said. "Now talk."

"How about we start by you telling me what you remember," I said.

"No damn way," he said.

"I'm going to take a guess. If I'm right, you have to tell me everything," I said, not waiting for him to agree. "Friday night you felt sick, probably didn't go to work. The next thing you remember is waking up, not in your house, naked, miles from home."

"Who put you up to this?" he asked. "Did you do something to me?"

"I'm not through. You had blood on your hands and fur or feathers in your mouth?"

He pulled a gun from his waist and pointed it at me, tears running down his face.

"What'd you do? I have a family," he said.

"Put the gun away, Joe. I'm the least of your problems. I'll help you if I can, but I need you to tell me what you know. It's not safe for me to tell you some things," I said.

"Safe? From what? We're in my truck."

"Just tell me."

"Yeah. It pretty much went like you said. I wasn't feeling good, so Jen slept in Sienna's room. I woke up in a ditch next to a corn field, naked. That's not the worst of it. I'd eaten an entire rabbit, guts and all. It was all there when I threw it up," he said. "You know how hard it is to get home when you're naked and ten miles from home?"

"Sounds messed up," I agreed.

He continued, talking in a far-away, monotone. "When I got home. I thought someone had broken into my house. The bedroom was torn up and my partner Sandy was still there talking with Jen. They thought I'd been abducted. I told them about waking up in the field."

"What about last night?"

"I didn't go home last night," he said.

"Slept in the truck?"

"I tried. I had a crazy dream."

"Dream?" I asked.

"I was running through fields, hunting," he said. "I had four legs."

"You're wondering if it really was a dream, aren't you?"

He didn't answer other than to take another long pull on the whiskey. We continued to drive for another twenty minutes, Joe giving terse directional changes until we pulled up to an old farmhouse on the edge of town.

"Don't say I didn't warn you," he said as he jumped out, slamming the door behind him, stalking toward the back door of the dilapidated building. I got out and followed him.

"Josepho. I asked myself who would be visiting Nanna so late in the evening," she said, grabbing his face in her hands. She was speaking a dialect of Spanish that I couldn't place, but her words were easy enough to understand. I chuckled at her reference to the early hour. "And you've brought a friend. No? Come in."

An invisible force stopped me from entering the home, holding me back. Initially, Joe and his grandmother didn't notice and I allowed my spirit to inspect the protection. It was nothing I'd ever come into contact with, but I could sense that unraveling it would not be particularly difficult. I also understood that I would alarm Joe's grandmother if I did.

"What is this? You bring a brujo to my home?" she asked, stopping short and turning toward me.

"Nanna. Felix is like you. He's no witch. He made me come here," Felix said.

"You speak of things you do not understand. Be gone, brujo, or I will cast you to hell," she said. At least she said something close to that. The more excited she became, the fewer words I understood.

I felt an updraft of wind behind me and the familiar sensation of Maggie's claws latching onto my shoulder as she folded her wings and landed.

"Heya, Maggie," I said as she rubbed her beak against the side of my face. I'd always considered it a sign of affection, although it could just as easily have been her way of cleaning rotten meat from her beak.

"Ancient one," Nanna said. "Welcome." She was clearly talking to Maggie, but her barrier dropped all the same. Maggie lifted from my shoulders as I took a step toward the door.

"Come by tomorrow. I'll pick up meat," I called after her.

"Caaw," she called back, but kept flying.

"Sit, Josepho. You are sick, no?" she asked as we entered the well-lit kitchen. "Why have you come to Nanna?"

"Tell her, Joe," I said.

"Tell her what?"

I slid the wide silver ring from my left ring finger. I held it out for Nanna to inspect, but didn't give it to her. She looked warily from the ring back to me.

"Hold your hands out, Joe," I said.

He shook his head, but made a cup with his hands and held them out anyway. I dropped my ring into his outstretched hands. For a moment, he let it rest there, but no more than twenty seconds later, he dropped the ring to the floor, shaking his hands out as if they had been burned.

"Josepho, what is this about?" Nanna asked, leaning over to

pick up the ring, turning it over in her hands.

"He was bitten," I said.

"Hombre lobo," she said, not asking. "Did you turn?"

He sat heavily in a kitchen chair. "I... I don't know. Yes. Maybe."

"Does Jennifer know?" she asked. When she said the name it sounded more like yennifer.

"He didn't go home last night. I'm sure she's worried about him. He changed last night too," I said.

"What is your role in this?" she asked.

"I was there when he was bitten, but could not help him."

The old woman shook her head. She'd seen too much in her long life. "There is no medicine for the lobo."

"Talk to me, Nanna. What are you saying?" Joe asked.

"We must talk, Josepho," she said.

"The wolf who bit you was a werewolf, Lozano," I said. "Nobody broke into your home, but you already know that. It was you, Joe."

"I thought werewolves only changed at a full moon," he said.

"Hombre lobo learn to change at will," Nanna said. "But you will lose your soul to the lobo. Josepho, you must leave before this happens, for the sake of your family."

NO REGRETS

I'd left Joe to talk with his grandmother, choosing instead to sit on her front porch. The conversation had turned into a train wreck and I didn't have anything to add. Her assessment, while cold, was exactly what I'd come to understand – there was no such thing as a good lycan. The romantic notion of a noble beast, struggling against his inner rage, calmed by the damsel, didn't jive with the limited reading I'd done. I'd hoped that Nanna, being a Virarica Shaman would have some ancient wisdom. Turns out, she did. It just wasn't what either Joe or I wanted to hear.

The back door of the old house slammed open and Joe's angry voice yelled something I didn't recognize. I got up and jogged over to the gravel lane only to see Joe's truck accelerating out of the drive onto the asphalt highway. Without so much as a look in my direction, he tore down the highway, abandoning me at his grandmother's house.

I looked over and saw Nanna standing in the doorway backlit by the weak light of her back porch.

"What happened?" I asked, walking up to her.

"He is upset," she said.

"Right. You know of nothing that can help him?" I asked.

"It is too late for Josepho," she said. "Hombre lobo does not care for the character of his soul. It will devour everything within him."

"I can't believe you're giving up on him," I said. "He's your blood."

"He is not my blood. If he were, he would be dead," she said.

"Explain that?"

"Stupid brujo. It is your kind who created the lobo and now your creation has turned on you. Be gone and do not return," she said and slammed the door between us.

Not only was she unwilling to help Joe, but she wouldn't even explain the simplest detail of what was going on. So far, I was batting a hundred percent at finding jackasses in this town. It completely flew in the face of my experience with Judy and the girls. Geez, I missed them.

I pulled out my phone and was gratified to find plenty of service bars here on the edge of town. I pulled up a car-service app and punched in Nanna's address. A thirty-minute wait and thirty-five dollars would bring someone to out, eventually.

The headlights of a sub-compact approached and sped past just as I was getting cold. The driver hit the brakes and turned around a hundred feet after passing me. I climbed into the tiny back seat and had to push fast-food trash out of my way. I'd wondered why the driver had a low rating, but this far out in the country, I was just glad someone agreed to come for me.

"Felix Slade," I said, giving a quick wave to the driver.

"Angela Feland. Friends call me Angel," the woman replied. I returned her smile in the rear-view mirror.

"Thanks for coming so far out. My ride took off without me."

"Better fare coming out here and my little pony gets great mileage," she said, patting the dashboard. I followed her hand. The dashboard was covered with small plush toys – dragons, unicorns, squirrels and bunnies. "You've long legs, I'll pull the seat up for you." She leaned over the center console and wrestled with the chair, finally getting it to move.

"Thanks," I said, stretching my legs out as much as the tiny vehicle would allow.

"We'll get you home in a jiffy."

My phone buzzed and I pulled it from my pocket. I'd received a text message from Amak.

AMAK: We need to talk, Rose and Crown pub, midnight.

FELIX: What's up?

AMAK: Not on phone. Drinks on me.

FELIX: See you there.

"Angel. Do you know where the Rose and Crown pub is?" I asked.

"Sure. You want to go there?"

"If it's not too much hassle," I said.

"You're the boss."

She pulled up to the bar about eleven thirty. Rose and Crown was in a two story yellow and green painted brick building with parking lot on all sides. Loud music spilled from the open front door and copious amounts of smoke rose from an outside terrace. I looked for Amak's Jeep, but from the back of the tiny vehicle I wasn't able to locate it.

"Thanks for the ride, Angel," I said, approving payment for the ride and giving her a five-star rating.

"I'll be around if you need a ride home," she called after me as I closed the door.

I thought it a good sign that I recognized the music spilling from the front door as I walked in. I hadn't even made it to the bar when something brushed my butt and a hand snaked around my waist. I wasn't surprised to see Amak had sidled up next to me.

"Showing up early makes you look eager," she purred into my ear, swaying her hips and bumping them into me as she steered me toward the bar. Her visage was back to the tall, sultry human and her light brown hair was cut close to her neck with a long wave pulled across the front. She was wearing high leather boots and a simple, sleeveless dark brown leather dress that barely made it to mid-thigh. I found it ironic that a troll projected a sense of style well beyond any capacity I might have.

"You had me at free drinks," I said.

She laughed and backed down on the slutty a little. "Hah, you're not such a stiff after all. What are you drinking?"

I smiled. "Irish Car Bomb."

Amak did a double take, and then turned to the bartender, a tall woman in a knee-length, frilly red dress, complete with corset. "Make that two, Rose," Amak said, voice raised.

"I see you found a kindred spirit, Amak," Rose replied as she started drawing a Guinness into one of two tumblers she'd set on the bar top.

"He's just flirting," Amak said. "You know how boys are."

Rose adjusted her corset and smiled. "I sure do." She finished the drinks off by dropping a double shot glass filled with whiskey and Irish cream in the center of each stout.

"Down the hatch, kids," Rose said, sliding them across the bar.

Amak knocked her glass against my own, slopping the whiskey and Irish cream into the Guinness. The drink was well named because as soon as the alcohols mixed they started blowing up. I was ready and tipped the glass back, catching the shot glass against my teeth as I finished it off. It burned all the way down, but in the best kind of way.

"Well, hell yeah!" Amak said, slapping me on the back.

"Something for the table?" Rose asked, smiling as I wiped tears from my cheeks.

I glanced at the rows of alcohol behind her, but my eyes were still watering. "Midlist scotch on ice?"

"Make it a double. Vodka cranberry for me." Amak led me to a table where three twenty-something men were seated, watching us approach.

"Heya, sweets," the largest of the three said.

"Beat it," she growled menacingly, her visage slipping momentarily as she did.

"What the heck? She's a monster," one of them said. The noise in the bar was such that I didn't think anyone else had heard, but it wasn't the sort of attention we needed.

"Hey, that wasn't nice," I said. "Maybe you should call it a night." I used my influence and pushed the suggestion at them.

They looked at each other and one by one stood up from the table. The big guy nodded. "Yeah, sorry, we were just leaving anyway."

"My hero." Amak flopped down in a newly vacant chair, her long legs proudly displayed as she put her feet up.

I took a seat next to her and tipped it back against the wall. "So what'd you want to talk about?"

"I thought you were just here for the drinks," she said.

A waitress set drinks down in front of us and picked up the previous occupant's empties, frowning at the lack of tip. I'd have rectified the tip situation, but I'd burned all my cash at the morgue.

"Right you are." I picked up the scotch and sipped it. The two shots in the car bomb were going to my head. I rested my head against the wall and closed my eyes.

"Isn't Rose great?" Amak asked. The table she'd chosen gave us a good view of the bar. Indeed, Rose was slinging drinks and chatting people up at a manic rate.

"Wait. Is she a...?"

"Her mom and mine are cousins," Amak said.

"Kinda bigger around the... you know... upstairs," I said.

"She's pretty, though, right?" Amak asked defensively.

"Sure. But, I'm probably not the right one to ask," I said. I immediately knew I was oversharing, but such was the nature of me and drinking.

Amak spun toward me, her face losing the witch's glamour. Fortunately, drinking had an additional 'I could give two craps' benefit for me and I just looked back passively at her gray face. Her brown hair had shifted to jet black and her forehead was a little higher. Probably the most prominent changes were the two tusks sticking up an inch from her lower jaw, dimpling her upper lip where they rested. Oh, that and her long, pointy ears.

"You got a problem with troll girls? You saying we can't be pretty!?"

Several people turned toward us, Amak's explosive tirade grabbing their attention.

I shrugged. "Sensitive much?"

"I thought you were gonna be cool, Slade, but you're just another bigot like all the rest of 'em," she said.

"Amak, you're drawing attention," Rose said. I hadn't even seen her leave the bar, but here she was.

"Slade here say we ain't pretty," she said.

"Pull it together, Amak." Rose pushed, her own glamour fading as she did. "If Felix Slade has a problem with us, that's his problem."

"I'm starting to think that pretty troll girls listen about as well as pretty human girls," I said. "And, by that I mean, not very well."

"Wait, what?" Amak asked, her face morphing back to strictly human.

"You asked me if Rose was pretty and I said I wasn't the right one to ask."

"Damn. Stop twisting your words. Say what you mean already," Amak said.

"I don't like the glamour. Sure, you fit the mold of what people say looks right, but it's too fake for me. What's wrong with those little tusky things? I kinda like 'em. Tough and cute all at the same time," I said. I really wished I had a better governor on my mouth when I was drinking. "And Rose, all I was saying was that, you know, all the pictures of trolls I've seen are skinnier on top. Nothing small there about Rose. I think you're both sexy as hell."

I slapped my hand over my mouth. Drinking didn't explain what I'd just said. Sure it was in my mind, but I don't care how much I'd had to drink. I just didn't talk like this.

"What was in the drink, Rose?" I asked.

She leaned into the table and planted a wet kiss on my cheek. "Nothing much, dear, just a little something to help loosen you up. I have to say, you should speak your mind more often." She turned and sashayed back to the bar.

"What do you want to know, Amak?" I wanted to get the inquisition out of the way. I'd known something was up when she'd called and offered drinks. Nothing in life was free, but after the weekend I'd had, I didn't mind that much. Not like I had anything to hide.

"I want to talk more about how you think I'm sexy," Amak said. "But, I'm supposed to ask about what happened at the morgue."

"How do you know about that?" I asked.

"We have someone there."

"Jeffery?"

She nodded.

"Yeah, well, you might be careful with that one. I think he might be working with a lycan I call Shaggy."

"Jeffery blames you. He said you busted the place up," she said.

"What were you doing there?"

"How do I know you're not on the wrong side of this?" I asked.

"I might be if you've got anything to do with the Whyte Wood Coven murders," she said.

"Why not ask Gabriella? She was there, too," I said.

"There's a lot of distrust between council members right now and nobody's sharing information with anyone."

"Who are you working for?" I asked.

"I report to Camille, but I get a lot of my orders from Liise Straightrod. You showing up caused quite a stir."

"Me? What do I have to do with it?"

"You don't think it's strange that a month after a wizard arrives in town, witches start getting killed?"

"You've been tracking me that long?" I asked.

"When Straightrod found out, she wanted to have you dumped in our dungeon right away. She said that you'd come to town to make trouble. And this was before Victoria Barrios was murdered, and before she knew you were a wizard," Amak said.

"How is that possible?" I asked. "I'd never heard of her before last week. Same with the Barrios family."

She raised an eyebrow. "You seem to be telling the truth. Let me ask directly. Are you making a play for Leotown? Is that why you came back?"

"I don't even know how someone makes a play for a city. My only skin in this game is finding that little girl who was caught in the crossfire." I was shading the truth, but whatever Rose slipped me allowed for it. Even though Gabriella and I weren't in a great place, I still held onto the feeling I'd had in the vision.

"Great." She looked relieved. Her glamour was fading, her eyes had lost their bright blue, dissolving to a muddy green and her hair was black again.

"Your spell. It's fading," I said.

"Nah. That's just you. Magical types eventually see through it if they're around me long enough," she said. "You haven't answered why you and the Whyte Wood witch were at the morgue."

I took a long drink from the scotch. I had to work to get the liquid around the single round ice cube.

"Not that big of an idea. I wanted to see if Clarita's mom's corpse had any residual of Shaggy under her fingernails," I said.

"Grisly work for a human," she said.

Rose appeared at the table, fresh drinks in hand. Her glamour faded enough that tusks jutted up from her lower jaw. I wanted to touch them, but fortunately had enough restraint to stop myself. She smiled at me, knowingly.

I returned her smile, wondering if her drinks also lowered my inhibitions. I picked up the fresh scotch, not really caring – a warning signal I completely missed.

"Thanks, Rose," I said and turned back to Amak. "We didn't get that far. Shaggy and crew interrupted us a couple minutes after we arrived."

She raised her glass to her second cousin and nodded appreciation. "Did you get your sample?"

"We were interrupted," I answered. I could feel the drink's affect trying to push me to answer the question more accurately.

"Wonder why Straightrod has such a stick up her ass for you?" Amak asked.

I sniggered then asked. "Did she put you up to this?"

"Drinks? No. That's Camille. Straightrod's on her shit list, too."

"You think this will get me off Camille's list?" I asked.

"Can't hurt. Best I can tell, we're on the same side on this one. You feel like dancing?"

"Not sure I'm in your league, but I'll give it a go," I said.

She grabbed my hand and dragged me into the middle of the floor where there were dozens of others having a good time. Amak was an amazing dancer. I suppose it had something to do with the fact that she was nearly a foot taller than me and had the grace of a ballerina. Pictures of trolls and actual experience with trolls were two completely different things. The pictures from the Benedictine monks showed dumb animals, with overemphasized eyebrows and snarling faces. Amak, with her hands raised high, twisting and turning in front of me was about as far away from those pictures as a being could be. She was unbelievably seductive, her narrow chest leading down to a small waist that flared out to wide hips and solid legs. If she had an ounce of fat on her, it was covered by her leather dress.

"You're staring, Felix," she purred as she wrapped her long arms around me and pulled me in close.

"Hard not to," I said.

"You know, that drink Rose gave you breaks down your inhibitions. You might end up hating yourself if you keep hanging around with me," she said.

I felt the truth and the lie in her words. No doubt, I was still riding high from the drinks. I couldn't imagine myself acting this way otherwise, but it wasn't all that. There was no denying my attraction to her non-complicated personality. I could feel her trying to put some distance between us.

"Been a pretty shitty day, Amak. Gotta be honest, you've been the best part of it," I said.

She leaned in to kiss me on the cheek and I turned into it. I suspected I was going to hate myself in the morning, but hell, in for a penny … Besides, even if she was a troll, she was crazy hot. I saw surprise in her eyes as we made contact, but she didn't hesitate and her hands came around to rest on my butt. We continued this way for the better part of twenty minutes, finally returning to our table, where fresh drinks waited.

I tipped the chair back again, resting my head against the wall and grabbed her hand. "I like you better when you're not beating on my cell door with a stick."

"I try to tell 'em you get more flies with honey, but nobody listens to the troll girl," she said.

I laughed. I knew she'd been sent to get information from me, but I felt I could read her. She lacked guile and I couldn't find it within me to condemn her for that. Besides, I argued with myself, it seemed like we were on the same side in all this.

"Want me to give you a ride home?" she asked.

"Either that or I can call my Angel. She said she'd come and fetch me," I said.

"Gabriella?"

I scoffed. "Red? No. Car service lady. I think we had a real connection." I drained the last of my scotch which didn't help the buzzing in my head.

Hopefully, Amak was in good enough shape to drive. She'd kept up with me drink for drink, but something told me she metabolized alcohol much faster than I did.

I woke the next morning to a pounding headache and the sound of banging on my plywood front door.

"Oooh," I groaned and tried to roll over. A heavy arm lay across me and I picked it up, recognizing the dark purple nail polish that Amak had been wearing the night before. I twisted my head too quickly, which sent fresh pain lancing through my eyes.

Amak's eyes were open and she was studying me.

"Shit," I said.

"I knew it," Amak said, pushing off from the bed. She was completely naked and, man, was she a sight. Her abs rippled as she stood and looked for her clothing.

The loud banging at the door continued.

"Did we?" I asked.

"Yes. Don't say it though," she said.

It caused me immeasurable pain to slide to the side of the bed, but my brain caught up with what she was thinking. I grabbed her arm as she leaned down to grab her leather dress from the floor.

"Say what? That you're ridiculously hot?" I asked.

"Don't try to take it back, Slade," she said. "I heard you."

"Shit just means I woke up and didn't remember anything. It's not like I have visitors very often. I'd sure like to remember it."

She looked at me, mistrust in her eyes. "You mean that?"

"That and what the hell was in those drinks? My head is pounding," I said. "It was an all-purpose, 'Oh-Shit.'"

I pulled the reluctant Amak onto the bed next to me and yelled, "Hold on!" at the front door.

"It's just that this is where I typically get the boot," she said.

I looked up into her face, inspecting my feelings. Beyond the drinks, I didn't feel any regret. I wasn't sure where last night put our relationship, but I wasn't about to ask her to leave, especially as vulnerable as she seemed.

"Let me see what's going on out there and then maybe we could get some breakfast," I said.

She grimaced. "You don't have to do that."

The knocking continued. This wasn't doing my hangover any favors.

"That's your call, but I hope you stay. If I don't get this door, my head's going to explode."

She grinned.

I pulled my jeans on and a t-shirt from the floor and made my way to the front door. When I pushed open the plywood, I wasn't overly surprised to see Red standing there.

"Hey, Gabriella. What's up?" I tried not to sound hostile, but wasn't sure I'd succeeded.

"Can I come in?" she asked, stepping forward, pushing me back.

"Uh, sure. Come on in."

"I just wanted to explain about yesterday," she said. "I should have told you about Brian."

"Who's there?" Amak called as she exited the bathroom. She'd pulled on one of my shirts and a pair of my jeans, which she'd rolled up to look like capris. I shook my head. I might not ever be able to wear those jeans again now that I knew what they could look like.

"Amak?" Gabriella asked, looking over to me. "Are you fricking kidding me?"

YARN AND A COMPASS

"You slept with a troll?" Gabriella hurled the question at me. "Have you no self-respect?"

My mind whirled, looking for a snappy comeback and finding nothing. Amak covered the distance between the bathroom and Gabriella in a flash. We were headed for dangerous territory.

"Whoa, turn down the volume," I said. My head was pounding and I didn't need this blowing up on me. "And a gentleman never tells, but I can say that I woke up warm and friendly-like this morning. What do you want, Red?"

"Hold on. I want to get back to the self-respect thing," Amak said.

"Time to let the adults talk," Gabriella said, placing her hand on Amak's chest. Just like before, Amak's eyes glazed over and the anger left her face. "Now go sit down."

"What the hell was that?" I asked.

"Trolls are lesser beings, Felix. We don't screw the help," she said. "You should be ashamed."

"Ashamed because I took advantage of her or ashamed because she's beneath you?"

"Take your pick, but I'm not arguing about this. I'm on my way to work. I wanted to see if you made any progress on Clarita and if you wanted a ride to City Impound," she said.

"No. I don't need a ride and yes, I made progress on Clarita. I think I can track Shaggy's location. I was hoping we could find where they're holding Clarita," I said. "And for your information, I enjoyed hanging out with Amak."

"How?"

"She's not complicated. We had drinks, danced, and she gave me a ride home. I don't see the big deal," I said.

"I meant - how can you track Shaggy? Your thing with Amak is your own," she said.

I patted my pants pocket and didn't find my Shaggy compass. "Amak, did you see that bottle I was carrying last night?" I asked.

"Check the bathroom." The glazed, blissful look on her face was disturbing. I headed for the bathroom and she called, "It's in the cabinet."

Sure enough, the Shaggy compass was right next to my toothpaste.

"Nice memory," I said when I got back to the living room.

"Like she had a choice," Gabriella said.

"Knock it off," I said. "Amak was more than a willing participant, as you'd know if you've been talking with Camille."

"Not what I meant. She's still under my compulsion," Gabriella said.

"Oh. Sorry. Although I think compulsion is creepy," I said.

"Can we call a truce?" she asked. "I feel bad about letting things get out of hand between us. And you're right, what you and Amak do isn't my business."

"Knock off compulsion spells when I'm around and we'll have a deal," I said.

"Fine." She flicked her hand at the space between her and Amak.

I handed her the jar with the cork and needle floating in the Shaggy tainted water. "I call it my Shaggy compass."

"What's it doing?" she asked.

"Always points at Shaggy. Doesn't tell us where he is right away, but with a map and a real compass, I can figure it out," I said.

"How?"

"Basic geometry. Go to work and I'll have this worked out by later this afternoon," I said.

"Be careful," she said. "Shaggy meant business yesterday."

I helped her back out of the plywood that covered my door.

When I reentered the apartment, Amak was waiting for me. "Thanks," she said.

"For?"

"Standing up for me. Never had a person do that."

"Then you haven't known very many good people."

She shrugged. "The witches aren't bad. They're scared we'll turn on them."

It was too deep of a conversation for my current physical shape. "My head is splitting," I said. "What'd Rose put in those drinks?" I poured two glasses of water, handed one to Amak and chugged my own.

"Did you mean what you said about how you wished you remembered last night, Slade?" Amak asked.

"Do you hang around with very many men? Of course I do, that's mostly the point."

"It's just most men are scared when they see the real me."

"Don't get me wrong. In the dungeon, when you were big and angry, you were scary. In the bar, when we were dancing and you let your guise down – pretty damn sexy," I said. "And my friends call me Felix."

Amak crossed the room and stood close in, definitely invading my personal space. I ran my hand down her long arm and looked up into her face. She'd dropped her glamour and stood exposed. Sure, there were a few things that set her apart from humans, but otherwise, she was just a very tall, extraordinarily fit, woman.

"Is everything a test with you?" I asked. "I'm not flinching here, Amak. I'm not sure what last night makes us, but it feels like you're trying to figure out if I can handle it."

"You're a strange one, Slade. The reason you can't remember last night is because I mixed a little something in your drink to let you forget," she said.

I pushed away from her. "You drugged me? Why? How's that different from what the witches do to you?"

"I don't like how human men treat me after we spend the night. Even though they can't really see me, they know," she said. "It's better for everyone this way."

"If you want to be my friend, you'll let me make that decision for myself. If I'm disgusted, I'd think you'd want to know that."

"Who said anything about being friends?" Amak asked as she

walked back to the bedroom.

"You're just using me?" I asked. "Shit. Two women in the same damn day. I must have sucker written on my face somewhere."

"Must have," she replied as she scooped up her leather dress in one hand and panties in the other.

She'd turned just enough and I reacted without thinking, which given our physical difference wasn't the smart play. I pushed her shoulders and she fell back onto the bed, roaring angrily. I pressed my advantage and jumped onto her, attempting to pin her arms. It was an ill-conceived move, showing how little I understood her strength. With a deft move and the grace of a leopard, she flipped both of us over.

"You have a death wish?" she growled. Her eyes had turned cat-like, something I'd failed to previously notice.

"Feel sorry for yourself, much?" I stared into her eyes with a challenge. So the effectiveness was pretty weak considering the fact that she was now on top of me, holding my arms to the bed.

She let go and pushed off, trying to extricate herself. I grabbed her legs and pulled her back on top of me.

"What are you doing, Slade?" she asked.

"Felix." I reached up and grabbed her waist, pulling her to me. She gave in a little and allowed her hands to come to rest on the bed on either side of my head.

"You really want to do this?"

"Lights on and everything, Amak," I said.

She lifted back up, still sitting on me and crossed her arms in front of her, grabbing my t-shirt and pulling upward, exposing her body from the waist up as she did. I followed the cloth with my hands, running them over her warm skin up to her small breasts. She groaned, tossing my shirt to the side. I pulled her down into a long kiss, tusks and all. Turns out, I just didn't notice them that much. As she kicked off my jeans, I found I could barely contain myself. It had been over a year (at least as far as I could remember) and she was every bit the woman - and then some. I ran my hands over her body, exploring her every curve and as I did, she rocked against me. Whatever mistrust she'd felt dissipated as the morning slipped by.

When we finally separated, I was exhausted and unable to move. Amak lay next to me for a few minutes, then got up and I heard the shower start. I slid out of bed, pulled on my pants for the second time that morning and padded out to the kitchen. I filled a kettle with water, put it on the stove to heat and then pulled out cups, coffee and single serve drip filters. By the time I had water boiling, Amak had re-emerged from the bathroom and was putting her own clothes on.

"I don't have much for breakfast, but I have homemade cookies," I said, pouring water over the coffee grounds and sliding the open bag of frozen cookies across the counter.

"I gotta get going," she said, biting into a cookie.

I wrapped a second cookie in a napkin. "You can take it to go."

"Damn, these are good," she said.

"Landlord made 'em. She's awesome."

"You know I'm going to report most of last night to Camille, right?" she asked.

I chuckled. "I'd like to be a fly on the wall for that."

She smiled back at me. "You're not what I expected from a wizard."

"I guess that makes us even," I said. She raised an eyebrow, but didn't ask for clarification. "Any chance you want to join us hunting Shaggy tonight?"

"You sure it won't piss off your girlfriend?" she asked.

"She's definitely not my girlfriend." I didn't know what to think of Gabriella at the moment.

"That's not what her scent says."

"Don't you have to get to work?" While I found her physical differences to be interesting, her ability to smell people's responses to each other kind of grossed me out.

She tipped the cup of coffee, finishing it in a single swallow and set it down on the counter.

"I do."

I followed her to the makeshift plywood door.

"I'll text you if I free up," she said.

"Later."

I checked the time on my phone. It was nine-thirty. I dialed city impound and talked to a clerk who must have been used to talking to irritated people. Or maybe she just preferred people to be irritated, I wasn't sure which. She obviously knew what I was trying to find out, but made me pose the question three different ways before she gave me a serious answer. I finally learned that if I showed up with three hundred dollars, I could have my truck back.

I fished in my wallet to find Angela's business card and punched her number into my phone.

"Angela Feland," she answered professionally. It worked against the image I had of the woman who'd driven me around.

"Angel. It's Felix Slade from last night. Do you have any availability today? I need to get my truck outta hock."

"Felix Slade. Wonderful. Yes, of course," she said, overly cheerily. "Text me your address, I'll leave right away."

"Perfect." I hung up and texted her my address. I had at least twenty minutes, so I pulled out the 'Taxonomy on Extraordinary Creatures' Gabriella and I had been looking through. I began re-familiarizing myself with what the Benedictines knew about werewolves.

Angel must have been closer than I'd expected, as I soon heard the crunch of gravel and the toot of a car horn. I stuffed my book into a leather shoulder bag and swallowed the rest of my coffee.

"Where to, boss?" Angela asked as I opened the passenger door. I slid the front seat back and sat in the chair next to her.

"I need an ATM and then to the city impound," I said.

She backed up and started down the hill toward the center of town. "Did you have a nice time at Rose and Crown last night?"

"Best time I've had in months," I said.

"You're definitely in a better mood than you were when I picked you up in the country last night," she said with a knowing grin. "I can read auras and yours is brighter today."

She was shading the truth in her statement. No doubt she believed she could read auras, but I suspected not as directly as she was implying. It wouldn't take a full witch to see that I was in a better mood than when I'd left Joe last night.

A few minutes later she pulled over to an ATM and I withdrew the cash I'd need to get the truck out of hock. I was burning through cash at an alarming rate and was tempted to go get my sixty bucks back from that blasted morgue tech.

"Here we are," she announced when we arrived at the gate to the impound lot.

"Looks like it's open this time," I said. "Thanks for the ride."

"Any time." She handed me her phone with a signature box displayed. I checked a nice tip, completed the transaction and worked to disentangle myself from the small car. She drove off with her hand out the window, waving.

The reception area for the impound lot was small and grimy. Nineteen seventies era dark wood paneling, a stained, drop ceiling with fluorescent lights, and the stench of old cigarettes assaulted my senses as I walked in. A heavy man in grease stained overalls sat on a stool behind the tall, chipped counter that separated staff from customers. His attention was on a hidden T.V. mounted beneath the counter, the sound of a laugh track filling the room.

I walked over, stood at the counter and looked at him, not wanting to interrupt his show. He was content to let me hang out indefinitely. I finally lost our battle of wills.

"I'm here to pick up my truck. I called earlier?" I said.

He pulled out a clipboard and handed it to me. "Fill it out," he said. I wanted to slug him. He'd let me stand there for five minutes. I filled in the information and pushed it back in his direction.

"Three hundred," he said, still not looking at me.

I placed the cash on the counter.

He scooped it up and held it, still watching his show.

"I'll need a receipt," I said.

Absentmindedly, he scrawled out a receipt and handed it to me. "Have a seat. We'll bring it right up."

I raised an eyebrow but didn't push it. I was in his domain and didn't need to cause trouble. I sat in one of the ugly orange-cushioned, metal chairs. The smell of things I didn't want to consider assaulted me as I did and I stood back up and paced.

When the sound of a commercial didn't pry him from his chair, I approached the counter again.

"If you give me the keys, I'll just grab it," I said.

"Can't. Insurance," he said, not looking up.

"Forty bucks?" I asked, pushing him mentally.

This got his attention and he looked squarely at me. "You trying to bribe a public official?"

"Look, Hal," I said, reading the nametag sewn into his overalls. "I just want my truck." I wasn't going to point out to him that he was far from being a public official.

He reached under the counter and I readied myself for action. Who knew what this guy might be packing under there. Fortunately, he only tossed my keys onto the counter.

"Leave your money on the counter. I'm just effing with you," he said.

I scooped up my keys, dropped two twenties in their place and walked out the back door into an empty mechanic's bay open to the yard. I scanned rows of tightly-packed vehicles and finally found my truck. Fortunately, it was on the end and not trapped, but I had to climb through the passenger's side to get in. I wasn't surprised to see the contents of my glovebox dumped onto the seat.

Finally, I backed out and made my way to the exit. Hal waved me down as I approached. He'd dropped a bar across the drive. I rolled the window down but didn't turn off the truck.

"What's up?" I asked.

"You're not cleared," he said. "There's a hold on your sheet."

"From who?"

"Doesn't matter. Get out of the truck," he said.

"No," I said. "Who has the hold?"

"That's not how this works." He pulled his puffy brown vest aside showing a pistol in his belt.

I wouldn't be effective pushing him again, so I did the next best thing. I waved my hand, undoing his belt. The weight of the gun pulled his pants to the ground.

"How'd you do that?" he stammered, frightened. I was impressed he actually attributed the action to me.

"I'm trying not to hurt you," I said. "Tell me who put a hold on the truck."

"Don't know. I received five hundred in an envelope," he said.

"Give me my forty bucks and open the damn gate," I said.

With shaking hands, he reached into his pocket and handed me the entire wad of bills. I peeled off forty and gave the rest back. I didn't want anything to do with his money, but I'd take mine back. I gassed my '77 Ford through the gate as he hastily opened it. It was more for show than effect as the truck made a lot more noise, but didn't go much faster. As it was I was frustrated that a little girl had been kidnapped and I had been entirely ineffective in finding her. That, however, was about to change.

First stop was the grocery. I needed food for Maggie. While I was there, I bought a few folding city maps of Leotown, along with a ball of yarn and a package of stick pins. I was disappointed, but not surprised, that I couldn't find a compass. It wasn't the sort of thing that attracted the attention of kids anymore, I guessed.

I ended up driving across town to a sporting goods store to find a compass. Back in the truck, I pulled my Shaggy compass out and set it next to the mundane compass. I wrote down Shaggy's direction and my cross streets. On the way back to the apartment I took several more readings.

By the time I got home it was noon. I pinned a Leotown map onto the wall behind my couch, then placed a pin at each location where I'd taken a reading on Shaggy. To each pin, I tied a six-foot piece of yarn and stretched them out according to the compass heading I'd taken. Individually, the accuracy of each reading wasn't great, but with the number of readings I'd taken, I had a darn good idea of where he'd spent the morning.

After clearing the books from the kitchen table, I spread a second Leotown map out. I circled the area my strings had narrowed and oriented the map to match the mundane compass. I placed the Shaggy compass on top of where my apartment was and pointed it at the neighborhood I'd circled. If the compass moved, he was changing locations. So far today, however, he hadn't.

Part of me wanted to rush right up to where Shaggy was hiding out, but I knew better. So far, I'd barely scraped by on our interactions. I needed to learn everything I could about lycan in order to get the best of Shaggy, but also to see if there was any way to help Lozano.

An hour later, a knock on my plywood front door startled me. I looked first at the Shaggy compass. The needle had moved, pointing more to the north than it had been. It was moving on a slow arc. Shaggy was on the move, but he wasn't at my front door. I checked my phone - four o'clock. The knocking came again.

"Just a minute," I called back.

"It's Andy."

Ah, new doors! I got up and pushed through the plywood. Andy had a quick smile and extended his hand.

"What happened to the door this time? And the garage is really messed up too."

"Police cut through the casing and siding to get in," I said as I peeled the plywood sheet back.

"That's a messed up way to break down a door," he said. "Sorry to say, we're looking at fifteen hundred, give or take."

"I really need it to look good. Landlord wasn't happy," I said.

"Yeah. Damn shame. Kelli filled me in. I can't believe they think you had anything to do with Clarita," he said.

"When can you get started?" I asked.

"Right now. I need half up front, though," he said. "I need to get supplies."

I handed him my credit card. "Just use this. We can square up later."

"You're pretty trusting, Mr. Slade," he said.

"Call me Felix and I'm a pretty good judge of people."

He waved the card at me as he turned back down the stairs.

"I'll have Kelli bring dinner over, that way I might be able to get you closed in by tonight. Back in a bit," he called over his shoulder as he jogged down the stairs.

I followed him down. I needed to check on Mrs. Willoughby. As I approached her door, a pungent smell assaulted me. I crouched defensively and turned slowly. It smelled of lycan, but somehow different - more toilet, less wet dog. Then it struck me. Shaggy or one of his crew had marked this house. My heart leapt into my throat and I lunged for Mrs. Willoughby's door.

TEAM DYSFUNCTION

"What's all the excitement, Felix?"

It had taken Mrs. Willoughby several minutes to answer her back door and I'd been on the edge of breaking it down when she finally arrived.

"You didn't answer. I was afraid..." I stopped talking. I couldn't tell her why I was concerned.

"It just takes me a few minutes to get around is all," she said.

"I wanted to see about your hand," I said. The smell of fresh baked bread wafted out and for a moment I was back in Judy's kitchen.

She smiled. "That's very thoughtful and your timing is perfect. I've just finished baking bread. Would you take a loaf with you?"

She laid her hand on the rickety kitchen table that was no bigger than a card table. I sat next to her and gently peeled off the gauze. The salve I'd applied had soaked in and the burn had lost much of its angry redness.

"That's quite an improvement, Mrs. Willoughby." I gently tugged at the edge of the wound to see how flexible it was.

"That's Katherine, Felix."

I opened the jar I'd left on her table and spread more on the wound. "I need to talk to you about something, Katherine."

"Oh dear, this sounds serious."

"Somehow I've become mixed up in something bad. There are people who are trying to hurt me," I said. "I'm moving out as soon as I can find another home."

"Is it drugs? You're such a nice young man. You shouldn't be getting involved in that sort of thing," she admonished.

"No. It's not drugs and I've not done anything wrong. Promise me you won't let strangers into your home," I said.

"Pish posh." She waved me off with her free hand. "If someone wants to break into my home, they will. I have nothing of value here."

"These people might hurt you to get at me," I said. "Please tell me you won't let anyone in."

"For seventy-two years I've taken care of myself," she said.

"Katherine, please."

"Yes, yes," she said, patting my hand.

"I'll try to find a new apartment by the end of the week," I said.

"You'll do no such thing," she said, giving me a warm smile. "I'll be careful, but you shouldn't run from your troubles. Face your problems head on. They will find you regardless. Might as well be on your terms."

I just sat there, looking at her dumbfounded. She was entirely right. I'd been in reactionary mode, waiting. Katherine stood up from the table and handed me a loaf of bread. It was still warm and uncut.

"You didn't need to," I said.

"True enough, but you didn't need to check on me either," she said. "I knew you'd be coming, so I made an extra loaf. Did your tall friend like the cookies?"

I thought about it for a minute. She had to be talking about Amak. "She said they were the best she'd had in years."

Mrs. Willoughby laughed softly. "Oh, I don't know about that, but it's nice of her to say." She had walked to the back door and was holding it open for me. "Now you get along. I don't want to hear about you leaving until I'm good and ready to kick you out."

I took my cue. "Be careful, Mrs. Willoughby."

Once I was on her back porch, I punched in Gabriella's phone number and headed for my truck.

"Hello, Felix," she answered after the third ring.

"Shaggy's on the move. Are you in a safe location?" I asked.

"I'm about to leave work," she said. "And how do you know he's on the move?"

"I'll pick you up. I might have an idea where they're keeping Clarita," I said.

"I'll text you the address of our condo. Meet me there in forty minutes," she said.

I hung up and dialed Lozano's cell.

"Lozano," he answered.

"You working?" I asked.

"Who's this?"

"Slade," I answered.

"What do you want?"

"I might have a line on the guy who bit you," I said.

"Just tell me where. I'll do the rest," he said.

"Doesn't work that way. He might be holding that little girl."

"I'll be extra careful," he said. I was surprised at the callousness in his voice.

"No. You want a shot at this guy, we do it my way. I don't want any more casualties," I said.

"I could just bring you back down to the station. Lieutenant Dukats figures you're good for the murders and kidnapping. I'm sure we could make something stick," he said.

"Shit, Lozano. I'm trying to help you and you're busting my balls. What's it going to be? You want in or what?" I asked.

The pause on the phone lasted long enough that I started to question if Lozano had hung up on me. He finally responded. "It's... You're right. I don't know what's going on. I just got suspended and Jen said she needs to talk. My whole damn world is falling apart." He sounded like he was about to break.

"Lozano, pull yourself together. We can figure this out," I said.

"How?" The pain in his voice wrecked me. "I'm turning into a fucking monster."

"You can't believe your grandmother," I said. "She doesn't know everything."

"You think there's a cure?"

"No. Maybe. I don't know. Maybe we could find something to help," I said. "You have to fight this thing."

"You suck at this; you know that? If this were AA, I'd be headed to the bar right now," he said.

"You in?"

"Yes. Where do you want to meet?"

"I'll send you a text," I said.

***

"Joe, meet Gabriella. Gabriella, meet Joe," I said as Gabriella climbed into the back of Joe's four-door pickup.

"You think this is a good idea?" Gabriella asked. "I can smell him from here."

"Joe is the officer Shaggy bit," I said. "He's got a lot invested in this."

"Crap. Sorry, Joe, that's a bad break," Gabriella said.

"What are you?" Joe asked. "You have a funny smell."

"Interesting. Does she smell like me?" I asked.

"I certainly hope not," Gabriella answered too quickly.

Joe looked at me, raised his eyebrows and laughed out loud. I hadn't intended to be funny, but it had broken the tension.

"Different, but there are similarities. For the record, you mostly smell like soap, Gabriella, but you both smell like my grandma. Are you a shaman?" he asked.

"Something like that," I said. "We're not supposed to talk about it."

"Or what? You keep saying that. Is there a club? It seems like I'm in it now," he said.

"I'm a witch. Slade's a wizard," Gabriella said. I didn't appreciate her outing me. "And, yeah. Think of it as an exclusive club. One where bad things happen to the families of people who talk about it."

We sat there for a moment as he stared at Gabriella. Finally, he responded. "Are you threatening my family?"

"Not me. And I've never seen it happen, but my previous coven leader has. It's real. Don't mess with it."

"That never works," Joe said. "Only criminals can keep secrets and even most of them can't."

"I'd agree with you, but have you ever heard of a witch who could actually do something real?" I said. "Did your Nanna actually ever show you her magic?"

"No. She's just a crazy old lady," he said.

"You just keep telling yourself that," I said. "The woman I met is a very powerful shaman. And, before you tell us we're all crazy, watch my hand." I ignited a small flaming wizard's ball.

He blinked a couple of times and then remembered to breathe. "What the hell?"

"That's magic, Joe. It gets worse. There are things that go bump in the night and now you're one of them," I said.

"That's not helping," he said.

"You need to take ownership of it, Joe," I said. "If you don't, you'll end up hurting your family, or worse."

He sighed. "At least I know why you smell like Nanna. Where are we headed?"

"Happy Hollow Boulevard and Dodge," I said.

Joe fired up the truck and did a U-Turn, which was quite a feat as his truck was about as long as it could get. As he did, I pulled the compass from my satchel and checked Shaggy's position. We were headed almost directly away from him - a good sign.

Twenty minutes later we'd arrived in a beautiful old neighborhood. There were heavily wooded areas to the west and large, well-maintained homes to the east, and a grassy boulevard separating two lanes of traffic.

"I need more details," Joe said as he pulled through the intersection I'd given him and onto a side street, parking behind an expensive sedan.

"I've been able to narrow it down to this." I placed a map on the console between us.

Gabriella unbuckled and leaned forward to get a better look.

"How did you get this?" Joe asked.

"Magic," I said.

He looked at me skeptically for a long minute, finally shrugging and looking back at the map. "You couldn't dial it in any better than this?"

"No, but Shaggy and his friends ride bikes. They shouldn't be too hard to find in this neighborhood," I said.

"So, what? You want me to drive around and look for a biker

gang on Happy Hollow?"

"Only inside this circle," I said, tracing my finger around a ten block radius.

He picked up his phone and dialed.

"Who are you calling?" Gabriella asked.

"My partner, Sandy. I'll see if there've been any complaints."

Gabriella and I listened to the one-sided conversation. Apparently, Sandy was concerned about his recent behavior and suspension and kept asking Lozano if everything was alright. After several minutes he finally hung up.

"Not a thing," he said. "If they're here, they're keeping a low profile."

I opened my bag and checked the compass. As far as I could tell, Shaggy hadn't moved much. Joe apparently caught what I was doing and grabbed my left arm.

"What's in the bag, Slade?" he asked, which got Gabriella's attention.

I was busted, so I pulled out the specimen jar complete with floating cork and needle. I set it on top of the map.

"I call it my Shaggy Compass," I said.

"What's it do?" he asked, picking it up.

"Points at the guy who bit you," I said.

"Bullshit," he said. "How does it work?"

"It's an enchantment, which is what I do," I said. "Trust me. This thing points at Shaggy."

"He's not lying," Gabriella said. "After the last few days, is it that much of a stretch for you?"

"So what? We just sit here and wait for him to come back?" Joe asked, ignoring Gabriella's question.

"You have a better idea?" I asked. "I'd hoped we'd be able to figure out exactly where Shaggy's hideout was from my map. But, at least we're close. Now, we just need to wait for Shaggy to come back and hopefully follow him to Clarita."

Joe tapped the top of the bottle. "We should just use your little toy here and go grab him."

"And then what?" Gabriella asked.

"Sweat him for the location of the girl."

"Even if we could grab him, he'd never talk," I said. "We've got nothing on him and believe me, he's not going down without a fight."

"I'm a cop. We carry guns."

"Guns don't stop werewolves for very long," Gabriella said. "Trust me."

"Guns stop everyone," Joe said, starting to get hot.

"Let's just wait. See if he shows up," I said. "There's a bar on Dodge. We can wait him out there."

"Fine," Joe agreed, pulling away from the curb.

My phone buzzed with an incoming text.

AMAK: What's the plan tonight?

SLADE: I'm with Gab and Lozano. Headed to Goldberg's on Dodge.

AMAK: Meet you there. Who's Lozano?

SLADE: Lozano's that cop who got bit.

"Who was that?" Joe asked.

"Amak. She's going to join us," I said.

"Another witch?"

"No, but she's in the know," I said. I wasn't about to tell him she was a troll.

"I don't see why you're dragging her into this," Gabriella said.

"What's your problem with Amak?" I asked.

"She reports to Camille. We don't need that kind of attention."

"We aren't in a position to turn down help," I said.

Joe pulled into a parking lot behind the bar.

"You guys going to fight all night?" he asked.

Gabriella opened her door and jumped out without answering and we followed her in through a back entrance. Goldberg's was more upscale than most bars I visited. The place looked like they catered to the dinner and casual drinks crowd more than the late night scene I was used to.

A waitress seated us at a booth and I slid in next to Joe, with Gabriella on the other side. I set the Shaggy compass on the table and used a grease marker to note where it currently pointed. I made another mark, roughly in the direction we'd come from.

"That look about right to you guys?" I asked.

"It hasn't moved," Joe agreed.

"Has a little. If he were close, it would have moved more," I said.

The waitress approached our table and only gave the specimen jar a cursory glance. I suspected she had more pressing things on her mind.

"We're expecting one more." I told her when it got around to me. "She'll have a Bleu Burger and I'll have your Blackstone. Two drafts with that."

"Soda and cranberry," Gabriella requested.

"Two Goldburgers. Tell your cook that I want 'em as rare as he'll go," Joe said.

"What if this compass of yours never moves?" Joe asked once the waitress had left.

"Patience. The compass works, but he might be holed up." I pulled out my notepad and recorded the heading.

"What are you doing?" Gabriella asked.

"That's how I got our current location. I recorded the heading and my location," I said.

"Triangulation," Joe said. "Same principal used to track a perp down with their cell phone."

I waved as I saw Amak enter the bar. She'd changed since I'd last seen her and was wearing form fitting black leggings and a loose dark green sweater. Blonde and lithe in her human form, she got plenty of attention. I stood as she approached the table.

"Seriously, Slade?" Gabriella asked. I wasn't sure what her problem was, so I ignored the comment.

"You mind?" Amak asked Gabriella before sitting next to her.

Gabriella pursed her lips. "Fine."

I heard a low, dangerous growl and turned to see Joe on the verge of coming across the table.

Amak took a step back. "What's going on, Slade?" She'd crouched defensively and was looking directly at Joe.

"Shit. Joe. Stop," I said, stepping between him and Amak.

"What is she?" he asked, through clenched teeth.

"She's a friend, Joe. And, you can't do this here," I said. "Get ahold of yourself."

"She smells," he replied, through the same clenched teeth.

"That's rich coming from you, mutt," Amak answered.

"You want some of this?" he asked.

"Anytime. Anywhere," she replied.

"This is stupid," I said. "We're trying to find a missing girl and you guys want to have a pissing contest?"

"Lycan and troll are mortal enemies. It's in their blood," Gabriella said. "I told you this was a bad idea."

"Knock it off, Joe. I shouldn't have surprised you, but I didn't know it'd be such a big deal." I considered it a good sign that he stopped growling. I slid back into the booth next to Joe and Amak slowly lowered herself in next to Gabriella.

"Aren't we a happy group," Amak said.

"I ordered you a burger," I said, trying to change the subject. "I got two different ones, you can choose."

"I'm sorry. I don't know what got hold of me," Joe said.

Amak nodded, looking at the table in front of him. "Several centuries of war between our people, for starters."

"Camille know where you're at tonight?" I asked.

"No. But I'll tell her if she asks," Amak said. I would have liked her to have said she wouldn't share the information.

"I told you," Gabriella said.

We were rescued by the waitress delivering our drinks.

"I got you a draft. Wasn't sure if you drank beer or not," I said.

Amak warily accepted the tall glass, still keeping an eye on Joe.

"It's moving," Gabriella said. The needle in the glass still pointed roughly south, but appeared to be moving east.

"Neat trick," Amak said. "So fill me in on the plan."

I explained the situation as we watched the compass move. Wherever Shaggy was going, it wasn't toward Happy Hollow.

***

"Talk about dysfunctional teams," Amak said. The two of us had settled on taking the first shift and sent Joe and Gabriella home.

I pulled my jacket closer around my shoulders. "Agreed." The temperature had dropped to forty degrees and Amak's jeep didn't have any doors. "Why didn't we get my truck? I'm freezing."

She pulled a blanket from the back and I gladly accepted it. I vowed to look into spells that would keep me warm as soon as I got a chance. We'd parked near enough to a street light that we could just see the needle within the jar. It had been moving all night.

At around one in the morning the sound of a motorcycle jogged me from my stupor.

"He's close," Amak said, starting the engine, but not turning on the lights.

I looked at the needle. It was swinging from right to left. She turned the jeep around in the street so we faced Happy Hollow Boulevard from the side street where we sat. Two motorcycles crossed in front of us doing thirty-five miles per hour and the needle followed right along with them. I didn't need to prompt her as she turned her lights on and pulled out.

The motorcycles had already disappeared, but that was the beauty of the compass, we didn't need line of sight to follow. We were both surprised as the needle swung wildly to the right as we drove. In the dark and not close to a street lamp, it looked like they'd driven into a heavily wooded area. Not at all what you'd expect from someone on a motorcycle.

"Drive on past. We'll circle back and go in on foot," I said.

Amak nodded her agreement and pulled into another side street. This section of Happy Hollow only had houses on the east side. The west side was a greenbelt that eventually joined with a golf course backing onto Leotown University.

My feet were numb with cold and it felt good to get out and walk. "Right through there," I whispered, pointing at a thickly wooded area. I pulled my phone out and looked at the map.

"What are you doing?" Amak asked.

"Need the address, just in case we have to call the cavalry," I said.

"This way." Amak found a seam in the dense overgrowth. I picked up the smell of engine exhaust, a telltale of the motorcycle's recent passage.

"I can't see very well," I said, stumbling on a rock.

"Hand on my shoulder," she whispered back.

I was surprised at how the urban neighborhood disappeared behind us and how quickly we'd transitioned to dense woods. The canopy of trees above was so tight that little light made it through. I desperately wanted to light up my ring, but there was no doubt in my mind that Shaggy was up ahead. My mind turned with different problems. What if we called the police – would they do something horrible to the girl before we could get to her? What if they had a guard patrolling the forest? What if we didn't find the girl?

WOLVES AT THE DOOR

Dim lights illuminated the eerie outline of a gothic structure - big for a house, small for a cathedral. I had no idea what we were looking at. All the same, I appreciated the small amount of light which made it easier to follow Amak without tripping as much.

Without warning, Amak sank to a crouch and I followed suit. She looked back at me with a finger on her lips, then pointed at her own eyes before pointing at the edge of a multivehicle garage on one side of the mansion. A man stood in shadow next to one of four motorcycles, puffing a cigarette. After a few minutes, he threw his head back and made a big point of sniffing the air. I hoped he hadn't made us already. I wasn't sure that trying to sneak up on werewolves was such a good idea. After a few minutes, he flicked his cigarette onto the ground and ground it out. With a final look, he disappeared around the side of the house.

I tried to see through the arched window openings. Whoever was in the building was occupying the first floor. Dark shapes moved in front of the windows but it was impossible to make out details.

"We've got to get closer," I whispered.

"Make sure your phone is off," Amak answered.

I turned away from the house and pulled my phone out, hiding it inside my coat. I'd missed a message.

GABRIELLA: What's going on?

ME: Shaggy just pulled into a creepy old house. 230 Happy Hollow. It's on the wrong side of the boulevard.

GABRIELLA: Any sign of Clarita?

ME: Not yet. Going in for a closer look. Looks like four lycan.

GABRIELLA: Wait for backup.

ME: Hold on. We're going to look for Clarita first. Don't want to spook 'em.

GABRIELLA: I'm calling Lozano.

ME: Fine.

"Let's go," I said to Amak, turning off my phone.

We crossed through a brick courtyard and stepped over a fallen iron fence, not stopping until our backs were against the cool stone blocks of the house. Amak didn't have to instruct me to remain still as we waited to see if we'd attracted any unwelcome attention. After a few minutes, we cautiously moved along the wall in the direction the werewolf had gone and came upon what was left of a breezeway connecting the garage to the house. If the structure had once been enclosed, it wasn't any longer. Most of the side walls had been cleared away. Only rusty, bent nails and an occasional piece of old wall or window frame hung crookedly from the old support posts, testifying to what used to stand here. The ground was clear except for leaves and masses of vegetation attempting to reclaim the structure.

It was two steps up to a side door, which was in surprisingly good shape. Initially, I felt it was due to the protection it received from the breezeway's mostly intact roof, but when I grabbed the handle, I knew better. The brass handle warmed to my touch, causing a not unpleasant exchange of energy.

"Magic," I whispered as lightly as I could. Amak looked at me with surprise.

I'd never found a lock I couldn't open, so I released the handle and waved my hand across where I suspected the lockset was located. It took me a few tries to home in on the tumblers and they finally moved on my command, but before they were able to seat themselves in their final position they simply stopped.

I tried a second time and experienced the same response. When I grabbed the knob again, it had warmed even more. I was certainly missing something.

"*Altum Visu*," I said, bringing up my second sight. The lock rippled with a warm, blue energy. I found it interesting that the signature was similar, although not identical, to my own. I wondered if that meant this lock had been crafted by a wizard.

Waving my hand again, I followed the progress of the lock's tumblers, this time adjusting for a jog in the mechanical path. I lifted the tumbler up onto a second track instead of allowing it to get trapped on the lower track which was a dead end. Triumphantly, I twisted the knob and swung the door open a fraction.

"*Finis*." I released the planar view.

I hesitated while opening the door, listening for movement on the other side. Once through, I closed the door and the two of us stood in a ten-foot square mud room. Broken shelves littered the slate floor and we carefully picked our way through the rubble.

I pointed to the right and entered the kitchen. It smelled of lycan, although not overly fresh. A breeze wafted in from an adjoining hallway and we crept along, entering an informal dining area that had once been enclosed in glass. Only now, the glass was missing and weeds were encroaching.

The sound of voices ahead caused us to freeze.

"What are we doing here, Brand?" I didn't recognize the voice. "I'm tired of playing babysitter."

"We've lived in worse crap holes." A female voice responded.

"You need to let me get an air-hammer tomorrow, Brand. That kid has no idea how to get through the door," the first voice said. "Maybe the boss will let us off the little shit if we can prove she can't do it."

"Damn it. Let me do her and we can get out of here," the female voice said.

"Nobody's killing the kid. Boss doesn't want her messed up either, so back off." Shaggy's voice was thick with alcohol. "Air hammer is a good idea, though. We'll get one tomorrow."

"You smell that?" It was the first voice we'd heard.

"What?" Shaggy asked, sniffing. "I don't smell anything." I shook my head in disbelief. The smell of stale smoke, urine and wet-dog was so overpowering I couldn't imagine how they could smell anything else.

I heard a noise from the kitchen so continued down the hallway and pushed through a swinging door. I briefly considered taking a staircase on our left, but moved through the dark room, deeper into the house. We hunkered down behind a caved in couch. I pulled out my phone and shot off a text.

ME: Clarita's in the house.

GABRIELLA: Stay put, we're coming.

"Well. What have we here? What kind of idiot troll would walk into a wolves' den?" Shaggy asked, flipping on the light. Amak stood to face him.

"And, it's a two for one sale! I didn't even smell the baby wizard."

"We've already called the cops. Just leave the girl and go," I said, thumbing 911 as a text message to Gabriella.

"Shouldn't take us too long to deal with you two," he said as two men entered from the hallway behind him.

He continued, yelling, "Sue, get the kid. We're on the bounce."

I didn't hesitate as they were bottled up in the doorway. "*Adoleret!*" I threw a thick stream of flame from my charged ruby ring into the center of the group. "On me!" I yelled as I barreled forward, following the flame's path.

Shaggy and one of the other lycan dove out of the way. The third, having been caught in mid-change, received the blast full in his chest. The half-man, half-beast howled in pain as I lowered my shoulder, bowling him over as we ran through. I caught the fleeting view of a woman running up the staircase we'd passed only a few minutes before.

"Clarita's upstairs," I said.

A heavy body crashed into me from behind and I fell to the ground. Amak and Shaggy rolled off the top of me, grappling and focused on each other. I didn't have time to think as the other, still-human lycan, lunged for me. "*Scutum.*" I raised the invisible barrier and deflected him off to the side. He adjusted, twisted and launched over me, landing on his feet.

For a moment, I watched as Shaggy and Amak battled it out, her strength easily a match for his own. I marveled at the speed with which they traded blows, then redirected my attention to my own attacker who'd been just as distracted as I had. He leered confidently and reached into his belt, withdrawing a long knife.

I twisted my right hand and released an old picture frame hanging on the wall. The motion of the large, falling object startled him and he jumped to the side. I used the distraction to move past him to the staircase, which he'd been blocking.

"*Adoleret.*" I fired a smaller ball of flame, which he easily dodged.

"Amak, the stairs," I yelled, backing into the stairwell that led to the second floor. I had no other plan other than to try to find Clarita and hope that help would arrive shortly.

"*Adoleret.*" I flamed off a concentrated cone, trying to conserve my rapidly depleting ring. "*Lucem!*" My silver ring burst forth with a brilliant, white light. Both Shaggy and the other lycan dived for cover, my ruse working as I'd hoped. Their instincts were so finely attuned to danger that they'd mistakenly believed the ring's light was another fireball.

Amak used the opportunity to jump past me onto the stairs. I pulled the door shut and waved my hand across it, snapping the rusted lockset back into place. This was a proud old house with heavy doors and I had some hope of holding both lycan back - until the first body hit. The sound of splintering wood was enough to spur us both to sprint up the stairs.

Two thirds of the way up, I heard the cracking sound of the door giving way. I spun around and launched a fireball down the stairs. A yip of pain and the crash of a body was welcome feedback as I resumed my flight.

"This way," Amak said, turning to the right. She'd transitioned to full-troll mode, her hips and legs wider and thicker. Probably more encouraging was that she'd grown almost a full foot in height and the look on her face was all business.

We dashed down a hallway as the woman Shaggy had called Sue and I'd dubbed 'Daphne' emerged from a room, dragging a terrified child behind her. As soon as Daphne spotted Amak, she tried to violently shove the little girl back toward the room, only succeeding in knocking her to the floor.

I had one good shot left in me, so I launched a cantaloupe-sized fireball slightly off-center of where Daphne stood, braced to fight. She dodged right, turned tail and ran away down the hall. From behind, I heard our pursuers clawing their way to the top of the stairs.

"Back stairs," I said, running up to the sobbing girl. "Clarita, please trust me. Gabriella sent me." I reached down and pulled her up. There was no way to gain her trust in this environment, but I sure as hell wasn't leaving her behind.

"*Scutum.*" I erected a shield in the hallway just as Shaggy and the other two male lycan arrived. It took everything I had to maintain the shield as I held the child and backed down the hallway. Amak placed her hand on my shoulder and helped guide me backward, recognizing my overloaded cognitive functioning.

"How long can you hold that shield, baby wizard?" Shaggy taunted. "Seems that you're running out of gas."

Sweat ran down my face as we continued to retreat.

"Down," Amak announced. "Step now." Her hand braced me as I made the stairs.

I slammed the door at the top of the stairs and flicked the lock, quenching the shield. The relief I felt warned me of the effort I'd expended. I turned and carefully jogged down the steps, the splintering of the door behind us spurring me on.

"Which way?" We'd arrived in a hallway with three doors - one directly ahead of us and two leading back into the house.

A dark wolf sprung from the staircase, ramming into me. I stumbled, falling to a knee as I turned protectively to shield Clarita from snapping jaws. Amak roared in fury. Her long arms grabbed the beast at its nape and she threw it back into another who'd just emerged from the same stairs.

"*Scutum.*" I hastily re-erected my shield, creating a barrier just in time as the wolves sprung.

"We need to come up with something," I said to Amak as she helped me to my feet. "My shield won't last much longer."

"Magic door," the small bundle I carried whispered in my ear, her chest shuddering as she drew breath. I dared a glance over my shoulder. Clarita was right, the arched door was identical to the side door from which we'd entered the house. Salvation was tantalizingly close, but there was no way I could redirect enough attention to open the door.

"I can't, sweetie," I said, "It's too much. Get ready, Amak, this is about to get bad."

The gray female wolf joined Shaggy and the two others. The crowded hallway was humming with anticipation.

"I'm going to enjoy this," Shaggy said as he started to change.

The shield sputtered. My heart sputtered with it. I had nothing more in the ring. Before it failed entirely, Clarita grasped my exposed wrist. Energy surged through my hand, renewing the shield's strength and then some. My shields had never visually coalesced before, but for a moment it appeared to gain the corporeal form of an ancient gladiator's shield. Elation spread through my being as Clarita's spirit joined with mine, something I'd never experienced before. Momentarily, tears blurred my vision and emotion threatened to overwhelm me.

I looked back at the door, wishing my arms were free so I could attempt the lock. I must have communicated my desire to Clarita, because she straightened her legs and slid to the ground. With my right hand free, I manipulated the tumblers, hoping the sequence was the same as the door I'd opened on the way into the house. A mechanical clunk gave me hope and I reached for the door handle. The door swung easily inward, revealing a dark alcove.

"Amak, Clarita. Go, now!" I'd momentarily forgotten I was channeling Clarita's power and was chagrined at the sudden loss of strength. Shaggy saw the opportunity and slammed into the shield, his pack joining him. The force knocked me into the doorframe and down to the floor.

Amak picked me up by my shoulders and pulled me to the side, slamming the door closed and inadvertently pinching off my connection to the shield. The whiplash of the improperly terminated spell washed across me like a violent sandstorm. My head reeling, I tried to stay attentive to the frenzied assault on the other side of the door. Amazingly, the door held fast.

Before my eyes adjusted to the darkness, an iron wall sconce flared to life with a bright yellow flame. It was followed by another sconce several feet down the passage and then another and another. The sequence continued, marching down a curving stone staircase. The whole thing reminded me of my recent incarceration in the witch's dungeon.

"You're trapped and you can't stay in there forever!" Shaggy yelled from the other side of the door, his voice muted. They'd given up on attempting to breech the door, for the moment, at least.

"Are you okay, Clarita?" I asked, ignoring him.

She shook her head to indicate she wasn't okay and held her arms up. I'd spent enough time babysitting to recognize the universal 'pick me up' request, which I honored. The child had to be far from okay. She'd watched her mother murdered and then been terrorized by werewolves.

"Gabriella is coming to help you. Do you remember her?" I asked.

She didn't answer, other than to bury her face into my neck. If it was Judy on the way, I would have been very confident that Clarita would receive much needed support and healing. I wasn't sure, at all, that the witches of Whyte Wood had the same nurturing capacity. Although, to be fair, they had been under extraordinary stress lately.

"Let's see if there's another way out," Amak said.

I followed her down the stairs, still holding Clarita in my arms. At the bottom, the stairs opened onto a stone hallway that had exactly one door. "Hopefully, that's our way out," I said approaching.

The hairs on the back of my neck stood on end as a chill breeze passed behind me. I spun with Clarita still in my arms, trying to identify where the sensation had come from.

"Bad place," Clarita whispered.

I was inclined to believe her and pulled my hand away from the door.

"What's wrong?" Amak asked.

"Something's off," I said. "Clarita feels it too."

Amak raised her eyebrows, but didn't push. "Are you sure help is on the way?"

When I looked at my phone, I found I'd received twenty messages from Gabriella, the tone of which quickly escalated to panic. I hit the redial.

"Felix. Do you have Clarita?" she asked.

"She's with us, but we're trapped in the house," I said.

"We can't find the house. The address you gave isn't real. There aren't any houses on that side," she said.

"It's hard to see. It is on the west side, just down from Davenport, half a block or less."

"Shit. There they go." I could hear Gabriella's voice, but she wasn't talking to me. The sound of the truck's engine accelerating roared in my ear. "Joe. There's another one coming out." I pulled the phone out five inches from my ear as the sound of a collision nearly deafened me. It was followed by the insistent ding-ding-ding of a car door opening while the engine was still on.

"Gabriella, what's going on?" I asked, running back up the stairs.

"Joe clipped one of 'em, but three others got away on their bikes. The one Joe hit took off into the woods and he ran after her," Gabriella said.

"Can you drive the truck?" I asked.

"What? Why?"

"Drive the truck in. There's a house – big... old... surrounded by trees. We need to help Joe, but I have Clarita and I need to get her out of here," I said.

"I'm putting you in the cup holder," Gabriella said, which explained the clunking sound that followed.

I looked at Amak.

"I heard," she said pulling the door open. Apparently, it only locked from one side.

My arms were tired from holding Clarita, but I toughed it out and jogged through the house, exiting into the breezeway.

"I'm going after Joe." Amak said, bounding off into the darkness as bright vehicle lights illuminated the entry. I picked my way across the fallen iron fence and ran over to the truck where Gabriella had already jumped out.

"Clarita, I've been so worried," she said, rushing up and reaching for the small girl. If I'd been worried about Gabriella's bond with Clarita, my fears were now gone. Clarita never hesitated, but turned and latched onto Gabriella, who stroked her hair comfortingly.

"Get in the truck and lock it. There's still a lycan loose," I said. "If it's the woman, it'll be the gray from the morgue."

Gabriella didn't waste any time, but ran around to the other side of the truck, crawling into the passenger's side with Clarita. I backed the truck around and locked the doors. Before I could decide what to do next, the gray wolf ran through my headlights, only to be tackled from behind by a charcoal gray wolf with a white blaze on its chest.

"Crap," I said, jumping from the vehicle. "*Lucem*." I stretched my hand forward illuminating the path the wolves' had taken. I followed the sound of growling, yipping and general all-out chaos.

"We have incoming." I startled as Amak caught me from behind.

"Where?"

"Shaggy doubled back," she said. "We need to defend the truck."

"Crap!" I spun and retraced my steps to Gabriella and Clarita.

We arrived only moments later to find a huge black wolf on its hind legs furiously attacking the passenger side. The truck's mirror was bouncing limply as Shaggy rammed the vehicle's side over and over again. The door's glass wouldn't withstand the battering much longer and I could only imagine the terror Clarita and Gabriella felt within the cab.

"*Rhamno*." I reached with my hand and clawed at the air, drawing roots from the ground to entwine Shaggy's legs.

Peripherally, I saw a shape interrupt the truck's headlights, bee-lining for our position. Amak let out a roar, charged forward and met a red wolf in mid-leap. Their bodies seemed to meld together as they violently collided. Sure enough, the party was now complete. A third, light brown wolf entered the fray. He raced around Amak, intent on mowing me over. I wasn't sure if or how long the vine spell would hold Shaggy, but it no longer mattered. I had to deal with the incoming wolf.

"*Adoloret.*" I fired a stream of fire from my ruby ring, but it gave out almost immediately. Fortunately, it diverted the wolf enough for me to twist out of its way. I was running out of offensive weapons.

"Get out of here!" I yelled, hoping that Gabriella would drive away.

The brown wolf regained his footing and turned back to me, snarling. My mind spun with possible defenses. I recalled that when holding Clarita, I'd been able to cast the shield spell without my ring. I'd filed the experience away, wanting to come back to it when I had time to experiment.

I dared a glance back to Shaggy. I'd slowed him down and he was spending his time tearing at the vines, but he was making progress. Amak seemed to be breaking even. The red and she were still engaged in what could only be described as a 'fur ball' in the full light of the truck's powerful headlights.

I felt, more than saw the brown lunge for me. "*Scutum.*" I instinctively raised the shield, deflecting the wolf. The force of his attack knocked me back onto the bricks of the weed covered drive. The shield sent him sliding across its surface, his snapping jaws passing within inches of my head. I scuttled back as he rounded on me again.

A deep throated howl broke from behind the brown, freezing him in place. I used the distraction to give us separation, choosing to slide my butt on the ground instead of wasting time standing. Shaggy, free from the roots, jumped in beside his pack mate, bumping him to the side possessively. The message was clear. Shaggy had claimed me as his kill.

One glance in Amak's direction told me that she had enough problems of her own and wouldn't be providing any further help. My skin crawled as Shaggy lifted his huge head and howled. If his intent was to intimidate me, it was working. He lowered his head, looking me in the eye, issuing a challenge. I knew I should have lowered my own gaze, but I didn't think it would matter. Shaggy intended to kill and no amount of bowing and scraping would change that.

The brown circled to my flank as I gained my feet and I watched him tense to spring. My time had come. No shield would save me from an attack on both sides. I might deflect Shaggy, but Fred would certainly come in from behind.

"*Adoleret.*" I concentrated on channeling power from the ground through the ruby ring. Time slowed to a crawl as, initially, nothing happened. Shaggy flew through the air, his gaping maw ready to lock on. Too late and too slow, I twisted out of the way when I felt my spirit connect with the earth. A familiar sense of home flooded my body and I pulled at the well of concentrated energy that presented itself. A brilliant stream of flame erupted from my hand and splashed into Shaggy's exposed breast. His snarling turned to yelps as he planted his paws on my chest and sprung away, knocking me over in the process.

I'd never channeled so much energy before. Most of it had come from the energy well I'd discovered and had simply passed through me. My own body's reserves were still depleting quickly. I rolled back to my feet and turned to face the brown, who'd backed off and was snarling from a distance, clearly concerned about being roasted. Shaggy, even though I'd scorched the fur from his chest, wasn't ready to be done and warily paced in front of me, psyching himself up for another attack.

A barked command spurred the brown to action. He rushed from the side, while Shaggy charged. "*Adoloret.*" I fired another impressive gout of fire, sweeping it in an arc that followed Shaggy. I caught his right shoulder and pushed my hands together, palms forward, channeling as much energy as I could summon. My personal reserves drained from my body like milk from a spilled glass. The effort, however, had not been for naught as Shaggy stumbled and dropped to the ground, the remains of his furry coat smoking. While I might have won the battle, I'd lost the war. I had nothing left for the brown. I fell to one knee, completely expended.

It was no surprise to me when huge paws caught me in the back, knocking me to the ground. The fetid stink of dog breath assaulting my nose as he snarled, standing on my back, his mouth inches from my ear. He was communicating domination as he prepared to rip into me.

Without warning, I was flipped over as the charcoal-coated wolf plowed into the brown's side and ripped him from my back. I tried to sit up, but only managed to pull my elbows beneath me. Daphne, the light gray, was back. She placed her paw possessively on my thigh. Her intent was clear. We would wait to see the outcome of this final battle. Shaggy had transformed back to human form and lay naked and unconscious - or dead.

The fight was quickly over as the charcoal wolf pinned the other to the ground, latching his jaws around the brown's neck. For several long moments, the two stood locked together, the charcoal wolf growling menacingly. Finally, the light brown whimpered and relaxed.

"What's the play, Slade?" Amak asked, approaching.

"Not sure. What of the red?" I asked.

"He found my silver blades offensive, I guess," she said, looking at Daphne, who was still pinning my leg to the ground.

"I think the charcoal is Joe," I said. "I'm hoping he can pull it together."

As if hearing me, the charcoal wolf lifted his head and howled. Daphne relaxed and removed her foot from my leg and sidled up next to Joe with her head lowered. The light brown carefully slid out from under Joe, showing the same deference.

"Looks like there's a new sheriff in town," Amak said as the three wolves ran off into the darkness.

The sound of sirens filled the night as police cruisers poured onto the property.

IRREVOCABLE

I lifted my head from the plain steel table as Dukats entered the interrogation room I'd occupied for the last six hours. Turns out the police aren't an ends-justify-the-means organization and my appearance at yet one more crime scene was just too suspicious.

"Do you want to explain this?" The green hanging folder she tossed onto the table neatly slid to a stop in front of me.

"What is it?" I asked, picking it up. Lieutenant Iveta Dukats was a skilled interrogator and I was sensing a 'gotcha' moment.

"You didn't tell me you owned the house where Clarita was being held," she said.

"Maybe that's because I don't," I said.

"That's not how the trust document reads," she said.

I opened the folder. The trust charter was mostly nonsense to me, but there was no mistaking that my name was listed next to several others with a reference to the property at 230 Happy Hollow.

"I've never seen this before," I said. "Where'd you get it?"

"That's not how this works, Slade," Dukats said. She had a severe face, framed by short-cut straight black hair. She leaned across the table and projected an aura of intimidation. "I ask the questions."

"Sounds like I need to talk to a lawyer," I said.

"You're not under arrest, Mr. Slade. I'd just think you'd want to clear your name," she said.

"From what?"

"Two murders, a kidnapping and a missing police officer. You're in this, Slade, I just don't know how deeply. But mark my words, I will," she said.

I wanted to sigh, but instead I took a deep breath. "Look at it from my side, Dukats. You get an anonymous tip that I'm involved in Benita Barrios' murder and then at six in the morning, come up with this paper that says I own the house where Clarita Barrios was being held. Don't you find *that* suspicious?" I stared defiantly back at her, our faces less than a foot apart. "And you got your killer. Haven't you checked his DNA or whatever you do?"

"We're not talking about him. We're talking about you," she said.

A knock at the door broke the tension, although I sensed a flash of anger from her at the interruption. She pushed back from the table and stalked over to the door, opening it a fraction. A young officer spoke in low tones and I watched as she received whatever the news was with sharp nods of her head.

"You're free to go, Mr. Slade," she snapped, turning back to me.

"What's going on?" I asked.

"Officer Lozano corroborated your story," she said. "Understand me, I don't believe in coincidence. You're wrapped up in this and I'm going to find out how. Officer Pandry will escort you out." She opened the door wider and nearly bowled over a young, uniformed officer who had the misfortune to be standing in her way.

I sighed in relief. Joe had figured out how to turn back into his human form, which gave me hope he wasn't the total loss his grandmother believed.

Pandry stepped into the room and placed a manila envelope on the table containing my house keys, phone and wallet. I wanted the document Dukats had shown me, so with a quick twist of my hand, the door handle wiggled. Pandry darted a look at it and as he did, I folded the papers from the file and slid them surreptitiously into the manila envelope.

"Lead on," I said, picking up the envelope.

The floor we were on looked much like any other office setup, manager's offices next to the windows and short-walled cubicles for the worker-bees. I caught Lozano's eye from across the room as I followed Pandry. He looked even rougher than the day before, his beard thicker, his eyes still bloodshot. Dukats and another plain clothes officer had pinned him in a cubicle and were questioning him. I didn't envy the morning he was set up for.

Once I made it to the street level, I pulled my phone out. I had messages from Amak and Gabriella. I dialed Gabriella back.

"Where are you?" Gabriella asked, not bothering with a greeting.

"Downtown at the police station. Lozano just showed up and sprung me," I said. "Where's Clarita?"

"Child Protective Services," Gabriella said. "I'm on my way over to pick her up now."

"Is she going to live with you?"

"I'm Clarita's godmother, Felix. Benita named me as her next of kin," she said.

"Were you that close?" I asked.

"Not really, but Benita didn't have anyone else. Clarita's a great kid and now she needs me."

"Gabriella, I need to say something that's really been bothering me. I'm sorry I freaked out at you about your boyfriend. I pushed something you weren't ready for," I said.

"Where's this coming from?" Gabriella asked.

"You've lost your sisters and now all this with Clarita. I was selfish. I'm sorry," I said. "I took advantage of you in a weak moment and then got mad when it didn't go my way."

"Thank you, Felix," she said. "Just so you know. It wasn't entirely one-sided."

Shit. I totally didn't need her to say that. We had a nice clean break. I'd cleared the air, said my sorries and was willing to leave things alone.

My mind spun with what to say next and I grabbed the only thing I could come up with. "You get breakfast yet?" I closed my eyes, shaking my head at my stupid response.

"Aren't you tired? You can't have gotten more sleep than me and I'm running on two or less," she said.

"Yeah, sorry," I said. "I'm not thinking straight. Call me after you get Clarita back to your house. I want to know you're both safe. Okay?"

"Will do." She ended the call.

I pulled up the car service app on my phone and sent a message to Angel. I didn't think she'd be up and going at six in the morning, but I felt loyal to her. I was surprised when she responded almost immediately, giving me an ETA of fifteen minutes.

I sat on a bench at the bus stop and read my messages from Amak. It wasn't much, other than she'd finally lost Joe's trail at three in the morning and, not finding me, had returned home. I worked at composing a synopsis of what I'd learned and sent it off. For reasons I couldn't immediately put my hands on, I didn't include the information about my supposed ownership of the dilapidated mansion on Happy Hollow Boulevard.

AMAK: Glad you're coming out okay. Feel like dancing tonight?

ME: Not sure. I'm exhausted. Headed home for sleep.

AMAK: Want me to tuck you in? I could be by in thirty minutes.

A small part of me thought that sounded like a good idea, but I knew better. I hadn't been getting much sleep and it was getting to me. At this point, I was just happy I wasn't going to wake up in the drunk tank next to Gorby again.

ME: Not this time, sweet cheeks. I need some real rest.

AMAK: Your loss.

ME: I'm sure I'll hate myself tomorrow.

I must have nodded off as a high pitched car horn startled me awake and I looked up to see Angel. She'd pulled up in front of the bus stop.

"Wakee, wakee," she called through the open window.

I smiled and slid into the passenger's seat. "Wasn't sure if you rolled this early or not. Thanks for coming to get me," I said.

"Only for my best customers," she said, patting the side of my leg. "Where to?"

"Home would be great," I said.

It was a short drive from downtown, but it didn't stop my eyes from closing along the way.

"Are you expecting visitors?" she asked as she pulled up.

A jolt of adrenaline soured my stomach and my eyes flew open. It took me a moment to recognize Andy's work truck.

"Just having a little work done," I said. "Thanks again, Angel. You're a life saver." I gave her a generous tip.

As I approached, I heard the sound of a drill-driver setting screws in the garage. I poked my head in and found Andy hard at work.

"You're getting an early start, aren't you?" I asked.

Andy looked up from his work and held his hand out to shake. "Didn't quite finish last night. Figured I'd get to things before work this morning."

I shook his hand. "All done on the apartment, then?"

He reached into his pocket and handed me a ring with keys and my credit card. "All set. I'll do a final coat of paint before I leave this morning, but otherwise you're ready to go."

"Thanks for getting on it so quickly," I said.

"Kelli said you found Clarita last night. Nice job," he said. "Darn shame what happened to her mom."

Unconsciously, I reached for my tender cheek where I'd been forced into a wall the night before. "Horrible," I agreed.

"Kelli's upset, says she wants to move. You know Benita's mother got killed too," he said. "They was all friends, y'know. Benita, Kelli and Gabriella. Thick as thieves. Got together after work and all that."

"I'm headed up for sleep," I said. "Thanks for getting to this."

"Christmas is coming. Appreciate having the work."

I jogged up the exterior stairs to the apartment and inspected the newly installed door. Andy had done a great job. With a coat of white paint, you'd be hard pressed to know it had been damaged. I waved my hand and opened the lock.

Ideally, I'd have enchanted the door with a shield, but I just didn't have the energy. I flopped on the bed and caught a whiff of Amak's bawdy perfume. I smiled just before passing out.

***

I rolled over and looked up at the ceiling. The October sun was low in the sky and without looking at my phone, I put the time at somewhere after three. I'd slept over eight hours and if not for needing to go to the restroom, I'd still be asleep. I rolled out of bed, did the needful and grabbed the plastic bag with Mrs. Willoughby's frozen cookies. When I got to the kitchen, I turned on the kettle and sat at the table, enjoying the quiet moment as much as I did the sweet cookies from Mrs. Willoughby.

I was surprised to see a text message from Gabriella. I'd figured she had her hands full with Clarita.

GABRIELLA: Still looking for breakfast?

She'd sent the message forty-five minutes ago.

ME: Offer still good? I just woke up.

GABRIELLA: Sure. Chatty Katty's in thirty?

ME: I'll be there. You sure they'll let me in?

GABRIELLA: Yes.

A shower, shave, and fresh clothes gave me a sense of renewed energy. I chose a dark-collared shirt over my standard t-shirt and splashed on a small amount of cologne. I was in dangerous territory, having started something with Amak, but rationalized I was simply going to get something to eat.

With leather coat in hand, I walked out the new door, surprised at how much better I felt after eight hours of uninterrupted sleep and a shower. It couldn't hurt that Shaggy was in jail, either. A nagging feeling that things weren't finished loomed over my afternoon. My visions had always come to pass.

The parking lot next to Chatty Katty's was full and I had to park down the street. Late afternoon seemed an unusual time for a restaurant to be this busy, but I'd agreed to meet Gabriella, so there was no turning back.

"Felix Slade!"

The foyer of the house was packed with people waiting for a table and I heard Mari's voice well before I saw her. Not deterred by the crowd, she maneuvered her way to me and I wondered if we were in for another showdown.

"Gabriella asked to meet me here," I said hesitantly.

Mari's hands shot out and she pulled me in for a warm embrace. Ordinarily, I'm not a hug-an-acquaintance type of person, but part of Mari's magic was the ability to sincerely communicate a feeling of belonging and acceptance. As I returned her embrace, I caught the eye of an elderly gentleman. He looked on approvingly, no doubt enjoying the overflow of Mari's gift. It was no wonder the home-turned-restaurant did so well.

"You do clean up well, my boy. And you smell so good!" She stepped back, holding me by my shoulders. I shifted uncomfortably as we'd become the center of attention for most of the patrons at the front of the restaurant. "The girls are already here. Right this way." She pulled me through the crowd.

As we walked, a fist-sized explosion of colorful lights quietly erupted a foot above a table to my right, catching my attention and slowing me down. The woman at the table clapped her hands together and bowed her head slightly as I passed. I nodded in response as Mari tugged me along. The scene repeated itself as small displays of fireworks lit many of the tabletops along our path and people stopped what they were doing, turning in their chairs to watch our progress.

"Here we are, Mr. Slade," Mari said, louder than I felt was necessary given the amount of attention we'd already garnered. Gabriella stood up and embraced me. As usual, she smelled amazing and was dressed in a dark red sweater that hung over form-fitting jeans.

"Sorry about all that," Gabriella whispered as we separated.

"How sweet," Mari said, beaming at us. "I just knew it."

I looked at her for clarification, but she seemed oblivious, so I sat in the plush bench seat opposite Gabriella and Clarita. Our booth was at the back of the house and looked out at the greenhouse garden in full bloom. I recognized many of the varieties of plants, having used them in my own enchantments. There were even more I couldn't easily identify. For a moment, I envisioned myself in the garden with my shoes off and toes sunk into the rich soil.

"Felix?" Gabriella asked, breaking me from my reverie.

"Yes?" I asked, looking from Gabriella to Mari.

"Mari was asking if you had any special requests. I think Belle might have something planned, however."

"You're welcome to tour the garden, Felix," Mari said. "I know Willow would love to show it to you."

"I'd like that," I said. "And whatever Belle has in mind is great. I'm starving. Thank you."

Clarita shuffled in the chair next to Gabriella and pulled on her sleeve. After a brief, whispered conversation, Gabriella looked from the girl to me. "Clarita would like to know if she could sit by you."

"I'd love it," I said. It struck me that I'd never actually seen Clarita's face before and even now, her long black hair occluded my view. She slumped down in her chair, slid to the floor and crawled under the table, only to slide up into the bench seat next to me. It wasn't lost on me that she'd chosen the side closest to the wall. "Hey, kiddo." I bumped her shoulder with my own and she rested against me.

Gabriella gave me a questioning look. "She's not generally this accepting of people she doesn't know well, but she wanted to see you when she woke up from her nap."

"We're buddies," I said, draping my arm protectively over the girl.

"I see that," The booth lit up with her warm smile. "There must be more to this story."

"A topic for another time?" I asked as I felt Clarita's small hand slide into my own. A spark of energy passed between us on contact. Originally, I'd been surprised that Gabriella would bring Clarita out after she'd been through such a horrible ordeal, but it was easy to see why she'd chosen to come. The witches of Leotown had shown up en masse and their subtle, yet powerful magic of love blanketed us. I was tempted to call forth my wizard's sight to get a better look.

"So, what's going on here? Did I miss a witch's holiday?"

"No, silly. They're celebrating Clarita's return and the capture of Victoria and Benita's murderer," she said.

"It's almost overwhelming. How did they know she was coming?"

"There are few secrets among witches."

Mari arrived and set water, iced tea, and chocolate milk on the table. Her eyes rested on Clarita for a moment before she flitted off just as quickly as she'd arrived.

With my free hand I pulled out the trust charter I'd snagged from Lieutenant Dukats and handed it to Gabriella. "Put your lawyer hat on for a minute?"

"Sure." She took the papers, studied them and set them down when our dinner arrived.

In front of me, Mari left a bowl of chili, a steaming hunk of cornbread and a small glass jar of honey with a wooden dipper sticking out the top. My mouth watered instantly. I would never have picked it off the menu, but sitting in front of me now, it seemed the natural choice.

"Oh, that's good," Gabriella said looking across the table. "You won't believe it's totally vegetarian, too, although not vegan."

Predictably, Gabriella had a salad with a slice of what I suspected was home-made bread and Clarita had a grilled cheese sandwich.

Gabriella handed the papers back to me. "Where'd you get these?"

I had to wait to answer as I'd already jammed a too-big spoonful of the chili into my mouth and couldn't talk. Finally, after a drink of tea, I explained how I'd borrowed it from the file Dukats had shown me.

"You can't always trust what the cops show you when they're investigating," she said. "Sure doesn't put you in a very good light."

"Dukats was quick to point that out," I said. "What I don't get is how I keep getting singled out in this. It's not like I have any ties to anyone here."

"You sure of that? That paper seems to suggest quite the opposite," she said.

I sipped my tea. "I couldn't make heads or tails of it, other than it has my name on it and the address of that old mansion."

"That's only a small part of it. You're looking at an irrevocable trust. Someone set it up quite a while ago and now some trustee is doing what's been ordered," she said.

"Like?"

"Normally, a trust like that is set up to dole out money to kids or keep up a property, but really it could be anything. We'd have to get a copy of it from the trustee to find out," she said.

"How do I go about doing that?"

"I know someone who works at the firm on the charter. Hang on," she said and pulled out her phone, dialing.

As she talked, I picked up Clarita's uneaten sandwich and waved it in front of her face. I'd been a few years younger than her when I'd lost my own parents and I still remembered feeling helpless. The world decided what was best for me and I'd been passed around like so much luggage. If she'd have me as a friend, I vowed I'd be there for her.

"You need to eat. You don't want to hurt Belle's feelings, do you?" I took a risk that she cared about the three witches who owned the restaurant. Clarita shook her head almost imperceptibly, but leaned forward and nibbled a bite from the sandwich in my hand. It must have tasted good because she took it back from me and continued eating. For the first time, I got an unobstructed view of her face, which reminded me of a little Gabriella.

Gabriella gave a surprised look at my having encouraged Clarita to eat and rewarded me with a smile as she talked nonsense into the phone. Finally, she stuffed the phone back into her purse.

"You're set up for a meeting at nine tomorrow morning with David Phibbly. He's the trustee. According to my friend, they're very interested in finally meeting you. This trust has been in place for over twenty years," she said. "I'd go with you, but I'm meeting with people to start planning the memorial and I need to look for a place for Clarita and me to live."

"Oh. I hope everything's okay with…" I realized I didn't know her boyfriend's name and I selfishly didn't want things to work out for them.

She smiled perversely. "Brian. Things are fine but his place isn't set up for family."

"You're doing a good thing. She needs you," I said. Clarita shuffled next to me and snuggled in closer. I couldn't explain why we had such an immediate connection, but I felt it too.

"She's certainly taken with you." Gabriella observed, smiling.

"When will you have the memorial?"

"End of next week on the new moon. It'd be nice to wait for the solstice, but that's just too far away."

Before I could respond, the sultry middle-aged Willow approached the table. "Mari said you might like a tour of the garden," she said, sliding in next to me on the bench. Her perfume was a little overpowering and I felt uncomfortable as her chest bumped my arm.

"It is beautiful," I said, unbalanced by a bit too much familiarity.

"It certainly is," she purred. "I've a few minutes, care to take a stroll?"

I looked to Gabriella for help, but she was smiling like the Cheshire cat.

"He's all yours, Willow," she said.

I released Clarita's hand as Willow stood from the bench and pulled on my elbow. She was clearly not taking no for an answer. At the last minute, Clarita scooted over and grasped my hand, holding her other arm up and giving the universal, 'pick me up' signal again. I swung her up and she wrapped her legs around my waist, laying her cheek on my shoulder.

"Looks like we're coming too," Gabriella said, following along in our wake.

"Lovely." Willow pushed open a swinging glass door into the green house. The aroma of flowers and peat joined with the already rich smells of the restaurant.

Upon crossing the threshold, I paused and knelt down, setting an unwilling Clarita onto the ground next to me. "Just for a minute," I reassured her. Grudgingly, she released my neck. Willow and Gabriella stopped and looked back at me questioningly. I unlaced my boots and pulled them off, folding my socks on top.

"What are you doing?" Gabriella asked.

"You can't ask me to walk through such a lush garden with my shoes on." I wrapped my arm around Clarita and pulled her up with me as I stood.

"You are no witch, but your magic comes from the earth?" Willow asked. She'd dropped the flirtatious façade and stared intently.

"It's true that I'm unable to join a witch's circle. I guess I've always believed all magic comes from the earth," I said.

"Oh moon and stars, no," Willow said, laughing. "A necromancer's power comes from the dead and dying. There are those who flirt with demons and those who worship the moon or the sun. There are many magics about. What *is* unusual is someone who has power outside of the witch's circle. I've only known one other like that."

I caught up to where Willow and Gabriella had stopped in front of an amazing array of ferns. I couldn't help but reach forward and run my hands across their tiny, pointed leaves. The plants fairly hummed in their lush habitat. I pushed a small amount of energy into the nearest plant, helping it expand its roots.

I was sure that neither Willow nor Gabriella could have noticed, but I'd forgotten about the little one who hung from my neck.

"You made it happy," Clarita whispered. If only I could do the same for her. According to Gabriella, she'd spoken few words since she'd been freed from her lycan captors.

We continued deeper into the greenhouse, past several long rows of relatively simple flowering plant varieties, many of which adorned the tables within the restaurant. Generations of witches had worked the soil I stood on and I felt their care. Plants carefully placed where they had received optimum care for decades. It wasn't a place of great power, but it was certainly a place of verdant fertility. A couple would not want to lie in here if they had no desire for a child.

As if reading my mind, Willow locked eyes with me and cocked an eyebrow, a subtle invitation that made my cheeks blush. She was easily twenty years my senior, but she might have been able to sway me in this place. I had too many irons in the fire already, but such was the power of the garden. I returned a smile and thought guiltily about my interactions with both Amak and Gabriella. Judy had raised me to work on one relationship at a time. Fortunately, Willow was simply offering and I could feel no offense being taken by my silent demurral.

"Monkshood? I've never seen so much," I said. It was a variety of wolfsbane with pretty little purple flowers that slumped forward like the hood of a monk.

"A recent addition," Willow said. "No doubt I don't need to tell you why."

"Not hardly," I laughed ironically. "I'd love to get a few starts of this. One of the lycan marked my landlord's entry. None too subtly either. I think that's over, but I'd rather be safe."

"Heavens yes. I'll cut several into a flat. It's too cold to plant outside, but if she'd keep them by her doors and windows, it would be very effective."

"I was thinking of building a garden box with a plastic cover," I said.

"I think you're still too late for that."

"I could talk to Mrs. Willoughby about keeping them," I said. "Unfortunately, she's unaware of the problem."

"As long as she doesn't make tea with them," Gabriella added, causing us all to laugh.

We followed Willow further back and she stopped to explain the next section. "Belle has grown finicky over time. She refuses to cook with herbs that come from anywhere else."

She waved her hand across a small field of rosemary, basil, thyme, garlic, green onions and many more. The fertility of the soil was considerably more depleted than the rest of the garden, most likely due to constant harvesting.

"How do you keep up with it?" I asked, closing my eyes as I focused on a rosemary plant that had been severely cut back. I pushed my magic into the plant and felt a wellspring of energy flow cleanly through my feet and out of my hands. I was surprised at how easily the magic flowed and how quickly the delicious herb leafed out, growing into a robust plant like its neighbors.

"Beautiful," Willow said, placing her hand on top of my own and gently grasping it. "May I join with you?"

It wasn't as cougarish of a proposition as it sounded. It was a familiar terminology that Judy's sisters used when making an impromptu circle. Unfortunately, I'd nearly killed a witch friend when she'd tried to bring me into a circle in North Carolina. It wasn't something I was willing to repeat.

"It doesn't work," I said, trying to keep things light. I didn't want to sound too emphatic.

"I don't see how that's possible. It would take me a few days to encourage that little plant to restore so much, yet you did it in moments. How much more so if we joined."

"No." I drew my hand back. The very idea terrified me. I could hardly face my family in North Carolina for all the pain I'd caused. I wasn't about to repeat that here.

"Felix. You're being rude," Gabriella said.

"I need to leave," I said. I transferred Clarita over to Gabriella and was grateful that neither made a fuss.

"It's nothing," Willow said. I sensed her trying to sooth me, but my fear response pushed me and I couldn't accept it. I ran through the garden and grabbed my shoes. There was a side exit, which I took, sprinting for my truck. Winded, I threw the boots into the truck, started it up and drove away, my bare feet freezing on the pedals.

ALL ABOUT TRUST

I awoke suddenly at four o'clock the next morning, having only fallen asleep two hours previous. After running out on dinner, I'd grabbed a burger and then set about cleaning the apartment, a task I reserved for times when my mind was too occupied for anything else.

Violent banging on my front door spurred me to action and I stumbled from bed, grateful that I'd cleaned up and didn't have to pick my way around a mess. With a wave of my hand, I unlocked the door and opened it to Amak, who swung a clenched fist clumsily, recognizing too late I'd opened up. I dodged her awkward swing as she twisted, falling into me. The smell of booze followed her across the threshold like a tsunami.

"Whoa, hold on there, killer," I said, catching her.

"Booty call!" she announced, wrapping her arms around me awkwardly as we fell into the apartment.

"Shhh, you'll wake my landlady," I said, swinging the door closed with my foot. I was grateful that Mrs. Willoughby took her hearing aids out at night and nothing short of a gas explosion would wake her. Amak pulled off her sequined top, tossed it to the side and pushed me onto the couch, following my progress and landing roughly on me.

As beautiful as I found Amak, we hadn't had the same night. She'd been drinking and was already in overdrive, ready to go. My baser instincts wanted to fulfil her expectations, but I was having a hard time catching up.

"Hold on, Amak," I said, between her rough kisses. The smell of alcohol wasn't doing much to encourage me.

"Playing hard to get?" Amak asked as her hands slid under my belt, searching.

"You're way ahead of me here," I said. "I just woke up." The irony of having this conversation with a woman, albeit a troll woman, was not lost on me.

"I just want to have fun. You can still pine after that witch if you want. I don't care," she said.

That got my attention. I pushed her back and scooted to the corner of the couch, disentangling.

"That's a horrible thing to say, Amak," I said. "I really like you, and I'd like to think…"

"What? You'd like to think we could be together? Don't make this more than it is, Slade. We have fun together. No strings. I thought you got that," she said.

"Is that how you see us?" I asked.

"Oh, don't get huffy. Humans have been taking advantage of trolls for millennia. I'm just being a realist," she said.

"I'd like to know *you*, Amak. I'm not plaything material," I said.

"You want to cuddle and talk it out?" she asked, waggling her eyebrows.

"You're drunk and you aren't listening."

"Gods, but you can be a buzz kill. Do you have any idea how much I have to drink to even get a buzz?" she asked.

I took my shirt off and handed it to her. "Put this on. I can't have a conversation with you if you're hanging out like that," I said.

She smiled at me mischievously and ran her fingers around her breasts suggestively. To my dismay, I was unable to take my eyes off her as she did. She ran her fingers down her firm stomach and when they reached the band of her leather skirt, I broke eye contact and stood, turning away.

"You smell like you're ready. Why are you holding back?" Amak had silently stood and her breath blew hot on my neck.

"I'm not that guy, Amak."

"You have feelings for that witch and you're still messing around. What would you have me think?" She wrapped her arms around my waist, her breasts pressing into my back. Fortunately, she kept her hands north of the danger zone.

"It's not as clear to me as it is to you, Amak. I think we could have something, it's just so confusing," I said. "What I know is that I don't want to lose you as a friend. If I just turn into your booty call, I won't be able to handle it."

She grabbed my shoulders and gently turned me around. She was still naked. Her glamour had faded so that I saw her as she really was – a gorgeous troll warrior. Her aura was no longer projecting lust as much as confusion and even hope.

"You're saying you just want to be friends?" she asked.

I shook my head, looking at the ground. "When you say it that way, it sounds terrible."

She gave her head a shake, confusion written across her face. "This is new territory for me."

I inspected her face to help me understand what she was saying, her eyes glistening in the dark of the apartment. I didn't want to hurt her, but this was a critical point in our relationship and I had to be honest.

"I don't know where our relationship is going, Amak. What I do know is that you've become important to me. I can't lose you."

"And, you'd give up sex for that?"

"Absolutely."

"You are an unusual man, Felix Slade. I've only known those who wanted a physical relationship and then tire of me and move on. Yet you, who see me as I am and desire to join with me physically, abstain from this to keep me as your friend."

"It'll sound less stupid to me when you have a shirt on and I've taken a cold shower," I said.

She stepped forward and slid her arms around my back, tipping her head over to rest her cheek on my own.

"You know. Trolls don't have the same hang-ups about sex and relationships. We could just be – I believe you call it – friends with benefits." She gently shook her chest, once again catching my eye.

I averted my gaze and tossed her my shirt again. "No. Stop. You're so naughty."

"How does this work?" she asked, pulling the shirt over her head. "Should I leave?"

"You shouldn't drive in your condition. Stay here tonight."

"And, what happens when your girlfriend shows up in the morning?"

"One of the benefits of being friends. We can have all the sleepovers we want. Are you hungry? I still have these frozen cookies from Mrs. Willoughby," I said.

"No. Sleep is probably a good idea."

I pulled a blanket and pillow from the closet and tossed them on the couch. "You take my bed, you're too long for the couch."

"Nah. This'll work just fine." Amak fell onto the couch, dangling her legs off the end and pulling the blanket over her shoulders.

"Seriously, it's not a problem," I said.

"Go to bed, Slade," she said, rolling over. I smiled. The woman could change gears faster than a Nascar driver.

"'Night." I turned off the hall light on my way back to bed.

***

Buzzing woke me from a deep sleep and I tried to turn over, but a long arm lay across my chest, inhibiting movement. At some point in the night, Amak had joined me in the bed. The presence of my shirt on her sleeping form reassured me that we hadn't done anything more than sleep. Gently, I moved her arm so I could retrieve my phone. It was just after eight and I'd missed a call from Gabriella. When I entered the security code, I discovered I'd also missed more than a few texts as well. I dialed her back and slid out of bed.

"Did you remember your appointment with Phibbly?" She didn't bother greeting me.

"Who?" I asked. The name sounded vaguely familiar, but I couldn't place it.

"At the bank. You're meeting him at nine," she said.

"Crap, I totally forgot," I said.

"Are you okay? You ran out of Chatty Katty's pretty fast last night. Willow and the sisters were concerned," she said.

"I can't talk about it."

There was a long pause before she continued. "That bad?"

"Just painful," I said. "I'll apologize to the sisters. It wasn't Willow's fault."

"Everyone has baggage, Felix. Willow was concerned for you more than anything else. She's very perceptive. You don't need to apologize."

"I feel like a heel. I knew she was reaching out to me and I rejected her."

"Then talk to her. She won't pry, but don't let it fester."

"When did you get so wise?"

"It's easier when I'm not involved. And you better get rolling," she said.

"Thanks for the call, Gabriella. I'll talk to you later," I said, hanging up.

I had only forty-five minutes to get cleaned up and to the bank for my meeting with David Phibbly, trust administrator. I jumped in the shower and was toweling off when Amak knocked on the bathroom door.

"Just a minute." I wrapped the towel around my waist and opened the door. "It's all yours." I gestured grandly to the tiny bathroom.

"You're up early. Do you have plans for the morning?"

"Banking," I said, squeezing past her into the hallway.

Amak straightened as I spoke and turned to me. "Slade, I hate to ask, but does this have anything to do with 230 Happy Hollow?"

"That's quite a leap from banking to that old run-down mansion."

"Don't mess with me. Does it?"

"Who wants to know?"

"Liise Straightrod compelled me to ask," she said. "I can't leave without getting an answer I believe."

"Do the witches really have that much control over you?"

"She does, yes. Please tell me," she said, her eyes begging me not to.

"I'm not much of a secret keeper, Amak. I've learned that my name is on a trust and it has something to do with that old mansion. I'm going to talk with them about it."

"I can't let you go," she said.

"What do you mean?"

"I'm to detain you and call Liise," she said. "I'm to use whatever force or tricks work."

"Wait, what? Has Liise compelled you to sleep with me to get information? I thought it was Camille who was asking for information."

"Camille asked for information, but Liise compelled me to use whatever means were necessary."

"Camille knew this?"

"No. Camille would never go that far."

"But, she'd still use her power to command you," I said hotly.

"Witches and trolls have been enemies for centuries. My service to the witches is voluntary as part of a truce. Their control of us is a condition of that truce," she said.

"That's too much. It's slavery," I said.

"My mother wouldn't like what's being done, but I don't know if she'd break the truce just because one witch is abusing her power," she said. I filed that little bit of information away. I needed to meet her mother.

"So what do we need to do?"

"I can't let you go this morning," she said.

"Fine. I won't go," I said. "I don't really want to anyway. How about some breakfast?"

She smiled, stress draining out of her face. "Do you have anything?"

"Steak and eggs," I said. "Take a shower, I'll have it up by the time you're out."

"Promise me you won't leave before I get out," she said.

"I promise. On our friendship, I'll be waiting for you."

She turned and started removing her clothing. I pulled the door closed behind me, dressed quickly and got to work in the kitchen. If I were going to make my meeting, I'd need to hustle.

Fifteen minutes later, Amak walked into the kitchen, wearing another pair of my jeans and a clean t-shirt. I mentally noted that I needed to purchase more clothing if I was going to be sharing at this level in the future.

"As promised," I said, sliding plates of scrambled eggs and steak onto the table.

"This smells delicious," she said. "I can't believe you're being such a good sport."

"Coffee?" I asked.

"Water would be good," she said, digging in.

I got up from the table and pulled a cardboard bottle of salt from a shelf and poured it on the ground, completing a spell circle behind Amak.

"What are you…?"

"*Sphaera.*" A translucent bubble popped into existence, separating us.

"…up to?" She completed her sentence, her voice taking on the tinny characteristics caused by communicating through the impervious spell wall.

"Sorry for the deception, but I can't let Liise Straightrod decide what I can and cannot do. I promise I'll be back as soon as I can. Feel free to eat my eggs," I said.

"Do not leave, Slade. The consequences will be grave. Straightrod is up to something."

"What's it got to do with me?"

"I don't know. I just know she wants you and Gabriella dead."

"Would you kill me if she required it?"

"No. There are limits," she said.

"Do you believe you can get out of my spell circle?"

"No."

"Good. I'll see you in an hour or so," I said. "Enjoy the eggs."

I waved to her over my back as I walked out the front door, locking it behind me.

I was five minutes late for my appointment.

"Can I help you?" An older woman, seated at a reception desk asked as I entered through the second set of double doors.

"I've an appointment with David Phibbly," I said.

"I'll let him know you're here." She smiled a practiced smile and lifted the receiver on her phone, cradling it on her shoulder and gesturing at a row of empty seats.

Several minutes later, I heard the ding of an elevator. A weasely looking man with salt and pepper hair and a narrow build walked purposefully in my direction. As he arrived, he adjusted his round wire-framed glasses, making eye contact with me. I stood and pushed down a strong feeling of being underdressed and out of place.

"Mr. Slade?" The man managed to sound both raspy and nasal as he stood in front of me.

"Yes." I offered my hand. The disgust at my gesture rolled off the man in waves as he forced a smile. It occurred to me that sensitivity to people's feelings wasn't always an advantage.

"David Phibbly. If you'll follow me, we've gathered in my office." He shook my proffered hand with a single pump and let go, turning back to the elevator doors from which he'd exited.

It was an uncomfortable ride up. Phibbly stared forward, not making eye contact as we rode quietly in the elevator. When it stopped, he took a practiced step back, bowed slightly at the waist and gestured with an open palm toward the door. "After you, Mr. Slade."

I walked into an open, low-cubicle environment where ten middle-aged women busily worked in front of computer terminals. Phibbly caught up and guided me past offices along the outer wall. As I looked into each of the offices, I noticed they were predominately occupied by older men in suits. It felt like I'd been transported back to a nineteen fifties black-and-white movie. As we entered Phibbly's office, I was surprised to see two women in conservative business suits already seated at a round table.

"Aimee Bestmun." A blonde-haired woman offered her hand.

"Kim Munstel." The other offered as they both stood.

"Felix Slade." I shook their hands and gathered a quick read. Bestmun was absolutely roiling with curiosity, where Munstel was calm with an undercurrent of concern.

"On behalf of Leotown Bank and Trust, we'd like to welcome

you, Mr. Slade," Phibbly said as we sat. "How may we help you today?"

I pulled the paper from my pocket and slid it onto the table. "I was hoping you would clear up a mystery for me relating to the property at 230 Happy Hollow Boulevard."

Phibbly picked up the paper, looked at it briefly and then handed it to Bestmun. "Do you have an interest in making a claim on the property?"

I felt three sets of eyes looking at me intently, hanging on my answer.

"I don't know. I'm not familiar with it, but a friend suggested I should talk to you," I said, looking to Kim for support.

"There's a test." Bestmun blurted, unable to contain herself.

"Aimee. That's not the procedure," Phibbly corrected.

"What kind of test?" I asked still looking at Kim.

"There are three tests," Kim answered. Again, I felt her concern surface. She made a sudden decision.

"Kim!" Phibbly objected.

"No, David. There is a higher responsibility than this charter. Mr. Slade needs to know what he's getting into."

"There is *no* higher responsibility than the law," Phibbly stated emphatically.

"The first step is simple, Mr. Slade," Kim said. "We need to verify your identity. We need a driver's license or passport and a social security card or birth certificate."

Gabriella had warned me that they might ask to verify my identity and I'd brought my birth certificate and driver's license. I slid them across the table. Aimee stood wordlessly, scooped them up and walked from the room.

"The second is a blood test to be administered by Mr. Phibbly. It is a non-standard test we, quite frankly, don't understand. But, as David has correctly pointed out, the agreement of the trust charter must be fulfilled and this is clearly spelled out."

"Only if he is making a claim," Phibbly corrected.

My curiosity was piqued and while I felt the warning from Kim, I wanted to know what was at the end of this rabbit hole.

"What do you need to hear from me?" I turned to Phibbly.

For the first time in our conversation, he smiled, steepling his fingers together as he responded. "Something along the lines of – I claim Tenebris Manerium."

"Dark Manor," I said mostly to myself, translating the Latin phrase.

"There is danger," Kim interjected.

"Kim! Please remove yourself from this meeting," Phibbly said.

"I'd like to request that Ms. Munstel stay," I said as she started to rise.

Phibbly exchanged a look with Kim and she sat again. "My apologies," she said.

The tension was interrupted as Aimee Bestmun returned, placing my license and birth certificate on the table next to me.

"And?" Phibbly asked, turning his attention to Bestmun.

"We are indeed talking with Felix Slade, third son of Atronia Baltazoss. Father is listed as Egils Slade." She sat back into her chair. "At least that's how the birth certificate reads. Mr. Slade, will you consent to a background check to verify the authenticity of this information?"

My mind reeled. Third son? As little as I knew of my parents, I'd always thought I was an only child.

"Mr. Slade?" Phibbly pushed, sliding a paper and pen in front of me. "Consent?"

I tried reading the paper, but couldn't make sense of it. My mind did not want to read the words while I was still processing what I'd just heard. I scrawled my signature, desperate for nuggets of information on my family.

"And the claim for Tenebris?" He placed a small crystal phial on the table in front of me. His smile broadened, like a spider anticipating a fly's approach. I'd intended to question Kim of the danger, but my mind refused to stop spinning with questions about my family.

"Yes. I claim Tenebris Manerium."

I wasn't sure if everyone could feel the wave of magic that pulsed from the phial, but the room grew silent as they all considered me.

"The first of two tests requires a blood sample," he said, pulling the pointed stopper from the top of the ornate bottle. "Your finger?"

A compulsion resonated that required my participation. It wasn't from Phibbly and I suspected it was the enchantment on the bottle. I had the capacity to resist, but the suggestion that I might learn about my family was enough. I held my finger out as he pulled on latex gloves.

"This is barbaric," Kim said. "We should never have agreed to administer this trust."

"Why? What happens if things don't work out?" I asked as Phibbly jabbed my finger, squeezing it harder than was required to make blood flow.

"Those who have passed the blood test have never returned to this office," Kim said.

"How many have passed?"

"You'll make four," Phibbly said, releasing my hand and stoppering the bottle. A green glow emanated from the bottle. "And there you go. You're who you say you are."

"I thought you had to run a background check," I said.

"That's for the government. The charter doesn't require anything but this bottle to proceed," Phibbly said, managing a patronizing tone.

"What's the next test?" I asked.

"Simple. There's a large crystal jar in the basement of the house. A companion to this one. When you bring it back, we combine them. If all goes well, you become a probationary owner of the property."

"Probationary? What does that mean?"

"It's a relatively simple term, I'm sure you'll understand," he said patronizingly. "There is a three-year probationary period where you're given full use of the property and an allowance for maintenance."

"After three years?"

"The house and assets of the trust are transferred to you in their entirety."

"What's the allowance?"

"It is quite generous. The trust will reimburse up to thirty thousand dollars in approved expenses."

"Who approves?" The man emanated deception. What was he lying about?

"The trust specifies a list of approved categories. But, to answer your question, it would be my responsibility," he said.

Kim Munstel sat forward in her chair. "The trust also pays real estate taxes, insurance, and has a provision for emergencies, like flood or fire."

"What is the value of the trust as it stands today?" I asked.

"Ahh, of course. I'm surprised it took so long to get to this," Phibbly said with a disapproving pout.

"He passed the identity test. He has a right to know," Kim said.

Phibbly sighed, rolling his eyes. "Fine. Excluding the actual land and structure at 230 Happy Hollow, the assets were last valued at twenty-eight million, four hundred twenty thousand."

"That's a lot," I said. "Just one thing, though. Do you want to explain to me how Leotown Police ended up with a copy of this trust at a particularly inconvenient moment?"

"I'm sure I have no idea," Phibbly replied, the lie as apparent as the nose on his face.

"Are you saying the details of this trust aren't confidential? Or are you saying Leotown Bank and Trust isn't capable of keeping these details secret?"

"What are you implying?"

"A simple question asked," I said.

"I have no way of knowing how this information came into the possession of the police. Perhaps there was an old copy floating around that we were unaware of."

"I'd hate to think my parents chose to trust the wrong bank," I said.

"Your mother set it up and I assure you, we are most trustworthy," Phibbly said.

I'd made my point and wasn't prepared to push it any further.

"All this is mine if I simply retrieve a bottle from the basement?"

"That about sums it up," he said. "Aimee would be happy to accompany you there now if you'd like."

"Now?"

"Our instructions are to accompany claimants to the property and escort them to the basement and then leave. When they return with the bottle, the three-year process for transferring ownership begins."

"And, you've done this three times previously? No one has returned?" I asked looking at the blonde trust officer.

"Me? No, this would be my first time," Aimee said.

"Fine. Let's do it then," I said. "I just have to make a quick stop at home to take care of something."

As I stood, Kim grabbed my arm. "You can walk away from this, Mr. Slade. Don't be blinded by the money."

"If it were just that, I would." At least I hoped I would.

SHADES OF THE PAST

"Wait here, I'll be right back"

Aimee Bestmun parked on the street next to my apartment and looked out her window expectantly.

"Take your time," she said with a smile. "This beats paperwork any day."

I jogged past Amak's Jeep and up the stairs to my apartment. I was unusually proud of the fact that for once, I was returning to my apartment and the door hadn't been ripped from its hinges while I was gone. I swiped the locks open and found Amak asleep in the kitchen chair with her legs propped up on the table.

"Wakee, wakee," I said as I approached.

"Heya, sweet cheeks. What's shaking?" she asked. "Did you have a nice meeting?"

"You know bankers…"

"Not really."

"*Finis*." I dropped the spell circle that contained her.

"Locking me in there was pretty clever," she said. "And your eggs were a little dry."

"Sorry, I was in a hurry," I said.

"What'd you learn at the bank?"

I knew we were in dangerous territory as she would just report whatever I said back to Camille and Liise Straightrod. I was starting to believe one of them – or both - meant me harm.

"I might have a claim on that mansion where the lycan were holding Clarita," I said.

"You really need to stop telling me this stuff," Amak said.

"You asked."

"What part of compulsion don't you get?"

"I get it, but I'm also not willing to lie to you."

She shook her head. "You need to get more comfortable with

it."

"Can you hold on a minute? I need to grab something from the truck."

"Sure."

I turned, ran back down to the truck, started it up and pulled into the drive, parking behind her Jeep. I looked up to the apartment where she was watching me through the window. I gave her a friendly wave, tossed my keys into the front seat and jogged over to where Aimee Bestmun still sat in her car.

"Probably be best if we got moving," I said as I jumped into the passenger side of her vehicle.

"What's going on?"

"You're driving, right? So let's go." I pushed a sense of urgency into my words.

As she put the car into gear and sped away, I caught a glimpse of Amak bounding down the stairs, three at a time, a wide smile on her face. I wondered if she'd chase us all the way over to the house or if she even knew where we were going.

**

"Slow down. It's coming up on the right," I instructed.

"What? I don't see anything."

"Seriously, slow down a lot!" I said. Aimee drove like a crazy person, which wasn't uncommon in my circle of people, but her little car would never make the turn at this speed without taking damage. "It's right there." I pointed at a gap in the vegetation that had a much more pronounced separation than it did a few days ago. Several dozen police vehicles had opened things up nicely.

"It might have been better if we'd brought your truck," she said.

"We can park on a side street and walk in if you'd prefer," I said.

"No. I got this." She bumped over the curb, flipped on her headlights and followed the newly-formed ruts created by emergency vehicles.

"Take it slow," I put my hands on the dash to brace myself.

"There are limbs down everywhere."

"Look, pal. I grew up on a farm. I got this."

A few minutes later we pulled up to the house.

"Are you going to accompany me the whole way?" I asked.

"My instructions are to follow you into the basement and wait until you enter the single door. Once you're in, I'm to return without entering the room," she said.

"Easy enough."

"Really? It sounds pretty cloak and dagger to me."

"Wrong genre. Think Dungeons and Dragons."

She gave me a quizzical look. I avoided her questions by hopping out of the car.

"Wait," she called after me. Her spiked heels sank into the soft dirt as she tried to follow. "What did you mean by that?" She grabbed my arm to steady herself.

"We're just around the corner." I guided her toward the breezeway entry Amak and I had entered two nights before.

"Let me find the right key," she said, pulling a ring full of keys from her purse.

"Sure. I'll just see if it's locked," I said, waving my hand across the door and slid the tumblers into place, following the now familiar pattern. I pushed the door open.

"That should have been locked." She followed me into the empty mudroom, her heels clacking on the hard slate tile.

"I'm guessing it's through here," I said, walking into the rundown kitchen.

"Are you sure?" She hustled to keep up with me, her narrow skirt constraining the length of her stride. I wasn't purposefully being annoying, but my mind was consumed with what Clarita and I had both felt in the basement of the house. "Wait up," she called after me. I'd already made it to the room where we'd first run into the lycan.

"Almost there." I encouraged her, waiting by a door I knew led to the small hallway where we'd been trapped and Clarita had saved us all by energizing my spells.

"I'm not sure why they haven't torn this crap hole down," she said, catching up. "The land would be worth a fortune. Drop a million-dollar home on this and you could sell it for double that."

"Is that what you'd do?"

"If I had the money. We run into this all the time, though - property that people don't want to part with. I just don't understand being nostalgic about a wreck like this. I say bulldoze it and cash in."

"Maybe," I said, pushing through to the expected hallway. There were four doors, one being the magical door to the basement. It was closed, just like I'd left it.

"What happened here?" she asked. "Is that blood?"

I hadn't even noticed the blood stains on the floor and smears on the wall, too focused on the task. "You have a key for this door too?"

"Don't you? The instructions say that you have to open both doors and I'm to turn my back as you do," she said.

"Shouldn't you turn around then?"

"Really? You're not going to let me watch?"

"Wouldn't want to break the agreement," I said and twirled my finger at her. She pursed her lips, but turned around all the same.

This lock was definitely old hat, mirroring the lock leading into the mudroom. I slid the tumblers across and pushed the door open, stepping in so the sconces would start lighting.

"Did you get it?"

"One second." I watched as the lights ignited around the corner on the way down the stairs. "Yup, we're good." She turned and looked on with surprise.

"How'd those get lit?"

"I think they're all connected. I just had to light one of 'em," I lied.

She gave me a dubious look. "Dungeons and Dragons indeed."

We walked down the stairs together, Aimee using my shoulder for balance on the worn steps. I was surprised by their lack of dust or debris. I wondered if that was due to how the passage was constructed or if there was magic at work. I leaned toward the latter. If I knew a cleaning spell, I'd certainly have used it on the entire house, not just down here.

"Look at that. A second door, just like you said." I feigned ignorance.

"I'm not supposed to say anything, but Kim wants me to remind you that you don't have to go through with this," she said. "You can still walk away."

"Tell her thank you, but this is important to me," I said.

She turned around without my prompting. "Okay, do your thing, Mr. Slade."

I placed my hand on the door handle. Like the doors above, this handle felt familiar in my grip. "*Altum Visu,*" I fired up my second sight. The door and the entire wall in front of me absolutely writhed with the same bluish energy signature I'd seen in the breezeway door. It was as familiar to me as my own face in the mirror. I wondered if this deep connection was because my family had some part in the construction of this place. My heart raced at the possibility.

The magical lock on this door was considerably more complex than the two upstairs. There were multiple paths for the magical tumblers to travel. I instinctively understood that there was only one correct path and to make a wrong turn would shut the door down. It wasn't a problem, though. I knew the pattern just like I recognized the bluish energy signature. I pulled the tumblers along the pattern as if I'd been doing it all my life. Turning the handle, I pushed the heavy wooden door inward.

"*Finis.*" I dropped my second sight.

Wizard's fire ignited in ornate iron sconces in sequence around the room - or, more accurately, laboratory. When the final sconce lit, a fire popped to life in the stone fireplace on the back wall. An ornately carved desk sat to one side of the hearth, and floor-to-ceiling bookshelves filled with leather-bound tomes covered the rest of the back wall. While the air smelled stale, the polished stone surfaces of the work tables appeared completely devoid of dust. A silver cauldron rested on a heating element as if the resident wizard had left only days before.

"Why does this feel so familiar?" I asked, mostly to myself.

"You opened the door!" Aimee had turned around and was peering into the room.

"You should leave, Aimee." With my words, I pushed a sense of foreboding at her. I might have overdone it, as her face turn ashen and she quickly retreated, her back hitting the stone wall.

"I have to see you step through the door," she mumbled.

I stepped over the threshold and turned back to her. "Good enough?" The sound of her heels on the stone stairs was the only evidence she'd been there with me. The lights in the hallway extinguished as I heard the door at the top of the stair clack shut.

"Well, that's something," I said to myself.

As I walked into the room, past the lab tables, my eye fell on a pile of bones on the floor. A mostly-rotted human skeleton was on the floor in front of the fireplace and in its boney fingers was a crystal like the one in Phibbly's picture. The skeleton was enough of a warning. I wasn't about to grab the jar just yet. I walked around the desk and plopped down in the leather chair, pulling my phone out. I wanted to call Gabriella and get her read on the situation, but she had enough going on with Clarita and the memorial tonight. I dialed up Amak.

"Something's been bugging me. You sound a lot less troll-like than you did when we first met. What's that about?" I asked, when she picked up the phone.

"That's pretty random. And nice job ducking me at your apartment. You know I'm going to have to up my game," she said. "So what gave me away?"

"I'd say it was the lack of growling, snorting and use of single syllable words," I said.

"Would you believe it's easier to be scary when everyone thinks you're a single-minded killer?" she asked.

"That's hot. Totally had me fooled," I said.

"You're weird, Slade. You sure you're not up for a booty call?"

"No. I just wanted to talk to someone," I said.

"You good then?"

"Yeah. Thanks." I hung up. She was right. I am strange.

I leaned back in the chair and closed my eyes. The familiar

smell of the leather brought a long-forgotten memory to the surface. I was remembering the face of a woman I believed to be my mother. Her long black hair fell around my face as she leaned down to give me a kiss. I smiled at the powerful memory of the love she'd shared with me in that moment.

I breathed deeply and turned my head back into the chair. The memory had been triggered by the faint scent left behind by the previous occupant. It was hard not to take the memory as a sign. If I wanted to know more about my mother, I was going to have to see this test through. I looked over at the corpse.

"So what was your story?" I asked as if it would reply.

My eye caught something new. A silver band, two inches wide had been inscribed into the floor and formed a circle six feet in diameter around the corpse. Upon closer inspection, I discovered faint etched runes in the silver. I knelt and ran my fingers across the surface. It was warm to the touch and my senses revealed that the silver ran deep into the floor. Whoever had created the circle hadn't been messing around. Silver was a powerful medium and would make a strong barrier.

I thought about the two uses I knew of for a spell circle. The first was to bind a wizard to the earth and provide protection. The wizard would cast the circle while sitting within it. This practice had become something of a routine for me when I wanted to recharge. The other purpose of the circle was to trap something, usually a spirit or demon. The wizard remained outside the circle, like I'd done to Amak.

"Is that what you did?" I asked the circle's occupant. "You summoned a circle and what...?" I was missing something. There was no reason for someone to die inside a circle. I supposed they could starve to death or run out of water, but nothing physical or magical could touch them while they were inside. I looked at the skeleton and wondered if whoever it had been had perished in the circle for something as mundane as dehydration.

"You're no help... screw it!" I said and reached down, grabbing the crystal jar from the boney hand.

Not unexpectedly, a cold breeze blew across my back and one

by one the lights along the wall extinguished. I turned and sprinted for the door, but it slammed in front of me. A cold presence passed behind me and the hairs on my neck stood on end in the light breeze. I spun around, not finding anything.

"Who's there?" I asked as the final sconce on the wall extinguished. Instinctively, I moved back to the fireplace, the only light remaining in the room.

The sound of metal dragging along the stone floor echoed through the room. I peered into the darkness, trying to identify its origin. An occasional spark traced along the floor, the only hint of its location.

"*Lucem,*" I shouted as I mentally chastised myself for being so riled up. Light from my left hand ring burst forth and I swept it across the room, looking for what was making the noise. A tall shape darted behind the table, but when my light reached its position, I was unable to find anything.

"*Altum Visu,*" I cast the planar view.

"Shit!" I exclaimed to no one. My wizard's site had exposed four indistinct, lumbering shapes closing on my position. The closest was dragging an ethereal sword which it lifted as it approached.

"*Adoloret,*" I launched a gout of flame across the ten feet that separated us. To my horror, the flame simply dissipated, causing no damage.

It wasn't as if I didn't know what was happening. It was too obvious of an answer to take safety in the silver circle. Sure, I'd be safe, but I suspected the shades would simply wait me out. I wasn't going down without a fight. I ran toward the door that led into the hall, hoping I could unlock it and escape. I placed my hand on the first table and vaulted over it, my legs knocking the silver cauldron on the ground. I leapt over the second table and placed my hands on the door, looking for the handle that appeared to no longer exist. My wizard's sight clearly showed the lock, but when I attempted to move the tumblers, they lifted and immediately fell back.

The spirits had reoriented and were once again slowly closing on my position. I could outrun and out maneuver them. But if I couldn't escape the room. Even that small advantage wouldn't help.

"*Scutum*," I projected the shield in front of me and pushed it into the closest figure. Too late, I realized the spirit wielded a dagger and my shield hadn't stopped its slashing strike. The skin on my forearm was laid open as if cut by a fillet knife.

"Damn you!" I cursed, quenching the shield and scuttling away. The spirit cackled in response.

I ripped a strip from my shirt as I took refuge along the side wall, tying a quick compress around the wound. If I survived, that was sure to be a nasty wound. I wracked my brain, trying to come up with a plan that didn't involve me using the silver circle. I jumped over the desk and pulled the drawers open, spilling their contents on the floor. If only I could find salt or something else that was useful against the undead. Of course, there was nothing helpful.

I scooted around the desk, avoiding the approaching shades. I wasn't completely sure what would happen if they reached me. Would they really kill me? The slash to my arm was throbbing and still a good example of what I wanted to avoid. I pulled my phone out and redialed Amak. No dial-tone, no dialing. It wasn't a huge surprise. Spirits, specters, shades, ghosts and just about anything south of the grave had the capacity to interrupt electronics.

As my ring's light bounced around the room, a glint on the wall caught my eye. An ornamental sword hung on the center pillar supporting a double-arched entry to an alcove I'd yet to inspect. The odd thing was that it reflected the light from my ring even in the mystic plane. Ordinarily, a steel sword would barely even register, much less reflect a wizard's light.

I vaulted over the lab tables again, throwing miscellaneous and probably impossible to replace equipment to the floor as I did. I wrapped my free hand around the grip of the sword and tugged it from the wall. Initially, it resisted, but I pushed my will into it and broke it free. The sword was lighter than I'd expected and warmed in the palm of my hand.

The shades were either getting faster or smarter. They'd left me little room to maneuver and I was forced to enter the alcove. I searched for an exit and found nothing. The shelves along the walls were filled with deteriorated spell components and bottles of indeterminate material - nothing I could utilize.

Unfortunately, I'd backed myself into the proverbial corner. I had no experience with a sword, but it no longer mattered. I focused my being and slashed into the closest spirit. It shrieked as the blade struck home, drawing a darkened stripe along its chest. Its scream echoed off the stone walls and I pushed my advantage, slashing into the next figure. A parry from my attacker deflected the sword, but I spun with a grace that was not my own and blocked its counter attack, forcing the spirit back. I slid down the wall to my left to intercept another that was trying to flank me.

I was too slow to fully defend against the third specter's thrust, but managed to deflect its blade so that it only grazed me. The burning of the blade as it dug a furrow across my thigh caused me to fear the damage a successful strike might do. This attacker, however, didn't get the chance for a second strike. It had overcommitted, obviously expecting to have buried its sword in my flesh. As it careened toward the wall, I brought my sword up, drawing through it with what could only be described as a naval-to-head split. A bright flash of light preceded it blinking from existence.

"Who's your daddy now?" I asked, turning back to the figure coming at me from the right.

I dodged a strike and twisted around the pillar, coming face to face with... well... more accurately, face to twisted bundle of glowing skin and bone... My sword was out of position and there was no time to do anything but react. I jammed the pommel up into what – I would stipulate - passed for its face and the shade pulled back, its graceful glide interrupted.

My neck hairs responded to a chill wind. The image of an enemy about to strike from behind lodged in my consciousness. Instinctively, I plunged the sword back in an underhanded arc.

The blade passed inches from my waist as I spun to face it. The sword pierced the center of the specter as it exploded with a bright light. And then, there were two.

Confidently, I stepped through the arch and into the main room, slashing the blade in front of me in an X pattern, making a very satisfying 'whoosh, whoosh' as the sword sliced the air.

"En garde, bitches," I said, pointing the blade at them. The spirits backed away and I lunged forward, dispatching them easily.

The sound of the hall door unlocking was accompanied by the lighting of the wall sconces. Fire and light once again jumped rhythmically around the room.

"*Finis*," I said, releasing my wizard's sight and dousing the light from my ring.

I hastily set the sword down on the nearest table and stepped back. It appeared that the magic of the sword had temporarily imbued me with instincts and fighting skills I really wasn't sure I wanted. At the moment, I wasn't overly interested in what other party tricks it might want to share.

I nearly jumped out of my skin when my phone rang, not bothering to check the caller id.

"Hello?" I asked.

"Slade! You gotta come over here. I need your help." Joe Lozano sounded panicked.

"What's going on, Joe?"

"Just come," he said. "I'm sending you the address."

"Be there in twenty," I pocketed the crystal jar and left the lab, shutting the door behind me as I ran up the stairs.

I pulled out my phone and was about to call Angela to see if she was available for a ride when I rounded the corner and saw Aimee Bestmun's car still parked out front. Worried that something bad might have happened to her, I sprinted toward the car, vaulting over the fallen iron fence.

"Are you okay?" I asked as I slapped my hands on the roof of her car, using it to slow myself down.

"You're bleeding," she said, pointing to my arm.

"Probably gonna get tetanus. Hit a nail," I lied. She had tears in her eyes and her mascara had run, leaving dark lines on her cheeks. "What's going on with you?"

"Damn Phibbly. He had me convinced you weren't coming back. He said something bad was going to happen to you."

"You mean when I got this?" I asked and showed her the jar I'd retrieved.

"You found it? We have to go back to the bank right now! You're fully vetted, if that's the right jar," she said.

"Would you believe I have something else I need to do?"

"More important than a twenty-eight-million-dollar trust?"

"Yeah, I think so. Would you mind dropping me at my apartment?"

GET OUT

"Thanks for the ride," I said, hopping out of Aimee Bestmun's car.

She rolled her window down to talk to me. "You really need to come to the bank, Mr. Slade. David will want to test this right away."

"Will he be less of a jackass?"

She smiled ironically. "Caught that, huh?"

"I'll come by tomorrow if I can." I turned to cross the street and noticed a 1950's vintage Chevy pickup truck parked next to the curb, a purple 'Chatty Katty's' logo emblazoned on the celery colored door. I suspected the visit wasn't a coincidence, so I made my way up the gravel driveway. Amak's Jeep was nowhere to be seen.

A flat of purple flowers sat on Mrs. Willoughby's back porch and I recognized Willow's curvy form in work jeans and colorful smock.

"I'm afraid I can't afford to buy anything." I heard Mrs. Willoughby explaining as I ran up to intervene.

"No, dear. I'm not selling them," Willow answered patiently.

"Oh, hello, Felix," Mrs. Willoughby looked at me. "I was just explaining to this young woman that I can't afford to buy her flowers."

"My fault, Ms. Willoughby. This is Willow. She's my friend and I asked her to come over." I gave Willow a smile. I hadn't asked her to come, but recognized the friendly gesture all the same.

"Oooh. Why didn't you say so?" Mrs. Willoughby said in her overly loud voice. "Come in, come in. And, call me Katherine, please." She shuffled out of the way, leaving the door open.

I picked up the flat of monkshood and followed Willow into the house.

"What a lovely home you have here, Katherine," Willow said.

"It's not much. But, my husband and I had so many fond memories here," she said. "Please sit. Would you care for a cookie?" She shuffled to the freezer and pulled a round tin out, setting it on the table.

It was close to lunch and I'd given my breakfast to Amak, so I gladly helped open the tin and fished out two cookies. I offered one to Willow, who turned it down and then to Mrs. Willoughby, who also turned it down. It didn't seem polite to put them back into the tin, so I held onto them.

"Could I look at your hand, Katherine?" I asked as she sat heavily in her chair.

She'd removed the bandage I'd put on and it looked to be drying out. "It's much better," she said. "That ointment works miracles."

I pulled the jar over from where we'd left it on the table. I suspected she hadn't been applying it by herself. "I think it needs at least one more go," I said.

"If you think that's best," she said. "Willow, that's an unusual name." She turned her attention to Willow. "What about these flowers? I'm afraid I didn't understand what you were saying."

"I run a local nursery and Felix suggested you might be willing to winter a few of my plants," she said. I'd wondered how she was selling the idea. "They like drafty locations, so it's best if they sit next to a window or door."

"Oh. I've never heard of that before," Mrs. Willoughby said.

"They're an unusual plant. But, gorgeous, don't you agree?"

"They certainly are. I'm surprised to see them blooming in October."

"I shouldn't have dropped by unannounced, but I was in the area and wanted to talk with Felix on another matter," she said.

"He's a good boy," she said.

I finished bandaging her hand. "I'm right here, Katherine."

"I know you are, dear." She patted my hand. "I'd be more than happy to look after your flowers. I'm afraid I've something of a brown thumb though."

"That's okay. Felix said he'd be willing to care for them if you are amenable," Willow grinned, knowing I had just stuffed an entire cookie in my mouth and was unable to talk.

"I'll have to stock up on cookies in that case."

Willow reached across the table and brushed crumbs from my cheek. "It sounds like a perfect arrangement."

***

"Thanks for coming over," I said after Willow and I extricated ourselves from Mrs. Willoughby's kitchen. "I'm sorry for running out on you last night."

"I'm the one who should be sorry," Willow said. "I took a liberty that wasn't mine to take."

I shoved my hands in my pockets. "You were being generous and inclusive. You couldn't know I'd react that way. You and your sisters have been nice to me."

"I felt your pain and fear, Felix. You were protecting me - I can only assume from yourself. When you're ready to talk about it, I'd like to be there for you." I looked into her face and saw caring and concern, something she hid under her normally sultry mask.

It wasn't a compulsion as much as a need when I stepped forward and hugged her. Willow's gift was compassion and she'd freely shown that to me. I felt the same warmth I had when I'd hugged Judy. Man, I really missed that.

"When I'm ready to talk, maybe we could take a walk in the garden together," I said.

"Sounds right," she said. "Although, I also wanted to talk to you about that." She'd shifted gears and her voice took on a more business like tone. "Gabriella suggested you might be looking for work. I would love to have someone of your talents help in the greenhouse."

I was taken aback. It was one thing to give me a tour, but quite another to invite me to work there. My involvement would reflect on Willow because a witch's garden was often deeply intertwined with their identity. "Are you sure?"

"Are you interested?" She picked up my hand, turned me

toward the driveway and started walking.

"Of course. I'd be honored," I said.

"Come by some morning next week and we'll work out hours and all that."

"Witch morning or mundane?"

"Eleven is still morning, isn't it?" She winked and her sultry façade slid back into place.

"I could do that," I said.

"Sounds grand. And, just so you know. If you don't finish the next meal Belle makes for you, there will be no safe place in Leotown for you to hide," she said and bustled off to her vintage truck.

I hopped into my own truck and was glad to see Amak had left my keys on the seat. I checked the address Joe had texted me and plugged it into my phone's GPS. I was afraid using the device wasn't an overly wizardly thing to do, but it sure beat cooking up an enchantment.

It wasn't a long drive to Lozano's house and when I pulled up, things were worse than I could have imagined. Joe and a dirty-blonde werewolf - both in human form - were standing in the yard while a woman tossed clothing out the front door onto an existing pile of miscellaneous home goods. A child cried from inside the house and several neighbors stood in their yards, looking on with concern.

"Back in your houses. There's nothing to see," Joe said.

"I'm calling the cops," a neighbor woman shouted.

"I am the cops. It's just a misunderstanding," he said.

"There's no misunderstanding!" The woman I presumed was Joe's wife, Jennifer, yelled from the cement stoop. "You try to bring that slut into my house, I'll rip your nuts off."

"She doesn't mean it. She wasn't threatening anyone," Joe addressed the curious neighbors. He held his hands in front of him defensively, partially offsetting his reassuring words. "About time you got here." He turned, looking at me. He was even rougher looking than the last time I'd seen him.

"What's going on?" I asked.

"Jen. She's gone off the deep end and is kicking me out of the house," he said, apparently loud enough for her to hear.

"You think I'm crazy? You rip up my bed, trash my house and bring that… that… *puta* home and you're calling me loco?"

"Got it," I said. "How about you have Daphne there head down to the corner market or something and we try to have a chat with Jen? Maybe we could calm things down a little."

"You want calm. Tell him to get his crap off my lawn and beat it." Joe's wife stomped inside and slammed the door.

"My name's not Daphne." The dirty-blonde lycan said. "It's Susan."

"Daphne works better with Shaggy," I said. "But have it your way, Sue."

She lunged at me and Joe caught her at the last moment.

"What are you doing? Don't we have enough problems without you starting something else?" Lozano asked.

"What gives? Why isn't she in jail?" I asked.

"She wasn't responsible for most of what went down," he said.

"Bullshit," I said. "She kidnapped Clarita, probably helped kill her mom, too."

"I didn't do any of that," the girl said. "I turned on the last full moon, just like Joe."

"You were ready to kill that little girl. I heard you."

"I'd have done anything to get out of that house. Do you know what it means not to be alpha in a pack?"

"What are we even talking about?"

"Listen to her, Slade," Lozano said.

"Alpha can do what he wants, when he wants," she said. "It's not even considered rape, because I consented to it. I couldn't say no."

"It doesn't excuse terrifying a little girl and almost killing her," I said.

"Next time you're in that situation, you can make whatever call you want. I can live with myself."

"What's she even doing here, Joe?"

He took a deep breath. "I apparently became alpha when we

took down Shaggy."

"Well, you look like shit. Have you thought about shaving and taking a shower? Your eyes are all bloodshot too," I said.

"It's been a crazy couple of weeks. You have no idea what it's like to wake up in a different place every day. And, you didn't seem to mind my help last night." The pitch of his voice had risen and he'd slipped into a defensive posture.

"Feel sorry for yourself much? Put yourself into Jen's shoes on this. After everything she's seen in the last few days, you show up here with another woman, looking completely strung out. I'm kind of with Jen in this. You aren't thinking straight."

"Sue is my responsibility. I can't leave her alone," he said.

"Jen and your kids are your responsibility, too and you're going to lose them if you don't pull it together. What's going on with work?"

"I'm back on modified assignment starting Saturday for two weeks. After that I'm back in, as long as I don't have any other incidents."

"Then let's focus on that. What's going on with Daphne and Fred in that case?"

Joe's arm caught Sue before she could jump me, but it didn't stop her from taking a swipe.

"Don't do that, Slade," he warned. "You're making it worse."

"I think I'm starting to see the problem."

"What would you do?" He asked, looking at Sue. I promised myself I'd make an effort to call her by her real name. "I need a safe place for Susan. Becoming alpha means I have responsibilities."

"Like having her move in with your wife? I'd definitely cross that one off my list."

"Someone needs to look after her, she hasn't been a... you know..."

"Lycan," I helped.

"Right. Lycan. Sue has been a lycan for as long as I have," he said. "She's scared."

"No way. I'm not playing babysitter. She's a fricking time

bomb. And, why haven't the cops shown up? Surely, someone called this in."

"Response time in this neighborhood is a couple of hours."

"First things first. Let me see if I can talk to Jen," I said.

I made my way over to the pile of Joe's belongings and up the cement steps, knocking on the door.

"Go away!" Jen yelled from inside, causing renewed crying from a child.

"Give me five minutes," I said as calmly as possible. "If you still want me to leave after that, I'll make sure Joe goes with me."

"Forget it." Her voice had lost much of its energy.

"It's reasonable, Jennifer. There are things going on that you need to know about," I said.

That must have gotten her attention because she pulled the door open violently. "What?" For a small, mundane woman, she projected a significant amount of energy. And it hit me that I had the blood line wrong. Nanna wasn't Joe's grandmother at all.

"Is Nanna your grandmother?"

"What are you talking about?"

"Something she said. Is she?"

"Yes. What's this got to do with Joe?"

"May I come in? I think some things are better not shared with neighbors." I said.

"You have four minutes." She stepped back, allowing me into the house and shutting the door.

"Do your children speak Spanish?"

"A little, not really. Is this really what you want to talk about?"

"Joe is Hombre Lobo," I said.

"Get out!" She pointed at the door.

"Think about it. When did things come off the tracks? It was the full moon after he was attacked at Victoria Barrios's house."

"You're not actually asking me to believe this is about him becoming a werewolf. You're crazier than he is," she said.

"Talk to your Nanna. She knows the truth," I said. "This isn't about a woman, it's about Joe's survival."

"You need to leave," she said.

"I will. But, you need to call your Nanna. Better yet, drive out there and talk to her. She can't lie to you in person," I said.

"What do you know about Nanna?"

"You feel the truth in my words and it scares you. Talk to your Nanna, but when she says Joe can't be saved, don't listen. I don't buy it," I said.

"Your time is up."

I opened the door. "Joe has my number if you want to talk."

"Why do you think I'll be talking to him?"

"Because Joe is an honorable man." She was in no mood to hear anything else, so I moved through the doorway.

"What happened?" Joe asked, still standing on the sidewalk next to his truck.

"You're going to need to give her time to cool down. I'll help you load your stuff in the truck," I said.

"This is my house," he said defiantly.

I picked up an armful of clothing and walked it over to his truck as he watched.

"Not tonight and it's going to rain," I said.

Joe shook his head and pulled the cover back on the bed of his pickup. "I really want to kill that bastard for biting me! He's lucky he's in jail."

"Where'd Daphne go?" The moment I said it, I realized I'd already broken my promise.

"Her name is Susan and she's just up the street."

"Hang on a second," I said. I pulled out my phone and called Leotown Bank and Trust. Joe continued throwing his possessions into the truck bed.

"David Phibbly, please," I said.

"He's not available right now. May I take a message?" A woman informed me after I'd already been transferred twice.

"No. How about Kim Munstel?"

"I'll try her for you. One moment." I tapped my foot and looked at the ground, not making eye contact with Joe.

"Who may I say is calling?"

"Felix Slade," I said.

Only a few moments passed when Kim answered. "Kim Munstel. How may I help you, Mr. Slade?"

"I was trying to get ahold of Phibbly. I have a question about the trust," I said.

"Sure. I can help with that," she answered.

"Once I pass the test, how long before I can take possession?"

"I'm not sure, but I can read through the trust and get you an answer. David said something about inspections," she replied.

"I'm coming over to the bank right now. Will you be there?"

"I will."

"Would you see if you can find Phibbly?"

"I'll do my best," she said.

I hung up and noticed that Joe had finished loading his truck. "What was that about?"

I ignored his question and handed him my apartment keys. "Take Daphne to my apartment. Make sure she behaves herself. I have something I need to take care of. And what happened to the light brown wolf?"

He glared at my reference to Daphne. "Jerry is lying low. You don't need to worry about him," he said. "You're not going to tell me what you talked to Jennifer about?"

"Baby steps. We'll talk tonight," I said and walked over to my truck.

"Seriously?"

"And, keep Daphne out of my stuff." I hopped in my truck and drove off.

I dialed Gabriella.

"How busy are you?" I asked when she picked up.

"Why?"

"I might need some lawyerly help."

"Are you in jail again?" She asked.

I laughed. "No. I'm getting some resistance from Phibbly. I think it might be because I don't talk lawyer."

"He's good, but I've heard he can be a stickler for detail. That's actually a good thing for a trust administrator," she said.

"He lied to me today."

"That doesn't sound like him. About what?" Gabriella asked.

"I asked him if he knew how the police came up with the trust document. He said he didn't."

"You're sure he lied about that? How would he even know you were being held by the police?"

"I don't know. He definitely lied though," I said.

"What do you think that's about?"

"There was a test I had to pass to prove my family lineage."

"What kind of test?"

"A dangerous one. You remember how I told you the lycan were trying to get Clarita to open a door in the mansion?"

"Yeah.... What's this have to do with Clarita?"

"Test required I open that door. There were bad things in that basement. I think someone has been trying their best to get me out of the way. Things that I believe Phibbly thought would kill me. "

"You're serious."

"I am. There were three other claimants listed on that trust and not one of them has returned from the mansion after being vetted by the bank. At least one of them was still dead in the basement. Phibbly thought I'd be number four."

"What do you need from me?"

"I guess I just wanted to talk it out. I think that old mansion is wrapped up in this mess." I said as I pulled into the bank's parking lot. "Ahh, shit."

"What?"

"Fred's here," I said.

"The red lycan Amak was fighting with last night?"

"The same," I said. Fred was seated on his motorcycle in a parking spot next to the front door watching me as I pulled in.

"Get out of there," she said.

"I'll call you back," I said and hung up.

"Turn around, slick," the man growled as I approached.

"Probably not," I said, making a bee-line for the door.

With preternatural speed, he jumped from his motorcycle and blocked my passage into the bank. I pulled up short, inches from his face. The wet-dog smell and foul breath assaulted my nose as he jabbed his finger into my forehead. "You're not listening."

I swatted his hand from my head, which was, of course, the wrong thing to do. It can't be overstated just how quickly a lycan moves. My hand barely made contact before he'd grabbed my wrist and pulled it behind my back.

"What's going on out here?"

The automated door to the bank opened behind us and a uniformed guard stood in the entry.

"Back inside," Fred growled, momentarily loosening his grip. I used the distraction to release energy from my thumb ring. It was the same ring I'd underutilized on my first encounter with Shaggy and I wasn't about to make that mistake again. I dumped the entire energy store into the lycan's midsection and he dropped like a rock.

The older guard looked from the fallen lycan to me and back. "Not sure what his problem was," I said. "But he said he had a gun. Any chance you have cuffs on you?" I pushed a suggestion on him that I was probably an officer of the law and he bought it enough to hand me the cuffs. I pulled the gun from the lycan's belt, laid it on the ground and then cuffed his hands behind his back.

"Get inside." The guard's hands shook as he pulled keys from his pocket. I stepped over the lycan and into the foyer. The guard pulled the door closed and flipped the lock. "Heather, I'm placing Pine West on lockdown. I've detained an armed man who assaulted a customer," he said into a radio he'd pulled from his belt.

"I'll just be upstairs. I have business in the trust department," I said, pushing him once again so that he wouldn't try to keep me from leaving the foyer.

"Hello?" I said. The receptionist tore her attention away from the front door and looked at me, confused.

"Mr. Slade," I heard from behind me. I turned to see Kim Munstel approaching. "Welcome back, I was told we shouldn't expect to see you."

"Oh?"

"Yes. David said you wouldn't be coming after all."

"Weird. Is he in his office?"

"I'll take you up." She led me to the elevator and we rode up to the third floor.

"Knock, knock," I said as we arrived at Phibbly's office. He looked up from his desk, startled, as recognition set in.

"Kim, would you give us a moment?" he asked.

"Certainly," she said, looking at me for agreement. I nodded and she retreated down the hallway.

I closed the door behind me as I stepped into Phibbly's office. "What do you know about all this, Mr. Phibbly?"

"I'm quite sure I don't know what you're talking about."

"You need to come up with a new line. That's the second time you've lied to me today. You're involved in two murders and the kidnapping of a six-year-old girl. How long are you going to keep your job when that gets out?" I asked.

"That's not true. I've nothing to do with any of that," he said.

"Maybe not, but you called someone when you heard I'd retrieved the jar. Whoever that was, they sent one of their killers to ambush me in front of the bank. Your guard has him in custody and I'm sure the cops are on their way. Whoever tried to kill me is linking you to the murders so you can take the fall," I said.

"That's preposterous."

"Maybe," I agreed and pulled the jar from my pocket and set it on the desk. "Regardless, it's time to finish the test, Phibbly."

Phibbly looked at me, the blood draining from his face. To his credit, his hands were solid as a rock as he dialed the phone. "Kim, could you bring the Tenebris file?"

Moments later, she knocked gently on the door before opening it. "Is that it?" She set a file box on Phibbly's conference table and nodded at the jar I'd put on his desk.

"We'll soon see," Phibbly said, rising from his chair.

"I've been reading the charter," Kim said. "It says we place the smaller phial that was activated with the applicant's blood into the larger jar retrieved from the mansion. If the jar is authentic, it should turn a bright blue. Is it a chemical reaction? I've never seen a paternity test like this."

"Must be." Phibbly removed the still glowing green phial from the file box and dropped it into the carved crystal jar in his hand. The glowing green showed through the jar as if it was simply glass, which I suspected it was.

"What does that mean?" Munstel asked.

"Looks like it wasn't a good match. I'm sorry, Mr. Slade. It doesn't appear to be your lucky day. I'm sorry for your trouble," he said. "Kim, would you escort Mr. Slade to the lobby?"

"Odd," I said. "But that's not the jar I brought in."

"How's that?" he asked.

I'd felt a wave of unusual energy from him when he'd stood up from the desk and it had prompted me to pay closer attention. I didn't actually see him switch the jars, but he'd shuffled his hands in such a way that it didn't take much of a guess.

"*Altum Visu*," I said, waving my hands in front of my eyes.

"What's going on?" Munstel asked.

"It's all right, Kim." I scanned Phibbly's office. As I suspected, the jar had a unique magical signature which was easy to pick up with my wizard's sight. "I think you'll find my jar in the fern."

"*Finis*," I said. Strictly speaking, I wasn't supposed to cast spells in front of mundanes, but wizard's sight wasn't a particularly obvious spell.

Neither Kim nor Phibbly moved, so I took a quick step over to the potted plant and retrieved the jar. It had been a nice bit of sleight of hand on Phibbly's part.

"What happened to your eyes?" Kim asked.

"Are our conversations confidential if I'm a customer?" I asked.

"Of course," Kim replied.

"I'd ask that you keep what you saw to yourself in that case." I set the jar on the table. "Let's give that one a try."

"David. What's the meaning of this?" Kim asked.

"Just do it," he sighed, his cocky attitude deflating.

A bright blue glow emanated from the jar as it was combined with the green glowing phial containing my blood.

"That's it!" Kim exclaimed. "It's blue. It's magic." She clasped her hand over her mouth as realization sunk in.

"Maybe we could avoid using that word, eh?" I asked.

"Really?" she whispered.

"What now?" I ignored her question. "When do I take possession?"

"It's immediate," Kim said. "I read the charter through this morning. There's no provision for inspections. Mr. Slade, you're now the proud, probationary owner of the property at 230 Happy Hollow Boulevard."

MONEY PIT

"This is a nice upgrade from the interrogation room," I said as I was dropped off at an office where Lieutenant Dukats sat behind her desk. "Does this mean I'm not under arrest?"

The police had arrived at the bank shortly after I'd finished up my business with Phibbly and Munstel. One thing had led to another and after a call to the station, Dukats had requested a visit.

"We're still checking your story. According to bank personnel, you were assaulted on your way to a meeting," she said. "There's more to it though, isn't there."

"Joe Lozano should be able to identify this guy as being one of Clarita Barrios' kidnappers," I said.

"You know we take a dim view of vigilantes, right? You need to leave the police work to us."

"I was assaulted," I said. "If it weren't for that guard, I might have been shot."

"Don't play me, Slade," she said. "We both know the guard wasn't physically capable of taking that man down. I haven't looked at the bank's video yet, but I'd be willing to bet when I do, your story falls apart. Fill me in. What's really going on?"

"You wouldn't believe me if I told you," I said. I mentally face palmed, realizing my statement was chum in the water for a curious mind like Dukats'.

"You don't think I know this has an occult angle? I've been to your apartment, Slade."

"I really can't say anything about that," I said.

"I'll bet you wouldn't be surprised to learn I've received a call from the Feds. They insist we keep Flaeger in solitary and I suspect they're going to want me to do the same with Bothelman."

"Bothelman?"

"The gentleman you claim assaulted you outside of Leotown Bank and Trust," she said. "Both Flaeger and Bothelman lit up AFIS like a Christmas tree. The thing is, they read more like muscle for hire than they do brains."

"I've no idea what AFIS is or why you're telling me this."

"National fingerprinting database. And I'm telling you this because you need my help. You're in over your head, Slade. Feds are about to take this case and my Captain is going to shut it down. Bad guys are behind bars, case closed."

"If you know all this, why'd you drag me down here?"

"Because there's something brewing out there and it's about to boil over - all over my city," she said.

"I hope you're wrong, Lieutenant. Shaggy was bad news and I'd hate to think there's more where that came from," I said.

"You're free to go, Mr. Slade," she said.

"You don't need Joe to clear me?"

"He already did."

I stood up. "I don't suppose I could get a ride back to my truck?"

"You're at the center of this thing, Slade. Put me on speed dial and I'll see you get a ride," Dukats said.

***

I pulled a slice of pizza from the box on the broken coffee table in my living room. Joe and Daphne had ordered in and were on their third pie.

"You guys always eat this much?"

"Shifting takes a lot of energy," Joe said.

"Sue, you mind telling me what you were doing with Clarita at the mansion?"

She looked at Joe. "Go ahead," he said. "He's not going to make trouble. Right Felix?"

"I don't know, Joe. She helped kidnap a six-year-old girl and wanted to kill her," I said.

"I did not help kidnap her," she said. "I didn't even know I was a werewolf when that happened."

"But, you don't deny you wanted to kill her. I was there, remember?"

She looked at me with sadness in her eyes. "Your world is so simple, everything so black and white."

"When it comes to six-year-old girls, it sure is," I said.

"How about we try to stay on track," Joe said. "Sue, what were you doing with the girl?"

"We were supposed to get her to open the door to the basement."

"Did she try?"

Daphne ... no Susan ... nodded and dropped her head. "She did. Brand did. We all did. That door was stuck with more than rust. Mostly she just cried, though."

"Go figure. She'd just seen her mother murdered and was being held by werewolves," I said.

"Look pal. We all have baggage. If you hadn't noticed, our lives just got ripped apart too."

I sighed. She wasn't wrong. At some level, she had been victimized here, just as Jennifer and Joe had been. "How'd you meet Shaggy... er Brand?" I asked, trying to soften my voice.

"I waitress at a diner on I-35. He came in one night. I guess I have a thing for bad-boys. One thing led to another and we were sleeping off our party when he must have shifted and bit me. I woke up and after that, I had a hard time saying no to him," she said. "Look, I knew it was fucked up, but what could I do? I think he grabbed me so I could look after the girl. I guess he thought all women have a soft spot for kids."

"Guess he was wrong." I still wasn't ready to forgive her for threatening to kill Clarita. It felt like she was telling the truth, although, she and Joe were both hard to read.

"I've lived a crappy life and never wanted kids, so tough shit," she said.

"Tell me what you talked to Jennifer about?" Joe asked, changing subjects.

"I told her you're lycan and she should talk to her

grandmother," I said.

"You told her? She's got to be freaking out. I can't believe you did that without talking to me." He rose from his chair, tossing a piece of pizza back into the box. Sue stood with him.

"Calm down, Joe. How'd you think it was going to go? You trash the house, then disappear and when you finally show back up, it's with another woman. You need to understand. This isn't a disease you take a pill for. Lycan don't get better. They ruin the lives of people around them."

Joe took my standing up as a provocative move and placed his hands on my chest.

My heart raced as I looked into eyes which had changed from brown to yellow. A low growl emanated from his chest. "It wasn't your decision." He pushed me backward and I stumbled, almost falling back into the chair.

"No? You called me, Joe. If you want to screw up your life without me, go ahead. It's already a train-wreck. I just happen to hold out hope that you might be able to beat the odds. But you're not doing that without the help of your wife and even your grandmother. If you want to have it out, let's get after it. Better with me than Jennifer."

I stood completely still as he picked up a lamp and tossed it into the wall, roaring as he did. I could see the war within him. He wanted to respond physically, but was holding back, at least for now.

"You're pushing me," he said, his eyes returning to brown.

"No more than when you argue with your wife. You really think you're ready to be in the same room with her?"

He sat heavily in the chair and rested his head in his hands. "No. You're right. I was ready to rip your head off just then. What am I going to do?"

"You're not alone, Joe. The first thing we need to do is get Jennifer on board, but you can't push her. If she'll let you back in, then she sets the pace. For now, we need to wait for her to talk to Nanna and hope she reaches out," I said.

"And, if she doesn't?"

"We'll deal with it." I pulled a book from my shelf that had a few references to lycan and handed it to him.

"What's this?" He opened the book and started paging through it. "I can't read anything. It's in a foreign language."

"Welcome to my world. It's time to learn how to read Latin. The good news is, most of it isn't about werewolves, so you won't have too much to transcribe."

"How am I supposed to do that?"

"Oh, come on. Can you read Spanish?"

"Sure."

"Latin isn't that far off. Use the internet. Google will do the translation for you, but you'd be better off learning how to read it. All the material I have is Latin."

"We don't need moldy old books to tell us what it's like to be werewolves," Sue snapped. "We're living it."

"And doing a bang-up job." I turned on her. "Your first act as a werewolf was to participate in a kidnapping and your second was to beg to kill a child so you could get on with your life." It was a low blow, but I was tired of her woe-is-me attitude.

She jumped back up and swung, landing a blow on my cheek. I saw stars and stumbled in the cluttered space, but didn't go down. "Shit."

"Sit down, Sue," Joe growled. "Knock it off, Felix. You can't keep poking her like that."

Her response seemed disproportionate, but he had a point. I wasn't holding back my anger in a volatile environment and I'd received a quick lesson in etiquette.

"You're welcome to my apartment for a couple of nights. After that, you need to figure out something else," I said, nursing my jaw.

"Where are you going?" Joe asked as I started stuffing books into my satchel.

"I'll be around," I said. There was no way I was going to feel safe sleeping in an apartment with two werewolves. "Just lock up when you leave."

Once I was in the truck, I dialed Amak.

"Booty call?"

"You gotta stop that! It's not easy for me to say no to you," I said, meaning every word.

"What! The sex is good," she said.

"And, I never know if you're being compelled to do it or not," I said.

"I've had worse jobs."

"That's not helping," I said. "I'm headed over to Happy Hollow, want to do a sleepover?"

"I thought you said that was off the table," she said.

"Sex is off the table, but you're still my friend."

"I'll bring the booze; you get food. I'm thinking gyros," she said.

Thirty minutes later I pulled into the circular drive in front of the Tenebris Manerium with a bag full of gyros. I looked up at the canopy of trees as I stepped from the truck. The weak light of the late October sky a dull glow behind the leaves. Mentally, I added exterior lighting to a quickly growing list of repairs I had to fit within the thirty-thousand-dollar maintenance budget.

The sound of a beefy engine and blaring radio broke me from my contemplation. I turned to see the lights of Amak's Jeep bouncing along the entry lane as she avoided the many obstacles on her way in. I added clearing the lane to the top of my work list. It occurred to me that I might not own Tenebris Manerium as much as it now owned me.

"So is this place yours now?" Amak asked, swinging out of the Jeep onto the ground next to me. I appreciated that she was wearing loose sweats instead of the tight, revealing clothing she seemed to prefer.

"Who's asking?"

"Just me, but I can't guarantee Camille or Liise won't ask about it," she said.

"Everything you see here is mine," I said. "Such as it is."

"I love what you've done with the place," she laughed, wrapping a long arm around my shoulders as we walked toward the breezeway entrance. "It's so... so…"

"Gothic?" I asked, noticing the stone gargoyles staring down at us.

"If that means 'about to fall down,' then yeah, Gothic," she agreed. "I hope you brought a lot of gyros. I'm starving."

"I might not have thought very hard about how cold it was in October," I said as I pushed through the door into the mudroom.

"It'll be fifty tonight. If we snuggle, we'll stay warm." The brat waggled her eyebrows suggestively.

"If we keep it to snuggling," I said.

"Did you ever make it to the basement?" she asked. "That's the thing Liise was all worked up about, although I think she doesn't care quite so much now."

"What do you mean, she doesn't care?"

"I transferred a call from the bank to her today that I might have listened in on."

"From David Phibbly?"

"How'd you know?" she asked. "Anyway he told her that you'd been confirmed as the heir to this old dump. She pretty much lost her shit on him."

"What's her tie to Phibbly?"

"He's a witch. Part of Illuminaire," she said.

"You don't see a lot of male witches," I observed.

"Illuminaire has three of them. There are only two other male witches in the whole city," she said. "You know, I should have brought a chainsaw. We could have made a fire."

We'd made it into the kitchen and Amak was looking at the brick fireplace next to the oven, its hearth at waist level.

"You want to see what all the fuss is about?" I asked.

"Like you have to ask," she said, pulling a beer from the 12-pack she had under her arm. "Want one?" She handed me the beer she'd just pulled out.

I led her back through the solarium, its walls empty of glass and open to the back woods. I mentally added 'sealing breaches in the outside walls' to my fix-it list. We walked through the casual family room where we'd first hidden, listening to the plans of the kidnappers. Finally, we made our way over to the back staircase. I pushed through the lock on the first door and we went down the circular stone staircase to the main entry of the lab. I had to put the beer down to manage the more complex lock, but I finally got it open.

"I was thinking we could spend the night here," I said, setting the bag of gyros on the desk. I took one for myself and slid the bag in Amak's direction.

"How are your wounds?" I asked. "Aren't you worried about lycan infection?"

"Nah, they have no effect on me, aside from hurting that is," she said.

"Dukats seems to think capturing Shaggy was just the beginning. She's certain there's more to come." I leaned back in the leather chair that I was sure belonged to my mother. I dug into the gyro.

"Dukats?"

"Lieutenant with Leotown's finest," I said.

"I don't know. It seems to me that Shaggy was the bad news."

"Holy Shit!" I said, looking at the silver spell circle in front of the fireplace. The skeletal remains I'd taken the jar from were gone, the sword was replaced on the wall and the silver kettle I'd knocked from the lab table was once again sitting upright and in its original location. In fact, everything I'd upended during my fight with the shades was back in its original place.

"What?" Amak sat straighter and looked around, readying herself for action.

"I'm not sure. Someone's been here and cleaned up. There was a corpse on the ground when I left."

"You had to kill someone?"

"No. It was a skeleton, but it's gone now."

"Doesn't seem like the sort of thing I'd complain about," Amak said, grabbing a lab stool and rolling it over to the desk. "What do you want to do tomorrow? I'm off."

"I was thinking about getting someone out to look at electricity and heat. If I'm real ambitious, I might move my own lab equipment over," I said.

"Do you remember being here? According to Liise Straightrod, you lived here when you were really young," she said.

"Why would she tell you that?"

"She might not have known I was listening."

"You're a scamp." I tossed a french fry at her.

"You can't imagine how boring it gets out there in the country. Different groups of witches have meetings and my job is to make sure nobody breaks in or roughs anyone up. Which, of course, no one ever does because witches just don't get all that rowdy."

It felt good to just hang out and chat with someone. Later on, we found old blankets in a closet and stretched out in front of the fireplace. It wasn't as comfortable as a bed, but it was manageable. We finally drifted off to sleep sometime after midnight.

The next morning, I awoke refreshed but sore. Something about sleeping on the hard floor hadn't done me any good. Unfortunately, we didn't have running water, so I had to run outside to take care of business. I added yet another item to the ever-growing list of house maintenance tasks.

It was after eight in the morning, so I dialed Andy. "Good morning, Felix. Everything okay with those doors?"

"They're perfect, Andy," I said. "Any chance you have some time this morning to take a look at a few things?"

"You have more problems at your apartment?"

"No. I just came into a house and don't know how to get the power, water and all that turned on," I said. I was still outside, looking around at the property in the morning light. My eyes fell on a ramshackle greenhouse where most of the glass had fallen in. It was twenty feet from the back side of the house. Item number fifty-two on the repair list, I thought sarcastically.

"Sure, I can help. I'll have to bring my kid along. I've got babysitting duty while Kelli's at work," he said.

"No problem. I'll text you the address," I said.

I went inside and found Amak looking around the kitchen.

"No food in here, not even a can of beans," she complained. "And those darn werewolves made a heck of a mess in the front of the house."

"Let's go get some breakfast and a chainsaw," I said.

"In that order?"

We walked out and jumped into my truck. I noticed Maggie's silhouette and found her sitting atop one of the many gargoyles on the front of the house. I whistled at her and she nodded in acknowledgement, but didn't join us.

An hour later we returned with a new chainsaw, gas and oil. We set right to work clearing the entryway at the street. We cut back vegetation and freed the once proud stone pillars that bracketed the brick-paved driveway. At some point in time, a reckless driver must have veered off Happy Hollow and knocked one of them over. I pulled out a notepad and added the pillar to the list of items to be fixed.

About the time we'd finished clearing the entry, Andy pulled up in his work truck. A red haired, ten-year-old boy sat next to him, fidgeting.

"House is just down the road," I said. "You'll have to go around the back and in through the broken solarium attached to the dining room. The doors are all locked for some reason."

"I'll see what it's going to take to get your water on, but you'll want heat before we open the valves. Hard freeze is around the corner," he said.

"Could you make a list and see what needs to be done to, at least, get us limping along?"

"Sure can," he said and drove off down the lane.

Amak and I settled into a comfortable rhythm of work. We'd decided to concentrate on clearing the brick lane of the fallen trees. As we worked, we uncovered a bridge that spanned a dry creek bed and discovered that several of the six-inch thick planks were rotted. I began to wonder if we'd ever discover any good news related to the house. Two hours into it, Andy finally returned, rolling to a stop next to us.

"Looks like you're making good progress. What are you going to do with all that firewood?" He was looking at the back of my pickup that was now filled.

"No shortage of fireplaces," Amak said.

"True," Andy agreed. "I'd get someone out to inspect 'em before you burn, though. Critters like to build nests in abandoned fireplaces."

I pulled out my notepad and added it to the list.

"What's it going to take to get the water and electricity on?" I asked.

"Good news or bad?"

"Good," I said.

"You're on a well and the electrical looks relatively modern. Once you call the city for electricity, you'll probably get water too," he said. "Although, it'd be worth getting someone..."

"To inspect the well," I finished his sentence as I wrote down yet one more thing to do. "If that's the good news, then what's the bad?"

"Boiler looks shot. You could be looking at ten or twelve thousand to get it running," he said. "I also looked at your roof. There's another twenty thousand in that, although I could probably patch a few places enough to get you through the winter," he said.

"You're full of good news. What would it cost to have you patch it?"

"Six or seven hundred," he said.

"Let's do that," I said. "Any recommendation on a furnace company?"

"You want me to call 'em out?"

"Sure. Why not?"

FAMILY TIES

My phone rang as we stacked the third load of firewood onto racks in a wood shed next to the long garage. It was late in the afternoon and I was physically exhausted. I felt good about having cleared the lane all the way to the house, especially since Leotown Public Power had then been able to make it down the drive and work on our power issues. We now had lights and water. Even better, Andy's furnace company was coming out in the morning.

The caller id showed Gabriella.

"Heya," I answered. "What's shaking?"

"I was talking with Mari and she said you might be working for Willow. That true?"

"I'm going to talk to her on Monday, but it looks hopeful."

"Do you really need work now? I thought you came into an inheritance."

"According to Phibbly, I can draw some money to repair the property, but after looking around, that's not going to cover much," I said.

"How much?"

"Thirty thousand a year," I said.

"That sounds like a lot to me."

"This place is a wreck. It needs a new boiler, new roof and before we start heating, we have to close in the solarium. The house is totally open to the outside in the back," I said.

"Doesn't sound like the bank did a very good job of maintaining the property. Do you want me to look at the trust? There might be emergency provisions," she said.

"That'd be really nice," I said. "I don't have a copy of it, though."

"I'm close to the bank. If you call Phibbly and tell him that I'm your legal representative, he'll give me a copy," she said.

"I wouldn't count on it. Did you know he's a witch?"

"Of course I do. He's Illuminaire."

"Well, he tried to trick me when he figured out I was going to pass the stupid blood line tests," I said.

"That doesn't sound like him. He's a little odd, but we've always gotten along."

"Mind if I call Kim Munstel instead?"

"You should be able to talk to anyone in the department. This isn't a big ask," she said. "So Clarita and I were thinking about bringing you dinner tonight. Any interest?"

"Great, when?"

"Six thirty. She wants mac-n-cheese."

"Tell her I want extra cheese on mine." I placed the phone on my chest and looked at Amak who was pulling weeds out from around the shed. "Clarita and Gabriella are coming over for dinner. Are you in?"

"Do you think she wants me here?" Amak asked, eyebrows raised.

"I do. You're my friend. We're all friends and we can hang out together."

She smiled and shrugged her shoulders. "Sure. Extra meaty, if there's a choice."

I put the phone back to my ear. "I suppose you heard all that."

"You're not sleeping with Amak anymore?"

"No. Long story. I'm hoping you guys can play nice," I said.

"After what she did for Clarita, she's got a lifetime pass with me. I just don't know what you see in a troll," she said.

"A good hearted, beautiful, powerful woman not unlike yourself," I said. "Is Clarita going to be okay coming to Happy Hollow?"

"We'll play it by the ear, but she really wants to see you. I have a theory I want to pass by you, but I need to look at that trust first," she said.

"I'll call right away," I said.

"See you in a couple of hours."

"What now?" Amak asked.

"Feels like time for a beer run and maybe we could drop by my apartment for a shower and fresh clothes."

***

"You guys must be exhausted. I didn't even recognize the entrance," Gabriella commented as she set her bags on the rough-hewn table I'd found in the shop attached to the garage. Upon seeing me, Clarita had climbed into my arms, snuggling her head on my shoulder.

"Heya, kiddo," I whispered in her ear. "Glad you came over. I missed you." She hugged me tighter, but didn't otherwise respond.

Amak had set a fire in the kitchen fireplace. I'd retrieved a cooler from the garage and stocked it with long-necked beer, which I found preferable to Amak's inexpensive twelve-pack. The water was still running a rusty brown, but it was enough to get the toilets working. After exhaustively exploring the house, we couldn't find any leaks, which surprised me.

"I'm starved," Amak said as Gabriella placed large styrene bowls of steaming sides on the table. "Beer, Gabby?" Amak held out a bottle to her.

Gabriella winced at the nickname, but didn't correct her as she accepted the beer. "That'd be great." It was a simple act, but I smiled at the interaction. They were playing nice, if only for the moment.

"Have you found a place for you and Clarita, yet?" I asked, scooping a portion of mac-and-cheese onto a plate for Clarita.

"Not yet, but Brian's being a trooper about it," she said.

I could feel the shaded truth of her statement and raised an eyebrow as she spoke.

Before I could say anything, a tapping at one of the kitchen windows caught our attention. "Why don't you get after your dinner and I'll check that out," I said, placing Clarita on the bench next to me. Initially she resisted, but finally gave in.

I unlatched the vertically hinged window and swung it inward. I'd recognized the tapping and wasn't surprised when Maggie jumped onto the window sill. I was surprised, however, when she fluttered over to the end of the table, sinking her claws into the edge.

"Felix?" Amak asked, trying to assess the threat.

"She's okay, Amak. Maggie is a friend," I said.

Clarita, who had a habit of keeping her long hair in front of her face gave the crow a shy smile as Maggie nodded her head. I wasn't sure what to make of the exchange. Maggie's ways were still largely a mystery to me.

"What do you think of my new friends, Maggie?" I asked. I was pleased when she replied with a long cawwk and bobbed her head several times. "Clarita, Maggie really likes meat. If you pull some chicken from the bone and put on the table, it'll make her happy." I didn't have to prompt Clarita further and she offered hunks of chicken from my plate to a grateful Maggie.

"What have you heard from Joe?" Gabriella asked, once I'd sat back down.

"Not much today. Apparently, he's now alpha of his own little pack. At least that gray is following him. Her name is Susan Bluestein. There was another, Jerry something or other, but I haven't heard much about him," I said. "Joe and Susan stayed the night at my apartment, but when we went over for showers, they were gone and my keys were on the table. I hope he can pull it together."

"Odds aren't good," Gabriella said. "Especially if he keeps shifting. I was doing some reading at the Witches' Council Library today. There's a belief that every time they shift, they take on more characteristics of the lobo. Not evil, specifically, but not necessarily what we see as good."

"So, what did Phibbly say when you showed up?" I asked, changing the subject.

"No problems. He gave me a copy of the trust. It's a big document. I asked him about emergency provisions and he said repairs to plumbing, structure and roof were all covered outside of the maintenance allowance. He just needs two bids for any major item like that," she said. "Maybe you just got off to the wrong foot with him. He is a little odd. How about this? You give me bids for the furnace and roof and I'll get Phibbly to approve them."

"I can take 'em over to the bank, but maybe you could make a call once I do."

Gabriella pulled a thick sheaf of papers from her bag and laid it on the table.

"Is that the trust agreement?" I asked.

"Sure is. Something you said about those identity tests sounded odd. They were looking for people in the right blood line," she said, flipping through papers. "It got me to thinking. Why Clarita? Why did they have her working on that door to the basement?"

"How does looking through the trust help with that?" I asked.

Gabriella pointed to something on one of the pages. "Here it is. How much do you know about your lineage?"

"Nothing more than my mom and dad's names."

"Egils was your dad? Your brothers were Filip and Geoff and your sister was Sevena?"

The world became nothing more than a tunnel between us as my heart sped up and my hands started sweating. I found it difficult to breathe, much less talk. It was as if something was crushing my throat as she spoke.

"Felix? Are you okay?" Gabriella asked and I heard Maggie squawking. Breathing was becoming more difficult.

Clarita's small hand slid into my own, her tiny fingers interlacing with mine. Warmth spread from her hand and I felt the same connection I'd only experienced once before. I closed my eyes and concentrated on drawing comfort from her presence. The darkness around me lightened and the tightness on my throat loosened. The remnants of a spell cracked and broke away from me and the world returned.

"Felix, what was that?" Gabriella asked, still worried. Even Amak had a concerned look on her face.

"We're buddies," Clarita said, surprising everyone at the table. I wrapped my arm around her and pulled her in close. I could have cried at the joy I felt at our connection.

"A spell," I managed to squeak out. "Something was holding back my memories. Clarita helped me break it."

"As Clarita's guardian, I have access to her birth certificate. Her father is listed as Geoff Baltazoss. That's your brother's first name and mother's maiden name, which she never changed. The trust charter has a list of people who are possible claimants. Your name is listed just beneath Filip, Geoff and Sevena's. But they all have the Baltazoss last name."

"You're saying Clarita is my niece?"

"I think you already know the truth. I saw your face when she leaned into you. The two of you joined, didn't you?"

"We did something. I could feel her. I don't know how to describe it, but it felt like… it sounds stupid, but it felt like home."

Gabriella smiled. "That's a witch's circle. With people you trust, there's nothing more fulfilling. I can only imagine how it would be with family."

Maggie squawked loudly and fluttered out the window.

"Another beer?" Amak asked, pulling two from the cooler. It seemed like she'd become uncomfortable with all of the witch and wizard talk.

"Oh, hell yes!" I said, gratefully accepting one.

"Do you think all this bad stuff was about control of Happy Hollow?" Gabriella asked. "Not that I don't like your new digs here, but I don't see it."

"I can think of twenty-eight million reasons," I said.

Shock filled her face. "That's the value of this place?"

"No. That's just the liquid assets," I said.

"I suppose," she agreed. "But murder? Kidnapping? I don't know, it just felt like there was more going on than that."

"Lieutenant Dukats agrees with you," I said. "She's not buying Shaggy as the brains."

"What else could it be?" Gabriella asked.

"Witches aren't all love and flowers," Amak said.

"What's that?" Gabriella asked, turning on Amak, who flinched at the attention. It reminded me just how much I hated the hold witches had over trolls.

"It's not mine to tell, but there's more here than property," Amak said, looking down at the table.

"What are you talking about?" Gabriella asked.

"She's right. There's something I want you and Clarita to see," I said, standing up from the table.

"Where are we going?"

"To the basement," I said.

Clarita's hand grabbed my own and she pulled me down so my face was next to her own. "Bad things," she whispered.

"I sent them away," I whispered back, pulling her up so she could wrap her legs around my waist. I knew she could feel the truth in my words, but I felt her trepidation, nonetheless.

We made our way through the dining room slash solarium, which was now just one big room since the panes were all missing from the huge French doors and floor to ceiling windows. We passed through the family room and finally entered the back hallway, which joined the basement, the stairs leading up and the front and back of the house.

"This is the door Clarita was trying to open," I said. "Want to give it a try, Gabriella?"

"I don't see why not," she said and pulled on the handle.

"No. There's a wizard's lock on there. You need to manipulate the tumblers before it'll open. And, you might want to let go..."

"Ouch!" She shook her hand.

"Let me see." I inspected her hand with my free one. Her palm was red, but not burned. "I probably should have warned you. It has a deterrent against other attempts at entry, as you just figured out."

She glared at me and pulled her hand back.

"You want to give it a try, little monkey?" I asked. Clarita buried her face into my shoulder and shook her head no. "I'll show you, if you'd like. I think you can do it." She shook her head again and I chose not to push it.

I ran my hand across the surface, manipulated the lock and

pushed on the handle. As expected, it opened and the wall sconces lit the circular stone staircase going down into the basement.

"A dungeon?" Gabriella asked.

"Nothing so dark," I said walking down the stairs. I didn't even bother asking Clarita if she wanted to try the lab door's lock, as it was work, even for me. Moreover, when I tried to set Clarita down, she wouldn't cooperate and only held me tighter.

"*Altum Visu.*" I cast my wizard's sight and as I did, Clarita grabbed my wrist. I could feel her connection and I wondered if she was capable of seeing the same view I had of our surroundings. I moved quickly to open the door and dropped my wizard's sight.

"Would you look at that?" Gabriella whispered in awe as she entered the room. My eyes flitted up to the sword I'd used to dispatch the shades, the battle still fresh in my mind. "All those books and look at that circle. You're right, this would be priceless to the right people. You're saying Shaggy knew about this?"

"Amak and I heard Shaggy talking about how 'the boss' wouldn't let them leave until they got the door open. I think someone knew about this lab and wanted access."

"There must be a thousand books," she said staring at the back and side walls covered in book shelves. "Do you mind?" She'd crossed the room and put her hand on a narrow tome.

"Go ahead," I said, plopping in my mother's leather chair. Her face and long dark hair came easily to mind now. I had a memory of playing in this very room as she worked at the desk. I breathed in her scent mixed with old leather, relaxing with Clarita in my arms. "See, monkey? Bad guys are all gone." She nodded her head in agreement.

"You and Clarita could sublet my apartment over Mrs. Willoughby," I said. Gabriella was sitting on the floor, cross-legged, flipping through the book she'd pulled from the shelf.

"That'd be super. I'm having trouble finding a place," she said. "Did you know this book is an atlas of North American ley lines?"

"Ley lines?"

"Spiritual and mystical sites are believed to be joined through ley lines, like power couplings. Do you have a U.S. map handy?"

"No."

She stood and placed the book on the desk, opened to a page where several large lines intersected next to a river. "You think that's Leotown?" I asked.

"I'd need a map with more details on it, but I recognize the river pattern here." She pointed to a spot on the map.

"Makes sense. Where else are you going to find five covens in a single town, not to mention werewolves and trolls?"

"You'd be surprised," Amak said. She'd spread out the blankets and laid down in front of the fire.

"Liise Straightrod would kill to get her hands on these books," Gabriella said.

"Seriously?"

She looked up at me, her cheeks red with embarrassment. "No. It was a figure of speech. It's just that she's really into this kind of stuff."

***

When Monday morning finally came, I was exhausted and sore. I'd spent a few hours duct-taping heavy plastic sheeting over the empty wall of glass separating the dining room from the solarium. Now, instead of a strong breeze flowing into the dining area and out through the rest of the house, it was still. We could all get used to the constant flapping of the plastic if it meant the house would be warmer. My efforts paid off when the furnace guy showed up and started working on the heating system. He finally got to the point where he could fire up the boilers and the radiators were pushing out heat. Since the same system produced hot water for the house, we also had showers. Unfortunately, the bad news continued to roll in as the boilers were indeed shot and I was looking at eighteen thousand to fix them.

Leaving the insurmountable tasks behind for a while, Amak and I set out to move my things out of Mrs. Willoughby's house.

Besides, I had promised to visit her and help keep the wolfsbane plants alive. I might have bumped the priority of the move up a bit when I remembered Mrs. Willoughby's promise to keep a good stock of homemade cookies for my visits. She'd also agreed to transfer the lease to Gabriella, who was impatiently waiting for me to vacate. I offered, but Gabriella didn't want any help moving. Apparently, it was easier for her to hire a mover than explain our relationship to Brian. Perversely, I was pleased at that revelation.

"First things first," Belle said when I showed up at Chatty Katty's at noon for work. She'd pulled me into the restaurant's kitchen. "You're going to sit on this chair and eat. If you get up before you're finished, you might as well just keep walking."

"It's never been about the food, Belle," I said.

"Talk is cheap, wizard. Eat up." She slid a toasted club sandwich with a side of fries in front of me. I nodded my acceptance and dug in. It was delicious and I polished it off in only a few minutes.

"I thought I saw you come in," Willow said as she sashayed into the kitchen. "Are you satisfied, Belle?"

"He's allowed to live," she said dramatically, although I could feel the levity of her words.

"Word is, your financial situation has changed," Mari said as she bustled into the kitchen with a platter of dirty plates, setting it next to the dishwashing station. "You still need a job?"

"How do you know about that?"

"Biggest secrets travel fastest," Mari replied, loading plates onto a clean platter and bustling away.

"Don't mind her," Willow said. "We can go out back."

"Thank you for lunch, Belle. It was better than I deserve."

She shook her head ruefully. "Finally, a man who understands and he's twenty years my junior."

I chuckled at what I hoped was a joke and followed Willow out into her greenhouse. Instinctively, I pulled my shoes and socks off and breathed deeply upon entering the lush environment. The earth was rich with the magic of generations of witches who had cared for these plants.

"How long has your family owned this property?" I asked, following her deeper into the beds.

"If you're asking, I believe you have some idea already. There have been Kattys on this property since the mid eighteen hundreds. I knew your mother, Atronia, you know," she said. "I should have figured it out when you admitted to being a wizard."

I grabbed her arm to stop her progress. She pulled up and turned toward me. She was still in sultry mode and stepped in a little too close for my comfort. Even though she was older by a couple decades, I wasn't completely immune.

"Really?" I asked. "Would you tell me about her? I have so few memories," I said.

"She was a contradiction, as the best of us are. Many would describe her as a hard woman. But, she could show great kindness. We had a common love of plants, which brought us together from time to time. It was a shame when she disappeared."

"What do you know about that?" I asked.

"Not much. One day she was here, the next she was gone. I didn't put it together, that you were her son, until I heard about Tenebris Manerium. I imagine you know her last name was Baltazoss, not Slade, like your own." She took my hand to lead me further into the greenhouse. "But, enough of that. We'll have lots of time to talk, but we need to get to work. Mari has been burning through my rosemary like it's candy. I'd like to plant an additional fifteen. Have you ever worked with rooting hormone?"

TROUBLE IN PARADISE

"Hand me that hammer, would you?"

It was Friday afternoon and the sound of spraying water had interrupted a late lunch with Gabriella and Clarita.

"Shouldn't you call someone?" Gabriella asked, handing me the tool.

"Probably, but I used to pull pipe on the farm. It's not usually that hard, but this valve is frozen," I said.

"Can't you free it with… you know, that hand wavy thing you do?"

"I'm trying, but the rust is strong in this one." I looked back at her for acknowledgement. If she recognized my humorous reference, she wasn't letting on. I manipulated small objects with my hands, but rust-frozen valves weren't on the list. I tapped on the valve with the hammer and attempted to twist it with my free hand.

"Most people will be wearing black for the memorial," Gabriella said. "Do you need any help picking something out?"

There would be a new moon tomorrow night and the memorial was scheduled to start at eleven o'clock at the Leotown Botanic Gardens.

"Crap. Not going to happen," I said, giving up and flipping the breaker for the well to off. "Now, what was that again? You want to help me get dressed?" I deadpanned it as best as I could, but Gabriella understood my meaning.

"*Felix*. Clarita is here." She tried for scandalized, but it's difficult to lie to a wizard or a witch. "And you have an unresolved relationship with Amak."

"As do you, with Brian," I said.

"Not as much as you'd expect," she said.

"Why do things always break just before the weekend?" I

complained and then realized she'd said something interesting. "What's going on with Brian?"

"He's asking for space. What's been happening... it's a lot to take in. I don't blame him," she said.

"I do." I stepped closer, running my hand down her arm and gently grasping her hand. "You deserve better."

She pulled her hand away. "We're just taking a break, Felix."

"This doesn't have to be weird, Gabriella. If all the room you have for me is as a friend, I'm okay with that."

"Are you serious? What of Amak?"

"She doesn't think of me like that," I said. "She's offering a friends with benefits type of relationship."

"Sounds ideal. No commitment." Gabriella's mood quickly turned dark and the wave of sarcasm behind her words wouldn't have been lost on a mundane. "Is that what you want from me?" She turned and stormed over to the stairs that led out of the mechanical room, picking Clarita up. "Come on, Clarita, we're leaving."

"Hey." I called after her. "That's not fair." Somehow the train had come off the tracks and I had no idea what I'd said.

I dropped my hammer in the toolbox and ran up the wooden stairs after Gabriella. The mechanical room was off a small hallway which deposited us in the small hallway joining the dining room that had once been a solarium to the kitchen. I caught up with her as she was exchanging a greeting with Amak, who I didn't know was coming over.

Gabriella looked over her shoulder as she continued her retreat. "You were quick to judge how I treated trolls. What you're doing is despicable."

"Gabriella, wait," I said. But, it was too late, she had already hurried out of the room.

"Trouble in paradise?" Amak asked, chuckling.

"I don't know what I said."

Amak waved her hand up and down across my body. "Why are you all wet?"

"Sprung a leak in the basement. I tried to turn off the water to the rest of the house so I could keep the boiler running, but the damn valve is stuck. Want to give it a try?"

"Sure, but we're going to Rose and Crown tonight. All work and no play makes Amak a grumpy girl." She followed me back down to the basement mechanical room. "What valve?"

I picked up the hammer and pointed at the heavy copper pipe with the frozen, industrial-strength valve. Most men would be intimidated to have a female friend who was physically their superior. Not me. If anything, I was disappointed that she had no interest in pursuing a romantic relationship. But just like with Gabriella, I wasn't willing to lose a friend over it.

Amak grabbed the small iron wheel and braced her hips against the wall. The strain visibly transferred from her hands to her arms as every muscle grew taut. Her muscles were sinewy, not bulky like a bodybuilder's and when put to the task, they looked like iron bands. If ever there was a basis for the Amazon myth, Amak and her kind were certainly it.

She let go after a minute, breathing hard. "How hard do you want me to try? I could damage something."

"That's two-inch copper and an industrial fitting, don't hurt yourself," I said. "But, if you did break it, nothing changes. I'd just have to call a plumber anyway."

"Okay." She repositioned, locking her hips and feet against the stone wall and house support post. "It's all about leverage, Slade." For a moment, other than her knuckles turning bright white, nothing happened as she grappled with the stubborn plumbing fixture. The pipe's groaning was the first indication that something was happening and it was followed by a sharp cracking sound as Amak broke the valve's handwheel and stem free and water sprayed from the fitting.

"I thought you had the water off," Amak's laugh was infectious and I grabbed her hand, helping her out of the new fountain.

"It is," I said laughing as we danced out of the way. "The boiler is completely full and that valve is lower."

"Oh, crap. You're going to flood the basement."

"There's a valve on the boiler reservoir. I'll turn it off." I splashed my way over to the large water tank and easily twisted the new valve shut. "Furnace guy already replaced this one. I'll give him a call. He said he'd do emergency fixes."

I turned around to find Amak standing in front of me, her shirt in her hand. "Whoa. What are you doing?" I was working hard not to think of her in that light.

"Don't get your panties in a bunch, Slade. My shirt is soaking and I want to get it dry. Like you haven't seen all this." She gestured to her front.

"I don't think you know how distracting I find all that." I forced myself to look away.

"You just keep telling yourself that. I'm still holding out hope for those benefits and I don't mind playing dirty."

"Say the words 'long-term commitment,' troll girl, and I'm all in. I just can't go halfway," I said. Having feelings of love for two women and little hope of a future with either one was driving me nuts. I wasn't sure my heart could take it.

"You're a strange one, Slade. I've only met a few human men who had any interest in the real me and not a one of them had issues being playmates. Far as I could tell, that's all they wanted. But, you... you would become my mate, but won't share physically with me otherwise.

I'd turned away and was surprised by her wet arms wrapping around me from behind. I was immediately aware of her wet, naked breasts pressing into my back. Instead of playing naughty and reaching for me in a way that I would not have had the strength to resist, she just held me, her head coming to rest on my shoulder.

"I accept your proposal of friendship, Felix. My people's bonds are deep and I find in you a worthy companion. I am unable to give you what you want, as it is not for me to cleave to another. If it were otherwise, I might have allowed my heart to be open to you. My friendship is all that I may offer," she said.

"Does that have to do with your people's relationship with the witches?" I asked.

"I can't talk about that."

"I hate how they control you," I said. "What if I could find something that blocked their control?"

"Why would you do that? Your witch would be furious," she said.

"You saw her stomp out of here. She's clearly not my witch."

"You're reading that incorrectly."

***

I awoke the next morning to the sound of my phone ringing. Amak and I had spent the night at Rose and Crown and the pounding of my head had synchronized with the beat of the ring tone. That was just one of several reminders that I'd hit it too hard last night. I was unable to focus on the phone, but was pretty sure it was the furnace guy, ready to repair the broken valve.

"Slade," I answered, rolling out of bed. I shivered in the cold air of the unheated room.

"I'm twenty minutes out."

"What time is it?" I asked.

I must have caught him off guard because he guffawed into the phone. "One o'clock. Tough night?"

"Yeah, sorry," I said. "Do you need me to be here?"

"No, I think I know my way around well enough," he said. "I assume the problem's not too hard to find?"

"Yeah. Open your new valve by the boiler and look for a geyser."

"Understood. I'm sure I'll find it."

I'd promised the Katty sisters I'd help with the memorial and I needed to get going. They had a load of chairs and tables that needed to be hauled over to the gardens and set up. Even with two trucks, we'd have to take more than one trip.

After cleaning up to the best of my ability without running water, I grabbed my dress clothes and hopped in the truck. I ended up passing my furnace guy on the way out and gave him a friendly wave.

"Come here, you crazy kid," Willow said, walking up to me

after I'd backed up to the Katty sister's storage shed.

"What?" I asked.

She reached for my face and gently rubbed her thumbs across my closed eyelids. Cool relief and sense of calm spread from her touch as she chanted a simple spell. "Comfort for pain - we're thankful for lessening of strain."

"Where have you been all my life?" I asked, grateful for the relief from my headache.

"This afternoon will be hard enough."

She was right. The three sisters each had a daughter. Solstice, Cypress, and Dande had come home from college and were helping, but there was still plenty of work for the lot of us.

"Do I have to worry about nudity tonight?" Solstice, Dande and I had just finished setting up the last of the chairs and were taking a breather before starting in on the candles.

"No," Solstice said unconvincingly. I could tell she was questioning if I was a creeper or actually concerned.

"Are you serious? A new moon with all the free energy?" Dande was quick to correct her cousin. "Aunty Willow will be down to a lace skirt by midnight. I'd bet money on it."

"My Aunt Judy and her coven burned my eyes out more than once when I was growing up. Some things you just can't un-see."

The girls tittered, sharing a joke between them. I suspected they'd seen things they wished they hadn't as well.

It was well after six when we finished. The furnace guy had repaired the damage, but reiterated the fact that I was living on borrowed time. Regardless, I appreciated the hot shower. I'd promised Belle that I'd show up early to carry food in and left the house shortly after ten.

Parking near the gardens was impossible and I ended up a few blocks away. It was a crisp night, which put me in a good mood. The odds of random old-lady nudity diminished with every degree the mercury dropped, but with a hundred or so witches expected, I wasn't going to completely dodge the bullet. I looked to the sky and saw stars. I'd been holding out for a freak snowstorm and was disappointed at the cloudless sky.

A block out, my phone rang. I suspected it was Belle, wondering where I was. Even though I was early for the event, I was a few minutes later than I'd planned.

"Flaeger and Bothelman broke out of holding." It was Lozano, who hadn't communicated with me in over a week.

"I thought they were in federal custody," I said.

"Feds came for them this morning. When they arrived, both Flaeger and Bothelman were gone."

"How is that possible? And where have you been?"

"You've been a good friend, Slade, but it's not going to work out."

"What are you talking about? What's not going to work out?"

"I'm no good for Jennifer or the girls. Promise me you'll look in on 'em from time to time," he asked.

"You can fight this, Joe."

"You don't know what you're talking about. It's part of who I am now. I think it always has been."

"That's crazy talk. You were infected by Flaeger. This wasn't something you were born to," I said.

"Fate's a fickle dragon, Slade," he said. "Tell Jennifer I love her, would you?"

"No! You need to tell her yourself."

"Goodbye, Slade. Take care of yourself and don't underestimate Flaeger," Joe said and hung up the phone. I tried dialing him back, but he didn't answer.

I'd stopped walking, not trusting myself to have an intense conversation without tripping. I'd held out hope, but could hardly blame him. Everything I'd read said exactly what his wife's grandmother, Nanna, had said when we visited. There was no coming back from being bitten by a lycan. Joe was probably doing the best thing he could for Jennifer, but his family was being torn apart just as surely as if Shaggy had attacked them all.

My mind raced. If Shaggy was loose, he'd either skip town or try to tie up loose ends. Whoever had hired him seemed the most likely to have sprung him. My guess was 'the boss' would want him to finish what had been started. The question was, what was the end goal here? With my claim on Happy Hollow complete, there was no reason to go after Clarita. Unless...

I dialed Dukats. The phone rang quite a long time before she picked up.

"This better be good, Slade. It's late."

"You knew about Flaeger and you didn't think to call me?" I asked.

"Don't need you playing vigilante again," she said.

"Is that what you think? That I'm out chasing Flaeger? No. I'm going to a memorial service for Victoria and Benita Barrios, where his kidnapping victim, Clarita Barrios, is going to be. Flaeger could be coming here," I said.

"It's ten thirty. Isn't that unusually late for a memorial service? Where are you?" Dukats asked.

"Botanic Gardens. And, it's an unusual group of people."

"How long is the service? I'll send a cruiser."

"Probably wind down around two a.m. You need to be discreet, this crowd is expecting a private service."

"I get it, Slade. You can't be on the force in Leotown without understanding we have a religiously diverse crowd. The officers won't crash your party."

Religiously diverse. That was about as politically correct as anything I'd heard.

"Thank you, Dukats."

"Just leave Flaeger to us. You copy?"

"He's all yours. If I never see him again, it'll be too soon," I said and hung up.

I suddenly felt exposed on the darkened street and quickened my pace. I knew I was responding to the moment, but I still felt like there were eyes on me.

"You look like you've seen a ghost," Willow said as I approached the Katty's catering truck where she and the younger Kattys were unloading. Like her daughter, Cypress, she was dressed in a simple, lacy green dress.

"Is Gabriella here? I need to find her," I said.

"What is it, Felix?" Willow asked.

"Shaggy, the werewolf, has escaped from jail," I said. "I think Clarita and Gabriella could be in danger."

"Girls, finish up here and get inside," she instructed. "Do not worry, Felix. We've woven a spell of serenity and safety and we'll strengthen it with a hundred strong. No lycan will pass onto our hallowed ground tonight. Besides, they are at their weakest at the new moon."

"Gabriella?" I asked.

"Yes, of course. She and Clarita are making final arrangements in the courtyard."

Wordlessly, I ran off. I had to find them and make sure they were safe. Any other night, I would have loved navigating my way through the carefully planned paths and well-tended plants. Tonight, I cursed the lack of a straight route. I doubled back and forth along the sloped terraces, thick with full hedges.

In the end, I resorted to clambering down over the final rows, inadvertently tipping over a beautiful potted planter. I winced as I recognized what it contained: one of Willow's Solanaceae, or nightshade. It had been full of gorgeous and delicate deep purple flowers. I managed to save the pot but shredded much of the foliage.

"Felix. Stop! What are you doing? This ground is consecrated," Gabriella had turned, hearing my steps. A look of horror crossed her face at my clumsy approach.

She wasn't holding Clarita, nor could I find the six-year old anywhere as I rushed up. "Clarita. Where is she? There's danger," I said. It was all I could manage. The thought of either of them coming to harm again, was more than I could bear.

I felt Mari's presence before I saw her. A blanket of calm settled around me and I turned to see her, Clarita in her arms. "We're here, Felix. Everyone is safe."

Clarita lifted her arms, slipped from Mari's gasp and ran to me, scrabbling up into my arms. "Little monkey, you're so pretty tonight." My world seemed to fall back into whatever gear I'd slipped out of and I was once again able to breathe.

"What's this about?" Gabriella asked. She was broadcasting her annoyance at my entrance.

"Flaeger escaped." I was hoping Clarita wouldn't recognize his name.

"We're safe here tonight," Mari said, placing her hand on my shoulder. She wasn't as curvy as her sister Willow, but she was beautiful in her lacey, green gown. Mari probably wouldn't win any traditional beauty contests, but she had a depth of presence found only in strong women, those who didn't look to others to establish their self-worth. Through her touch, I felt her connection with the ground beneath us and caught a glimpse of the protections woven by the Katty women.

"*Altum Visu*," I said, waving my hand across my face. I turned slowly and took in the green-hued spell they'd cast. At its center, Mari stood, a beacon of bright green. Her family stood out at their various positions around the garden like lighthouses on a foggy night. I gasped at the breadth of their spell, it was spectacular. "*Finis.*"

"I talked with Lieutenant Dukats," I turned back to Gabriella. "She'll park a cruiser out front."

"We'll be okay, Felix," Gabriella said. She was still annoyed, but at least projecting it less.

"You look beautiful tonight." It was the only thing I could think to say and it was also very true. She was wearing a dark plum-colored gown with a deep red drape. She'd always dressed nicely, but this was an entirely new level. I smiled grimly. I was definitely not in this woman's league.

"Thank you. You look nice as well," she said and turned away.

"Want to help me with Willow's pretty plant, monkey? I don't need the boss upset with me." Clarita nodded and we set the tall vase-like pot back upright, scooping dirt back in with our hands. "Do not touch the leaves or the plant." I gently pulled her hand back as she reached for one of the remaining flowers. "Until you learn to protect your skin, moonshade can hurt you. Would you like to help me make it bloom again?" I grasped her hand and used my free hand to direct a small amount of energy. "When I knocked this beautiful plant over, I detached small tendrils of its roots holding it to the earth. We must repair those first, otherwise we'll stress it by asking for flowers. We worked with the plant and I purposely kept the energy transfer low. Clarita had an amazing reservoir, but this was a simple task and I wanted her to feel our connection to nature for as long as was practical.

"That's amazing!" Cypress and Dande must have been watching for some time. They were standing stock still, holding hands and watching us.

"Thank you. I couldn't afford Willow's wrath," I said. "What's really amazing is the spell you Katty's wrapped these gardens with. I've never seen anything of that scope before."

"You can see it?" Dande asked.

"He's a wizard, Dee," Cypress said as if that explained everything. "Mom said we need to respect Felix's space, but she said he's good in the greenhouse."

"Oooooohhhhh," Dande said and I got the distinct impression we weren't talking about gardening anymore.

"Felix Slade. I wasn't expecting to see you here tonight." I turned to see Camille, the leader of Illuminaire, accompanied by Amak. Camille was dressed in a simple dark brown gown. Her long blonde hair flowed freely down her back. Amak, on the other hand, was dressed in leggings and a loose smock.

I'd forgotten Camille's last name and kept it simple. "Good to see you again, Camille. I appreciate your help with Lieutenant Dukats. Your honesty saved me some jail time."

"Illuminaire holds the truth in high esteem and you were not guilty. Word is, you've claimed Tenebris Manerium," she said. Four foot ten inches and no more than eighty-five pounds. A casual observer would not have found the barefooted Camille physically impressive. Any time spent in her presence, however, quickly dispelled that misunderstanding. It wasn't hard to understand why she led the most powerful coven in Leotown.

"I've learned it's my family's home," I said.

"When Liise asked your lineage, you were unwilling to share that information. Why now?"

I looked to Amak and back to Camille. "You have been spying

on me, Camille. You already have this information."

"I've heard rumors, but I'd hardly call it spying." She wasn't lying and it startled me. I'd always assumed she and Liise Straightrod had been compelling Amak together.

I wanted to get into the conversation more deeply, but a stream of women began filing into the gardens. All ages and sizes, the woman mingled, chatting amiably, holding hands and even dancing. I smiled as I remembered how much I enjoyed the free spirited dance of a new moon. We would celebrate new life tonight, just as we would commit the memories of the deceased back to the earth. I'd have to find a better time to confront her about Amak's treatment.

Clarita chose that moment to climb back into my arms.

"Clarita? You're related? That must mean... Baltazoss." Camille took an unintentional step back as she read our auras. "I should have seen it before. Felix, you must take great care. This is not the place, but I fear you are in danger."

LEFT HAND

Something I should have expected, if I'd had any time to think about it, was how central Clarita was destined to be at this gathering. Whatever hesitancy the women had in approaching me was quickly overcome by their desire to see the child who had been rescued from danger. Clarita was an irresistible magnet for the horde of witches streaming into the gardens and we quickly became the head of an impromptu receiving line. I didn't mind, though. I'd grown up with witches very much like these ladies. They were mothers, teachers, lawyers, accountants, and small business owners - but that was how the world saw them. I saw them as caretakers of the world around them. No doubt when strength was required, they had plenty of that and more, but the common thread was their capacity for love and acceptance.

After thirty minutes of hugs and introductions, Gabriella approached. The divide between us was on simmer as she, too, was caught up in the spirit of the new moon celebration. "Mari and Belle would like Clarita to move to the center of the garden. We're about to start our ritual."

My heart skipped a beat. I knew better than to stand at the center of a witch's circle. I'd nearly killed two members of Judy's coven in North Carolina when I'd tried to join with them. I wasn't about to repeat the same mistake with the power of a hundred witches floating around. "Monkey. You need to go with Gabriella. I can't be part of this."

"It's okay, Felix. You can stand with her. We will be casting blessings and re-establishing our bonds with our mother, the Earth. No one will harm you." Gabriella projected calm and reassurance, but the idea was a non-starter. Under no circumstances would I stand at the center of that circle.

Whether she was just tired of hanging onto me or she felt my resolve, Clarita allowed me to put her down. "No. I'm not one of you and I cannot be in the circle. I know you're angry with me, but you need to understand that I would endanger everyone here if I did."

"Fine. I'll be happy to take Clarita." Her words were clipped. "And for the record, I'm only angry because you made me rethink how we're treating Amak, and then, I find out you're taking advantage of her when she's compelled." Gabriella spun on her heel and strode purposefully away.

My mind reeled as I tried to figure out what she was talking about. I'd cut off my physical relationship with Amak specifically because she was being compelled to be with me. I'd refused to settle for sex when Amak made it clear she wasn't interested in a future with me. I replayed the last conversation I'd had with Gabriella as I'd done so many times since we'd argued. I realized I'd admitted to learning that Amak was compelled, but I hadn't told Gabriella that I'd ended the intimacy. I raised my hand to stop Gabriella, but she was already ten feet away and my time had passed.

"You've the look of a man lost at sea." Amak threw an arm around my shoulders in a friendly gesture. "I saw food and alcohol on the tables above. If history is any judge, they'll be at this for hours and I know from experience it doesn't get any weirder for us if we're drinking."

From the corner of my eye, I caught a flash of red and turned to see David Phibbly in the crowd. He looked different than he had at work, now wearing what looked like a black priest's cassock. It was spectacularly non-creative for a witch. I had no experience with male witches, but he didn't seem to share the almost obsessively creative nature of his female counterparts. He'd been looking at me, but abruptly turned away as I caught his eye.

Amak and I wound our way through the crowd in search of alcohol. It became apparent that I wasn't going to get my wish. The night was not cold enough and my comfort level was evaporating as quickly as the clothing. I'd seen plenty of naked women at these celebrations and had come to accept it as their expression of freedom. Judy taught me to see beauty in all things and scolded me when I'd been embarrassed or critical of her naked sisters. Over time, I'd come to expect the display and I'd be a liar if I said I didn't somewhat enjoy it.

"You're doing better than I'd expected," Amak said. We'd taken a path up to where I'd set tables up with the Katty girls. "Is it creepy if I tell you that I can smell that you're turned on?"

I laughed. "Fifty women just took off their clothing. You'd have to question my sanity if I wasn't." I scanned the crowd of dancing witches and found Willow. As expected, she was down to just a lacy skirt and dancing gracefully, her hair flowing behind her as she joined hands with her sisters and nieces. I smiled at the joy of their shared moment.

"Some are pretty old." Amak interrupted my reverie. "I didn't think humans liked that."

"Best we start drinking."

There was no way for me to feel like I wasn't creeping on the women below. Judy had explained to me that it was good and natural to be turned on by the dancers and that I simply needed to mind my manners when I found myself in that situation. That was great in theory, but it was all a bit overwhelming, so I cast my planar view. It was as if someone turned on a very powerful light switch. Unlike most mundanes, each witch had their own aura or energy signature. Some were dim with a minimal display, others burned bright with every color in the spectrum.

My mind jumped to Clarita and Gabriella and I found myself worrying about them again. The protection spell surrounded us all but Camille's warning still soured my stomach. I searched for and easily found Clarita, her familiar brilliant blue hues standing out in a sea of every conceivable combination of colors. Similarly, I was able to find Gabriella just as easily, a deep rose colored pillar standing next to Clarita.

"Here, start drinking. They're safe for now. Someone would have to be crazy to attack a group of this size, especially on a new moon." Amak shoved a bottle in my hand.

I set the bottle on a nearby table, which was tricky due to my wizard's sight, and rolled a forty-pound rock from beside the path so it sat between us. "*Adoloret.*" I warmed the rock to several hundred degrees.

"What I wouldn't give to lay a slab of steak across that," Amak said wistfully, draining her beer. I was grateful for the warmth that emitted from the rock as I rocked my chair back, balancing against the edge of the table.

"A wizard has to add some value to the party," I said.

We sat in amiable silence as the witches continued with their rituals. I suppose I should have paid attention to the goings on, but I was just as happy to sit next to Amak and nurse a beer. Finally, well after midnight, the witches filtered their way up to the overlook where the tables were absolutely littered with candles, all igniting without warning as the first groups approached.

"Finally! Time for the feast. Catch you tomorrow?" Amak stood.

"Afternoon would be best."

She nodded and made her way over to Camille. I'd dropped my planar view some time back and now I didn't need it. The crescendo of their rituals had occurred right around midnight and as they'd finished, clothing had been restored. I warmed my rock up again, but kept the temperature in a safer range. It wouldn't do to burn an unwary reveler.

I was caught off guard when Clarita jumped me from behind, grabbing onto my neck. "Hey, monkey," I said. "I didn't know you were such a pretty dancer." I'd found it a positive sign that she had joined with Gabriella in a muted dance. It was something I would not be able to share with her.

"You might as well broadcast your lineage, Slade." Phibbly growled as he walked past. Arrogance rolled off the man in waves. As his cassock lifted in a light breeze, I caught a bright flash of red, as if he wore two sets of robes. Something was amiss. I wasn't sure what, but I could feel it. The night was far from over.

I found it difficult to relax as the tables filled with happy witches carrying plates loaded with potluck food and glasses filled with wine. I stood and carried Clarita over to the outside edge of the overlook, where a gravel path went up to an exit. I wasn't leaving, but the precaution made sense to me.

"Are you hungry? When the line settles, we could get something to eat," I said.

Clarita didn't respond. She still wasn't talking and lived very much inside her own world. I could hardly blame her. I hoped that getting past the memorial and all of the attention would eventually allow her to start to heal.

"Witches of Leotown." An amplified voice quieted the excited chatter of the crowd.

I took a step up the path. I wasn't messing around. If crap was coming, I was getting out of here with Clarita. The girl had lived through more than any child, or adult for that matter, should ever have to.

"Where are you going, Slade?" Phibbly had found me again and stood several feet above us on the path.

"Back off, Phibbly."

He held his hands up defensively.

"Witches of Leotown. If I may have your attention for a moment," The voice called again and I located the speaker. It was Felicia Terpsa, the fifty-something leader of the now defunct Whyte Wood coven. She stood on a stepstool, a conch-shell held next to her mouth. Camille stood with a small group of older witches, Amak at her side. She watched Felicia, her normally placid expression replaced with concern. "Tonight, on this new moon, I have an announcement to share with you.

She waited for the witches to quiet. "As you know, my coven was brutally attacked, my dear sisters murdered, and our very way of life threatened by unknown forces. You must also know that, as a result, Whyte Wood's numbers have fallen so much so that we are no longer a viable coven.

A murmur of concern undulated through the crowd. "These attacks have brought to the forefront just how vulnerable we are to the forces of evil. Even as I speak, there are demons in our midst. While her heart is in the right place, Camille has allowed

Senwe royalty to walk amongst us, a troll princess privy to our inner most workings and sacred rituals.

It wasn't hard to see where this was going. The good humor of the crowd started to turn a bad corner. Felicia was hitting a cord. "And tonight, the whelp of the Sorcerer Baltazoss is allowed to walk freely among us. This cannot be overlooked. Our very survival is at stake."

"Sit down, Felicia. We made peace with Baltazoss and Senwe both. And you have no standing here," Camille said. A wave power rolled over the crowd as she spoke.

"But I do, Camille. And I won't be quieted by the likes of you anymore." Felicia continued. "My sisters, it is time to show our true colors."

Dramatically, Felicia untied the dark green robe at her neck and it fell away, revealing a fire-engine red dress beneath. As she did, twenty witches stood and followed suit, stepping away from their friends and families and joining hands as they gathered around Felicia. I wasn't surprised to see Liise Straightrod and David Phibbly among their ranks, although Phibbly didn't move to join Felicia, choosing instead to block my escape route.

"Tonight, on this new moon, as high priestess of Whyte Wood coven, I declare our re-envisioned order. Sisters, there is room for all of you, but know this: we will no longer sit back and cower in the face of adversity. We will embrace our full selves, for we are now The Order of the Left Hand."

"You can't do this!" Gabriella had climbed up on a chair to address Felicia. "You're desecrating Victoria and Benita's memory. You have to stop."

"Sit down, Valverde." Felicia lifted her hand toward Gabriella. I couldn't see the magic, but I knew she'd been attacked as she stumbled backwards, falling into the crowd. "Take us not for fools and test not our mettle. The enemies of the sisterhood will be struck down for the good of all."

Gabriella appeared to be okay. Somehow she felt my eyes and turned to me, mouthing 'get out.' Moments later, the group erupted into madness and I recognized my cue. The train had seriously come off the tracks and I agreed with Gabriella. Clarita didn't need to be in the middle of it.

I turned to run up the path when I felt an arm on my shoulder. "Where are you going?" Phibbly spun me around.

"Get off, Phibbly," I said.

"Sorry, I believe the Left Hand has business to transact with you both," he said.

I grabbed his hand with my own and twisted. An electrical jolt rocked me backward as he fired a Taser into me. I lost control of my limbs and dropped Clarita on the ground as I toppled over. I was dazed and couldn't move a muscle. All I could do was watch as Phibbly stood over me, a sharp knife gleaming in his hand. I was starting to regain my faculties, but it would be too late. I looked to Clarita and willed her to run, but she'd received the same shock and lay unconscious.

Phibbly grinned manically as he raised the knife. "You're such an idiot, Slade. Thank you for making my job so easy." He swept the blade in a long arc toward my throat, no doubt so I could see my impending demise. Just as the blade was no more than a foot away, his arms went slack and he collapsed on top of me, a baseball-sized rock ricocheting off his head.

I shook my head trying to clear the cobwebs and attempted to roll Phibbly off. I struggled as my limbs regained feeling and strength, finally succeeding. The good news was that once I started to mend, the process rapidly progressed. I hastily looked around, catching Amak's eye. I nodded in acknowledgement and continued to look for threats. Not finding anything immediate, I checked Clarita's pulse and breathing. She was unconscious but breathing.

"*Vivi.*" It was a new spell I was learning and used a minimal amount of energy. It was painful, but I transferred a small portion of my life's energy into the little girl. Its effect was immediate and she stirred. I scooped her into my arms and stumbled up the path, every stride both painful and stronger than the last. By the time I made it to the service entrance, I was moving at full speed.

The street I found myself on was deserted and I rushed in the direction of the parking garage still several blocks away. I knew I'd done the right thing escaping with Clarita, but I couldn't help feeling I'd abandoned the good witches of Leotown. And while they outnumbered the Order of the Left Hand by at least four to one, most ordinary witches lacked offensive capabilities, preferring instead to focus on life affirming skills.

Hopefully, the spells the Katty sisters had woven across the gardens would be enough. I suspected those spells were the reason Phibbly had resorted to the Taser. I comforted myself, knowing that if the witches were down to physical attacks, Amak would certainly be quite a force to deal with.

"Felix…" I heard a faint voice in the distance and spun, trying to locate the source. I was in the open and holding Clarita. There was no place to hide as I was on a city block with storefronts on both sides, but of course, none of the shops were open. I was about to give up the search when I caught the flicker of a shape moving across the sky. Maggie. The great raven swooped down from her high position and landed on my shoulder just as Gabriella stumbled around the corner and into view.

"Gabriella!" I yelled. She was running toward me, her red cape flapping behind her. It was the scene from my vision and I was horrified as I watched it unfold. A wolf sprang from the shadows and bowled Gabriella over. Her beautiful gown was now a hindrance as she tumbled inelegantly from the impact.

"*Adoloret*." I fired twenty grape-sized fireballs at the wolf and rushed toward her, pulling Clarita along with me. Maggie squawked as I unweighted her, but she stuck to my shoulder all the same. I'd never had her act like this before. "Maggie, get out of here, this is bad."

The wolf pulled back at my onslaught, but before I could reach Gabriella, three more wolves trotted around the corner. I recognized Shaggy and Fred. As I made a move to close on Gabriella, Shaggy stepped forward and growled possessively. He started shaking and his limbs took on the consistency of gelatin. He wanted to talk and was transforming back into a human.

Each time Gabriella attempted to gain her feet, one of the

remaining wolves rushed her, so she sat on the ground in front of them. Clarita's little hand dug into my own, her fear of Shaggy transmitting through our connection.

"I'd have to say, you've done me quite a favor, Slade. I couldn't have gathered all the right people into the right place so easily. And now I'll be able to get out of this shithole you call a town." Shaggy stood naked in front of me.

"Back down, Shaggy. Nobody needs to get hurt," I said.

"Not even close. You need to get hurt. I owe you that at least. As for your witchy little friend here, I'll kill her nice and slow. She looks sooo delicious." He licked his lips. "Now, if you'd like to save the little one from harm, you can hand her over. Boss wants her alive and you dead, but was unspecific about what alive should look like. I'll leave that decision to you. I'm good either way."

There was no way I'd hand Clarita over to Shaggy while I was alive, so I prepared to defend against the wolves. I had a number of different ideas zip through my head, but none of them would work. They would all fail for the same reason. I couldn't move quickly enough to save everyone and that assumed I could muster enough power.

"I'll die first," I said.

"That's the idea."

The sound of a shotgun blast and the yelp of a wolf alerted us all to the entry of a new player. It was followed quickly by the sound of a second and a third. Shaggy spun to face the attack as Lozano, Daphne and a man I assumed was the light brown werewolf walked into view.

"You live a charmed life, Slade," Lozano said. "I got a call from Dukats on my way out of town and we decided to check in on things. Now why don't you leave while these guys are out?"

"You're dead, cop," Shaggy said.

"Nothing personal. Sue and I owed you this much. I'm calling it even," Lozano said. "I also owed the wizard and now my debts are paid."

Shaggy didn't immediately move, but seemed to consider Joe's words. "You'll leave town?"

"On my way right now," Lozano said. "The wizard and the girls are given safe passage to the truck. What happens tomorrow isn't my concern. We're headed south."

While they were talking, I'd made my way to Gabriella and helped her up.

"Done." Shaggy spat on the ground.

HOPE IN THE DARK

"Are you hurt?" I asked Gabriella as I helped her into the truck. "Were you bitten?"

"No. I don't think so. You should have left me," she said.

"Nah. I knew Joe was coming," I lied.

Maggie had kept a close watch on us until this point. Once I was in the truck, she fluttered off. It was unusual behavior for her, although for a raven, I wasn't sure what 'usual behavior' might be. I knew that flying around in the cold night was hard on her. If she showed up at the house, I'd need to make sure she had plenty of food to recharge.

"You did not," Gabriella said as she clipped Clarita into the center seatbelt.

"True enough. But, there was no way I was leaving you there. Not in your fancy dress and everything. What kind of hero runs out on a distressed damsel?"

"Is everything a joke to you?"

"I'm dead serious, Gabriella." I swiped my credit card in the parking garage's automated attendant and pulled onto the street. Even as relieved as she was to be alive, she was still pissed. It made no sense, but then for as much time as I'd spent around witches, women largely remained a mystery to me.

The streets were empty and we caught no hint of pursuit by Shaggy and his gang. I couldn't have been more relieved when we finally pulled into the drive at Happy Hollow.

"This isn't over," Gabriella said.

"Did you know Phibbly attempted to kill me tonight?"

"No way. I know he joined Felicia's Left Hand, but are you sure?" She was in complete disbelief. I recounted the events to her.

"They're making a play for Tenebris Manerium," I said. "There's something here they want. I believe they want to get me out of the way so they can use Clarita."

I picked Clarita's sleeping form up from the truck.

"Aren't you taking us back to the apartment?"

"Not tonight, please, Gabriella. They may want me dead, but they're coming for Clarita too," I said.

"And you can keep us safe?" she asked as I opened the breezeway door and led her into the kitchen.

"Much easier than if we're separated. I've enchanted every opening in this house with a protective spell."

I made my way into the family room and placed Clarita on the couch I'd cleaned, pulling a blanket over her.

"We can't hide forever," Gabriella said.

"Agreed. We definitely need a better plan." I led her back to the kitchen.

A tapping on the window alerted me to Maggie's arrival. I let her in and arranged several strips of meat and a pile of soybeans and rice on the counter for her.

"What is it with you and that bird?" Gabriella asked.

"She's my family," I said. "You mind if I get something off my chest? It's been killing me."

Gabriella pursed her lips. "What? Is this where you profess your unending love for me? I trusted you Felix and you let me down. I can't be with a man with such little respect for someone else."

"You're talking about Amak, right?"

I squared off with her, offering my wrists. She ignored my gesture, but stepped in and unleashed her fury. "Of course, I am! You're, oh so happy to hang me with *my* treatment of Amak, but what you're doing is worse!" she said.

"But, that's just the thing. We're not doing that," I said.

"It's rape to take advantage of her! Wait... what?"

"Well, we did do that. But, only once, well, twice technically. But, that's before I knew anything was up. I called it off when I realized she was being compelled."

"Then why is she still hanging around?"

"Because she's my friend. We talk and do stuff together, but it's all friend stuff."

"She's just your friend? I find that hard to believe."

"Yes. I told her I couldn't have a physical relationship with her without the emotional relationship. I'm not that kind of guy. Ask her for yourself," I said.

"I will." Her chest deflated just as her anger did.

"Gabriella. It's always been you. I've always wanted to be with you. If you're only available as a friend, I'll take it, but I would like more. If tonight has taught me anything, it's that life is short," I said.

"That's not fair," Gabriella said, her voice having lost its edge. She rested her balled-up fists on my chest and I pulled her into me.

"I don't want to be fair. I can't lose this time," I said.

She looked up into my eyes and I felt her earlier resistance drain away as our lips met. I marveled at how soft she felt and how she just seemed to melt into me. I could have kissed her forever, but unfortunately that's not the nature of my life. Abruptly, Maggie lifted off from the table, her long wings smacking me on the back of the head as she flew from the kitchen into the cloak room.

I laughed as Gabriella and I broke apart. My heart was a hundred times lighter, having resolved things with her. Now I felt I could take on the world.

"Where are you headed, Maggie? There are only coats in there," I said. I refused to let go of Gabriella's hand as I looked in the direction the wacky bird had flown. "She's never done that before. I guess she's not a big fan of kissing."

"No. She's not." A woman, wearing only my leather coat, walked out of the cloak room. She was rail thin, to the point of being gaunt and had long black hair. Her face was so familiar; I knew immediately who she was.

"Mom?" I crossed the room and pushed her hair out of her face. The woman looked so much like my early memories of her.

"Yeah, sure that's it. Dumbass," she said sarcastically. "Do I look like I'm fifty?"

"Sevena?" I asked. I was proud that I'd actually recalled her name.

"You're painfully dull sometimes," she said and opened the refrigerator, pulling beer and leftover Chinese food out. "I'm starving. You have no idea how much energy birds really use." She didn't even bother microwaving and got straight to eating.

Gabriella grabbed my hand again, sliding up behind me and wrapping her arm around my waist. I smiled. I might get obliterated tomorrow, but tonight I'd figured things out with Gabriella and everything was right with the world.

"You've been following me my whole life and tonight you decide to show yourself?" I asked, watching in horror as the ninety pound, five foot three woman threw back food like a football player.

"I need more. Can you get delivery? How about a pizza?"

"Way too late for that." I took a frozen burrito from the freezer and tossed it in the microwave. I looked at her, patiently waiting for a response.

"So... that basement. You opened the door?" she asked.

"Both of them," I answered.

"And the shades?"

"How do you know about the shades?"

"I made a claim, Felix."

"If you didn't defeat the shades, how did you get out?"

"There's a tunnel up to the greenhouse. I don't think Mom knew I knew about it," she said.

"That's horrible. Why would our mother make a trap that could kill us?"

"They killed Geoff," Maggie said. There was no way I could think of her as Sevena after all these years. "Those were his bones in the circle. I imagine you saw them. It's not like she didn't warn him. Mom told all of us not to come back. She said it would be too dangerous, but you know how things go. She put a spell on you that was supposed to block your memories so you wouldn't return."

"Why did she leave?"

"Yeah, sorry. Can't say. I've already told you too much. And, the only reason I'm in human form now is because you've really stepped in the shit this time. Mom doesn't want to see you dead."

"You're in contact with her?"

"Not for fifteen years, when she told me to watch over you. But, I think she's still out there. She'd be proud, you know. I don't think she thought any of us had it in us to take back Tenebris."

"Let me get this straight. You showed yourself because you want to help me out of a jam? What about everything else that's happened in the last weeks? I nearly died a million times."

"Don't be dramatic, Felix. I was prepared to swoop in and save you. Hah, see what I did there. Honestly, I had to change to stop you from getting too kissy-faced. It's one thing to play with trolls, it's another to be diddling witches," she said.

"Hey!" Gabriella objected. "There's been no diddling."

"Shit, Maggie. You've been here five minutes and you're already talking crap about my girlfriend?"

"I've always liked the name Maggie. And, she's your *girlfriend*?" Maggie asked. "Wizards and witches don't mix, little man."

I laughed at her characterization. I was nearly a foot taller than her. "Seems to me they do. Have you met Geoff's daughter?" I asked.

"The little girl is Geoff's?"

"Not only that, but her mother was a witch," I said.

"Seriously?" Maggie looked to Gabriella for confirmation. Of course, Gabriella was sitting back in her chair dreaming up ways to punch Maggie in the face. "Oh, get over it. It's not personal, our energy sometimes backfires on witches. They go boom. I'm sure you're a perfectly good diddle."

"At least I see where Felix gets it. You're an ass," Gabriella fired back.

Maggie smiled and looked at me. "You know? I think I'm going to like her."

"Don't be talking trash about witches. I've grown up in a witchy world and I wouldn't have made it without them," I said.

"At least that explains what the fuss is all about. If that little girl can open the house, they'll kill you and use her," Maggie said.

"Use her for what!?" I couldn't get a straight answer out of her about what was so damn important about the property at Happy Hollow.

"Remember that first night you were here when you were out pounding on the werewolves? How did you think you got enough power to flambé the big one?" She pulled out the burrito I'd microwaved for her.

"I don't know. I reached for it and it was there."

"What was?"

"A well of power," I said.

"How much of a well?"

"Don't know. I just pulled from it," I said.

"That well has more power in it than all the witches in Leotown will gather their entire lives. This property sits on top of every major ley-line in the region and our ancestors found a way to tap into it. If the wrong people ever got hold of it and had a wizard to channel it, it would be lights out for whoever they wanted to take on. And now you've opened it back up for business."

"Oh shit," I said.

"Right."

"So, exactly how did you figure out this little girl is Geoff's?" Maggie asked.

"You should see her aura," I said.

"His name is on the birth certificate," Gabriella said, annoyed.

Maggie raised her eyebrows. "There's more. You were too positive."

"We joined," I said.

"What!? That's horrible!" Maggie recoiled.

"You pervert! No! Like in a witches' circle. We shared energy," I said.

"Impossible."

"Maybe for you."

"What was it like?" Maggie tried to talk around the burrito that was too hot to swallow.

"Incredible. I've never felt anything like it. We were just

together spiritually. It changed me, Maggie. I can't lose her."

Maggie looked dumbfounded from me to Gabriella. "It's true. That's how we all feel when we form a circle. It's better with some than others, but the first time can be very intense. Clarita feels the same way about Felix."

"Is it healthy?" Maggie asked.

"It is with Felix. We don't ordinarily allow someone so young to join. They don't know how to deal with the emotions. Clarita's been through a lot though and neither of them would have survived if she hadn't initiated it. There is nothing bad about it either way," Gabriella explained patiently.

"So what was it you were doing in the car - reading each other's blood. Were you trying to join? I was hoping you weren't going to have sex," Maggie said.

"You've a filthy mind," Gabriella said. "There was nothing sexual about what we were doing. Surely you understand that there is no hiding from each other when holding each other's wrists."

"Oh that. Right. And check-mark on the filthy mind, you can't believe the things you see as a bird. People are at each other all the damn time," Maggie said.

"My point is that I trust Felix, especially where Clarita is concerned."

"Good, because we're going to need help. This is going to get ugly."

"Clarita is going to be long gone by that time," Gabriella said.

"Only if you're a fairy, because they're already here." Maggie said. Her words were followed almost immediately by a loud 'thawump' which shook the house, sprinkling dust down from the ceiling.

"What the hell?" I jumped from the kitchen table, ran to the mudroom and looked out the small, forward facing window. "It's fricking Felicia, Straightrod and their damn Left Hand."

"What are they doing?" Gabriella asked, crowding in next to me to look out the window.

Together, we watched a beach-ball sized stone rise from the

bed of a pickup truck. The eighty-pound boulder hurtled toward the front door as if thrown by an invisible hand. Their aim wasn't exact and the rock flew wide, striking one of the portico's pillars, which only slowed its progress. The impact was less violent than the first attempt, evidence of which was lying broken in front of the main entrance doors. The witches wouldn't have any trouble breaking in. Someone would figure out that only the doors and windows were enchanted against break-in. Those entrance points had become stronger than the surrounding structure. Nothing short of a spell circle would protect the entire house against a barrage of rocks and I'd never cast a shield anywhere near that big. One boulder through the front wall and the Left Hand would walk right into the house.

"Is this the effing middle-ages?" Maggie asked. "What's next? Boiling oil?"

"We've got to get out of here," I said. "This place is hardly a castle."

"And go out there with them?" Gabriella asked. "Can't we hole up in the lab?"

"This way," I said, running across the front of the house. I pulled my phone out and dialed Dukats. "Shit. They're blocking the signal. Try 911, Gabriella." I pushed through a hidden door in the paneling. We ran through to the back of the house and continued on to the family room where we'd left Clarita.

"Just going to have a little slumber party in the lab, monkey," I reassured her as I picked her from the couch. I shook my head angrily as I considered how much she'd been through in her short life. If I could end things tonight, I would.

Another boulder crashed into the front of the house. "We gotta move, Slade." Gabriella held the door to the back hallway open.

I rushed past her and swept my hand across the lock, opening the door to the stairwell. The three of us hustled down the stairs and I worked the tumblers on the door to the lab. I actually blew it the first time, but reset before I locked us out. I got the door open on the second attempt.

"You know what? I'm not doing this without food," Maggie

said and sprinted off.

"Are you nuts?" My angst was lost on her as she disappeared. "Don't open this door for anyone." I handed Clarita to Gabriella.

"You can't go," Gabriella said.

"You'll be safe down here. I can't lose Maggie - she's my only family. Don't open the door." Gabriella looked down, obviously not happy, but allowed the door to close.

I caught up with Maggie in the kitchen just as another boulder crashed into the house. "Classic horror flick mistake." She yelled over her shoulder as she pulled out the box of burritos and the baggie of Mrs. Willoughby's cookies from the freezer.

"Never split up." I finished for her. "So, what are we doing here?" As I spoke, a boulder struck, punching through the front wall and landing in the vicinity of living room.

"Grab the beer." She pointed at the remnants of a 12-pack Amak had left behind.

"Seriously? They're almost through." I couldn't believe she was looking to get drunk. I grabbed the box, regardless.

She didn't answer and with arms full of frozen food, pushed through the swinging kitchen door and jogged to the back of the house. A flash of my sister's skin, from a part of her body that shall remain nameless, reminded me she was wearing only my leather coat. I felt it was worth the risk to divert momentarily as we ran through the family room, for a pile of my clothing.

"Hold this." I pushed the pile into her arms and swept the lockset with my hands.

"Is it really that easy for you?" she asked. "Last time I opened this door, it took me fifteen minutes."

"How'd you get the lab open?" The sound of yelling and crashing in the front of the house spurred us through the door.

"Would you believe I didn't?" She looked at me impishly, a sly grin and laughing eyes telling me there was a story there.

"I don't follow. You were obviously in there after Geoff died. How else would you get in there?"

"Let's just say, I'm tricky," she said.

Gabriella pulled the door open as we approached. "Don't *ever* do that to me again, Slade." She poked her finger into my chest as we entered.

"Left Hand has broken through the front of the house." I set my load down on a table.

"You have anything to heat these up with?" Maggie held an unopened box of frozen calzones in front of my face, trying to get my attention.

"How can you eat at a time like this?" Gabriella asked.

"Survival. My metabolism is recovering from being a raven." She popped open a beer and chugged it. "Alcohol is pretty ideal. It translates into fat faster than anything."

"How about you put clothes on and I'll heat up the food." I handed her my smallest pair of running shorts and a thick t-shirt. She shrugged and dropped my coat on the floor. I closed my eyes - lest they be burned from my head - and turned away.

"Don't be such a baby. I know for a fact you've seen plenty of naked women," she said.

I shook my head. "This is wrong on so many levels," I mumbled to myself, pulling four calzones from the box and pushing heat into them.

"How long can we hold out down here?" Gabriella asked.

"No idea. We need to keep trying for a phone signal. No way will the Left Hand keep up their siege if cops show up," I said.

"If they try hard enough, a group that size will eventually be able to break through all of the protections," Maggie said. "Although I'm under the impression this lab is stronger than the rest of the house."

"It is. The walls not backed up to earth are all magically reinforced," I said.

"You have the sight?" Maggie asked.

"You don't?" I handed her the warmed calzones.

"Don't judge, we're all different. Damn, you're handy. These are so much better warm."

I felt Gabriella's hand on my waist and turned in her direction. "What's the plan?" she asked.

"Do you think that passage is still open to the greenhouse?" I asked, looking at Maggie.

"Should be."

"I say we wait them out. If they break through the upper door, then we take the back exit," I said. "I'll rig an alarm in the upper passage." I picked up Clarita, who had attached herself to my leg and carried her to the small alcove off the main room.

I'd brought the enchanting reagents from my lab at Mrs. Willoughby's and organized them in the alcove. I pulled a block of paraffin, two crow's feathers, a pinch of dog's hair and a handful of other items off the shelves. I gave them to Clarita to hold, then picked her up, bringing everything back out. I set Clarita and the components on the table top next to Mom's large silver cauldron.

"What are you doing?" Gabriella asked.

"We're making an alarm." I smiled at Clarita, hoping to distract her from the tension we were all feeling. "Now, don't touch the pot. It's going to get hot." I grabbed my spell book and looked for the enchantment I had in mind as Gabriella and Maggie pulled up stools.

One at a time, I handed the components to Clarita and had her drop them in the pot as the paraffin melted. "Now, for my least favorite part. We have to set the spell and that can only be done with the final ingredient - essence of wizard." Using a sharp, silvered knife, I quickly sliced into the palm of my hand. Clarita winced and reached for me. "Just a minute, monkey. I'm okay." I grabbed her hand and held the other over the cauldron, chanting "*Avem, avem...*" I hadn't thought about my connection with Clarita until I felt the surge of power through our hands. A puff of white smoke billowed upward as the spell set, the mixture turning into a clear frosting.

Clarita giggled.

I smiled despite the circumstances we found ourselves in and looked to Gabriella, who hadn't missed the moment. The girl who'd been traumatized to the point of not talking had found joy in the moment. It gave us hope.

DARKEST BEFORE DAWN

I hadn't expected to sleep, but the sound of chirping birds woke me. I was sitting in the leather chair, slumped over the desk, drooling on its wooden surface. I checked my phone. It had taken the Left Hand two hours to break through the upper door. I'd been hoping Felicia would give up and regroup, maybe come at us another day. Apparently, they were in this for the long haul. I looked over to the fireplace where Gabriella and Clarita were curled up on blankets, fast asleep. It seemed cruel to wake them, but we had to go.

"You ready for this?" Maggie asked. She didn't look like she'd slept at all.

"Are you?" I asked.

"Oh yeah. I needed some downtime, but I'm good to go. You know, we're going to have to make a stand, right? They'll just chase us wherever we go."

"You don't think we can get help from the police?"

"No. Bad things happen to people who bring locals into the affairs of witches and wizards," she answered.

I'd heard this from others, but no one could tell me specifically where those bad things came from. "What kind of bad things?"

"They get removed like they never existed or end up having a mysterious accident. No one knows who's behind it, but I've seen the results and you don't want any part of it."

"I can't fight a war with a six-year-old next to me," I said.

"The Left Hand is coming for her. You can't avoid it," she said.

Gabriella sat up and looked around. "Is that your alarm?" The cheerful sounds of the bird alarm were annoyingly loud.

"It's time to get going," Maggie said as she crossed the room and swiveled a bookcase away from the back wall. The ornate, round door looked like it would better fit in a Tolkien story.

"You'll need to open it, bro. It's a wizard's lock," Maggie said.

"Remind me to ask how you got out of here last time," I said as I cast my planar view and inspected the locking mechanism. It was every bit as complex as the lab's main door and I set to work moving the gears and tumblers into place. After a few minutes, the enchanted mechanism relented and I swung the door open. The passageway behind was only wide enough for a single person and too short to stand up in. The bricked walls gently curved into an arc, which formed the ceiling of the passage.

I sat in the entrance, holding the door open. "*Lucem*." I lit my ring and illuminated as much of the passage as I could. As far as I could see, it was in good repair. "Let's go. Maggie, you're last, make sure that door is closed behind you."

The floor of the passage was hard on the knees, but I could tell by the slope that we were rising rather quickly and wouldn't be crawling for long. At the end, the roof of the passage opened and I stood in a small room, just big enough for the four of us. I saw a ladder built into the wall and a trap door that led to the roof. I doused my ring and inspected the door in the mystical plane. It was one of the easy locks and I made quick work of it.

"Back into the passage. The door swings down and there could be junk on top," I said. Wordlessly, they all backed away.

I was glad I'd warned them. Once I released the brace, the door swung down and dirt, small rocks, glass and leaves poured through the new opening. I held the handle for a minute, staying quiet, concerned the falling detritus might have alerted someone. Not hearing anyone approach, I continued up the ladder. The sky was starting to lighten, although it was difficult to see through the thick canopy of the trees.

The opening was partially blocked by fallen branches and I cut my hand on a broken panel of glass that must have been part of the greenhouse as I tried to clear the debris. It took me a moment, but I pushed the limbs away enough so I could clamber out.

"Clear," I whispered.

Gabriella was next up the ladder, lifting Clarita to my waiting arms. Once out, Maggie pulled the trap door closed and we picked our way through the ramshackle structure. My thought was to work our way out the back of the property, find the golf course nearby and call for help once we had cell reception.

"You make me sick, Slade." Shaggy's growly voice caused my heart to sink. "The witches were sure you'd hide in your secret room, but I knew you'd run."

"Let the girls go. You can have me," I said, turning to his voice. He was flanked by the red wolf and the two others Lozano had shot. I knew lycan healed quickly, but that was ridiculous. They'd taken multiple shotgun blasts at close range not four hours previous. Clarita started crying, no doubt the voice of her mother's murderer too much for her.

"Bud, get the boss," he ordered and the smaller gray bounded off. "Boss said we can kill you all, as long as the kid makes it out. Hand her over and we'll make it quick.

Maggie stepped forward and pulled her shirt off, throwing it to the ground. Never taking her eyes off Shaggy or breaking stride, she closed the distance between them, wriggling out of her shorts along the way.

"Now, that's an option I hadn't considered. I like where your head's at," Shaggy leered at my sister. "Maybe a little more meat on those bones would be good, but..."

Maggie tipped her head as he spoke and I watched in horror as her body transformed not into a raven, but into that of a black panther. Before Shaggy could finish his sentence or react to the metamorphosis, she leapt. Too late, I pulled Clarita to me, trying to shield her eyes. Maggie had already locked on to Shaggy's throat, riding him to the ground, her powerful back claws digging into his soft stomach.

Fred and the remaining wolf pack jumped back, startled by the transformation. They quickly recovered and rushed forward in defense of their alpha.

"*Adoloret*." I released the energy from my ruby ring and sprayed a gout of fire over Maggie's back. She released Shaggy for a moment and looked at me, her green eyes glowing in the night and unspeakable things hanging from her mouth. Convinced I wasn't trying to barbeque her, she returned her attention to Shaggy as Fred and his buddy turned tail and ran.

"Felix. They're here," Gabriella said. I followed her eyes to the approaching mob. Twenty people, in blood red robes flapping around their legs, rounded the far corner of the house. As expected, Left Hand was led by Felicia and Liise Straightrod with Phibbly close on their heels.

"Join us, sister. As a member of Whyte Wood, your place is by my side," Felicia shouted from twenty feet away. "I'd meant to talk to you before now, but this meddling wizard was always nearby. I saw how he used your grief and fear to twist your mind. Do not let this sorcerer turn you from your own kind! Only The Order of the Left Hand can restore purity to our bloodlines, Gabriella! Choose wisely. Do not stand against your sisters."

"You're behind all of this? You killed Victoria and Benita? They. They were my sisters," Gabriella yelled back.

"They gave me no choice. We've been planning to take Tenebris Manerium for years and when Slade showed up, we had to advance our plans."

"If you want the property, I'll just give it to you." I wasn't thrilled to hand it over, but if it got us out of here alive, I was in. "You let the four of us walk out of here and you'll have my blood-oath that I'll sign it over to you."

"Sorry. We need Clarita," Liise Straightrod replied, stepping forward, standing even with Felicia.

"David? Is that possible?" Felicia asked.

"I'm sure I could figure it out. But don't we need the kid?" Phibbly asked.

"We've made it this far, we need to finish this," Liise Straightrod rounded on Felicia. "The girl isn't optional."

"Think about it, dear." Felicia stroked the side of Straightrod's angular face lovingly. "We'd have the property. We could spend our days learning to unlock it."

Straightrod batted Felicia's hand away. "You dumb bitch. You just can't seem to get it through your thick head. It's all about the girl - a witch from the Baltazoss line of wizards. Without her, this is just a house."

Felicia's face changed from concern to agony and she slumped forward. Straightrod stepped aside, allowing her to fall as she withdrew a long, thin knife, still wet with the witch's blood.

"There will be no compromise!" Straightrod flung the knife at Maggie, its flight obviously magically guided. If I could have anticipated the move, I might have been able to stop it. But the knife flew true and buried itself into my sister's side. She went limp and fell on top of Shaggy. "Kill them, but spare the girl."

I desperately wanted to run to Maggie, but the attack had begun in earnest. A great wind pushed through the trees, picking up debris as it swirled toward us. I had to turn away from my sister, shielding Clarita with my back.

"*Scutum!*" I brought up the shield. The onslaught was so powerful that the ring's energy drained at an alarming rate. Instinctively, I reached for the well of power I knew resided deep beneath my feet and was grateful when it responded to my call. With the additional power, I broadened the shield. I watched in amazement as the witch's spell also gained power. Small trees were ripped from the ground and hurled against the shield, which deflected them up and around us.

"Move over to Maggie," Gabriella yelled, the noise of the maelstrom so great I could barely hear her. We were close enough that I moved enough to stretch the protective bubble out to include my sister. Gabriella knelt down and pulled the heavy panther off Shaggy's corpse, inspecting her wound. "It's bad, Felix. She won't make it without help."

"I can't." I yelled back. "I'm barely holding on." The Left Hand's onslaught was intensifying. There was no doubt in my mind that if I let go, we'd be sandblasted into oblivion. Morbidly, I wondered how Straightrod thought Clarita would survive.

A small hand slipped into my own.

"No, Clarita," I said. "It's too dangerous." I would soon fail, but I'd use the last of my energy to shield her. I wasn't sure what would happen when I was completely expended and I couldn't risk being connected when that occurred. Straightrod knew I would never allow the child to die and was counting on simply burning me down. With twenty witches, even the power of the reservoir would not be enough. I couldn't channel the energy quickly enough to stand against their ever-strengthening storm.

"I'm losing it," I yelled to Gabriella. "Stay behind me."

Gabriella released Maggie and stood up, wrapping an arm around my waist and standing next to me. "My final act on this earth will not be to betray those who I love," she said, her lips inches from my ear.

I took a deep breath and stood firm, drawing energy even faster from the well beneath. It burned through me like lightning through the wires of a house struck in a storm. I knew I was in danger but I didn't care, too much relied on me.

We stood like this for what seemed like hours, but in reality, it was probably fifteen minutes. The witches had reached their peak and I was slowly, but surely losing ground.

"Felix. Look," Gabriella pointed to the trees not far from our position. Camille and the entire Katty clan had simply appeared next to the trees, looking for a way to get to us.

"They need a distraction," I said. "I can't let go of the shield." I was afraid that once down, I'd never get it back up.

A brilliant light, like a flare, lit up in the middle of the Left Hand and for a moment the storm lessened. When I turned back, Camille and the six Katty women had appeared next to my protective shield. I quickly opened it, allowing them to shelter within.

"Help Maggie!" I said. "That's my sister."

"You are holding them all?" Camille asked as the three older Kattys focused on Maggie.

"Not for long. I'm failing."

She grasped my hand and I felt the familiar request for joining.

"No! I can't," I said vehemently.

Camille considered me for a moment. "Then, what?"

Again, Clarita's small hand grabbed my own and I attempted to push her away. My strength was failing and she was so strong, I could no longer resist her. Temporary relief washed over me as we joined. I knew I'd end up burning her out just as badly as I had been, but for the moment, I appreciated the respite.

It was then that something quite unexpected occurred. Camille, having joined with Gabriella and the Katty sisters, both old and young, joined with Clarita.

"Nooo," I cried out. "You can't!"

"*Calm, child.*" Camille spoke to me. "*You're safe.*" It took me a moment to realize she was speaking to me in my mind.

"*You're in danger. Please let go,*" I replied, panicking.

"*You are not the first to feel this way. Trust us,*" Willow said. "*I know what you fear, but Clarita is protecting us. Can you not feel it?*"

I had no idea what I was feeling, aside from massive relief from the transfer of energy. "*The shield.*" I panicked again.

"*It's a lovely shield,*" Mari said. "*So strong.*"

"*Manly, really,*" Willow added.

I heard Cypress and Dande snigger.

"*Geez, patronize much?*" Solstice asked.

"*It's a good lesson, girls,*" Belle answered. "*Men often need reassurance.*"

"*Are you kidding? I'm right here,*" I said.

"*Indeed you are,*" Camille said. "*As are we, Felix. Are you so distracted as not to see you've not hurt us?*"

"*What do we do?*" I asked.

"*This is such a lovely spot. I would very much like to stay here for a while,*" Camille said.

"*Are you nuts? The Left Hand is attacking us.*"

"*So they are and yet, we are safe. It is an old lesson, Felix. Good will always triumph over evil. Today will be no different. How long do you think they can keep up such an attack? As with all storms, we simply need to wait and they will blow themselves out. They will lose much of their strength at dawn,*" Camille answered.

"*What of Maggie?*"

"*She slumbers,*" Willow answered. "*The knife hurt her badly, but she will not die.*"

With the support of the witches, maintaining the shield became an easy exercise. My mind wandered, wondering what Camille might have done if joining with me hadn't worked.

It wasn't long before the sun's light trickled through the leaves and dawn arrived. As predicted, the storm began losing its power and as it did, witches fell to their knees or stumbled away from the circle.

"I believe we are safe now. Thank you, Felix."

Camille dropped Clarita's hand and I released the spell.

"This isn't over," Liise shouted. It was an odd thing to say, since the storm abated completely as she said it. I knew what she meant, but her timing sucked.

"Rhamno." I flung a blackberry root from my pocket and cast my rooting spell at her, managing to catch Phibbly at the same moment. I walked toward them, Clarita and Gabriella at my side.

"Do you think we can't simply replay this attack any time we want?" Straightrod asked as I approached. "Your silly spell won't last and there's always tomorrow."

"Your coven has abandoned you," I said as the last of the red-robed witches disappeared around the corner of the house. "And you've killed your own sisters. For what? Greed? Power? You've lost your soul, Straightrod," I looked down at Felicia's dead body.

I laid my hands on the roots that entangled the evil pair and encouraged them to grow. I pushed the roots deeper into the earth and twisted them into two spires around the struggling witches. When I'd finished, they were completely encased, with only their faces visible.

"Hey, mister. Did your dogs run away?" I turned to see Amak carrying a large red wolf over her shoulder. Rose, Amak's shapely cousin, followed close behind, holding a gray wolf in much the same manner. They were both dressed in tight, stretchy pants and loose tunics. Each carried a long club in addition to the wolves, which they dropped unceremoniously in front of Straightrod and Phibbly.

"Amak!" I hugged her and then Rose.

"Looks like we missed all the fun," she said, looking out at the denuded area behind the house that had been torn up by the witches' powerful spell. The greenhouse's foundation was the only backyard feature remaining, other than dirt. Even the grass had been torn up.

"I'm going to check on Maggie," Gabriella said and walked back to where the Katty sisters were working on my sister.

"Maggie, as in the bird?" Amak asked.

"Long story." I pulled out my phone, dialing Lieutenant Dukats.

"What's going on, Slade? I've been fiedling calls about a freak storm in your neighborhood. A whole bunch of dirt and crap got dumped on the golf course. Owner thinks it's vandals," she said.

"Are those Feds still in town? You know, the ones who were looking for Shag... err Flaeger and Bothleman." I asked.

"I think so. Why? You have a line on the fugitives?"

"It's a long story. Call your Feds and tell 'em that and then let me know what you want me to do." I said.

"Tell me what you know and I'll pass it along." Dukats said.

"You make that call and then I'll tell you whatever you want."

She sighed, but hung up. Less than a minute later, my phone rang. I didn't recognize the number, but answered anyway. "Slade."

"This is Special Agent Dana Anderson with the Federal Bureau of Investigation. I just received a call from Lieutenant Dukats. She said you have information on the whereabouts of Brand Flaeger and Jerry Bothelman."

"I do. And, there's one more," I said.

"Tell me where they are and don't approach. They're extremely dangerous."

"How much do you know about these guys?" I asked. "Something's off with them. It's hard to explain over the phone."

"Don't say anything on the phone. What's your address?" she asked.

"I hope you have a van or something. We've made a mess of things over here," I recited my address.

There was a long pause on the phone. "I see."

EPILOGUE

At just after eight o'clock that morning a black van trundled into the back yard and two trench-coated people stepped out.

"Mulper and Anderson." The tall, thin man introduced himself. "Where's Flaeger?"

I pointed to the only remaining patch of grass in the backyard.

"I'll get a bag," the smaller female agent, who'd introduced herself to me on the phone as Anderson, replied.

"Make sure to get it all," Mulper instructed.

"I know," she said.

I'd tied up the red and gray lycan after they'd changed back to human form and had been guarding them ever since. Mulper slipped what appeared to be silver-lined leather collars around their necks and cuffed them both.

"What happened here?" he asked, pointing to the root cocoons which held Straightrod and Phibbly.

"Are you sure you want to know? It's pretty far out."

"Start from the beginning," he said. "Reader's Digest version is fine."

I recounted the story, starting with the previous night's memorial, leaving out as many of the details as I could without making the story sound ludicrous.

"You're a Baltazoss, then." It sounded more like a statement than a question.

"That's the rumor," I said.

"As far as we're concerned, you're in the clear. But don't be sharing any of this with outsiders. I'd hate to have to come back," he said as we pulled Phibbly and Straightrod from their prisons. "As for these two, I need to have a chat with them. Maybe you could help Dana bring that body bag back."

I left him with the two witches who immediately started

pleading their cases, blaming each other as they did. By the time we'd dragged Shaggy's remains back, they'd quieted and were staring at the ground.

"Special Agent Anderson will stay behind and negotiate with the locals. I'd like you to accompany her, so we can avoid any misunderstandings," Mulper said as he climbed into the van. He'd cuffed the witches, but hadn't loaded them with Shaggy's remains and the two lycan prisoners.

"You know, one of the werewolves got away."

Mulper had rolled the window down and the smell of wet dog was pouring from his window as he considered what I'd said.

"Isn't that always the case?" He quipped as he pulled away.

"Let me do the talking with Dukats," Anderson said as she pushed Phibbly and Straightrod toward the front of the house.

I wasn't overly surprised to be greeted by two police cruisers and a coroner's van as we crossed the brick courtyard in front of the house. Dukats was already out of the car and waiting impatiently for us.

"You want to tell me what happened?" she asked, looking to Anderson.

"There's a DB in the back. Felicia Therpsa. These two confessed to me already and I believe they're ready to give you a statement," Anderson said. "And I'm going to need a ride back to your station."

"Where are Flaeger and Bothelman?" Dukats asked. "And what happened to this house?" She was looking at the giant round hole in the living room wall, halfway between the front hall and the two-story picture windows.

"Flaeger and Bothelman are in federal custody. As for the house, I've no idea."

Dukats looked like she wanted to strangle Anderson, but didn't push it. She walked over to the cuffed Straightrod and Phibbly. They talked for several minutes and then she loaded them into her cruiser.

"Get what you needed?" Anderson asked.

"I don't buy any of this crap. You feds are covering something up. I've seen it before. Someone got to Straightrod and Phibbly. They just confessed to three murders and the kidnapping of Clarita Barrios," Dukats said angrily.

"Sounds like you have what you need," Anderson said. "I'd think you'd be happy to have them in custody."

Dukats harrumphed and walked away. "This isn't over for me."

"It never is," Anderson said.

***

When I made it back into the house, I found Clarita curled up on the floor with Maggie, the big cat's heavy, black paw lying protectively over the little girl. I'd read once that surviving stressful situations together formed deep and lasting bonds. Although it could have just been that Maggie in panther form, was both warm and soft.

Willow stood as I walked in. She'd stayed behind to watch over Maggie, but was ready to leave.

"How's your patient?" I asked, looking at my sister. From my perspective, she looked okay.

"She's tender, but appears to be in good shape. I'd rest easier if she'd transform, but she's being stubborn," Willow said.

"Where's Gabriella?"

Willow pointed to the bed I'd set up in the family room while I'd been working on the house. Last I'd seen Gabriella; she'd been stretched out on the couch.

"Why would she move?" I asked. "She was asleep."

Willow turned to leave. "You're a good man, Felix Slade, but you're none too bright where women are concerned."

I looked at her retreating form and wondered what I'd missed, replaying the conversation in my head. Realization dawned and I slid into bed next to Gabriella, pulling off my shirt. Still a bit uncertain, I hedged my bets by turning my back to her and staying on my side of the mattress. I was so tired. Lying down felt amazing and I started to drift off to sleep.

"Get over here." I heard her soft voice whisper in my ear and felt her hand slide over my ribs. I rolled toward her and ran my hand down her face, pushing her hair over her ear.

"Are you sure?" I asked.

"Shhhh," she said and pressed her lips into my own. "Now go to sleep." She rolled over and pulled my arm around her, snuggling in. I kissed the back of her neck and closed my eyes. We'd made it through and I could finally let my guard down.

It was dark and cold in the house when I awoke. I patted the bed, but Gabriella was gone. My heart sank, but I understood. She was coming off a relationship and I didn't want to be a rebound failure. Maggie's breath was shallow as she slept and I was just able to make out Clarita's tiny form, still asleep next to her.

I climbed out from under the covers and made my way into the kitchen to start coffee. Gabriella wasn't in the kitchen either. A quick check of my phone told me it was three in the morning. We'd slept for over twelve hours and I was starving. I opened the fridge and discovered what I already knew. We were without food. That wouldn't fly once people started to wake up, so I shot a text to Gabriella and let her know I was headed to the grocery.

About an hour later, I returned with loads of food. When I entered the kitchen, I found Gabriella sitting in a chair, wearing one of my dress shirts and a towel on her head, drinking coffee.

"Hey you," I said, unsure of my standing with her.

"Hey, yourself." She stood and took the bags from me, placing them on the counter.

I wasn't good with awkward so I bumbled on. "About last night... I...."

She approached and placed her index finger on my lips. "You're a good man, Felix Slade."

I'd been dumped enough times to know what was coming next and nodded in acceptance. Like Amak, I'd rather have Gabriella as a friend than an ex-lover. Although, in this case we'd skipped the latter.

"But you give up too easily," she continued and turned away from me. The shirt she'd borrowed was one of my least favorite. It was tight and filmy and, on her, it took on new life. She had nothing else beneath it and I forced my eyes off her perfectly formed and well-outlined posterior.

The distraction made me slow on the uptake. "Wait... what? This isn't a brush off?"

She pulled the towel from her hair, laid it on the counter, bent forward and quickly flipped her hair back and forth into some order. I was mesmerized watching her perform the simple task.

"No."

She stepped over to me and placed her hands on the sides of my face. I became aware of the fact that I had neither shaved nor showered this morning. She pulled me down and I slipped my hands around her, holding her to me as we kissed. She pushed me back into a kitchen chair and climbed onto my lap, straddling me. My excitement grew, but knew we couldn't risk starting something with Clarita so close.

"We can't do this here," I said, running my hands beneath her shirt, tracing the outlines of her body and enjoying her curves.

"I want to," she said, pushing her hands into the waistband of my pants. If she made it even an inch further, I wouldn't be able to stop.

"Clarita," I whispered.

Gabriella pulled her hand back and laid her cheek against my own. "Shit." I'd never heard her cuss before and found it adorable. That said, I think I would have found anything she did adorable. "You owe me a real date, then."

"A show, dinner and everything?" I asked, refusing to take my hands from her bottom, very much enjoying the intimate contact.

"I'd settle for dinner and everything," she said.

I heard a cat's chuffing and looked over to see Maggie standing in the entry to the kitchen, shaking her large cat's head slowly back and forth. Gabriella gracefully stepped off me. I grabbed her hand before she could run away, pulling her back for one more kiss. I felt a sense of elation when she acquiesced. The kiss caused Maggie to cough, which sounded more like she was throwing up than anything.

"You didn't have to come in, you know," I scolded. Maggie

padded across the room, rubbed her face across Gabriella's exposed thigh and slid in between us. I'd read that house cats did the same to scent mark their pride. "Any chance you're getting hungry? I have more groceries in the truck and I got some roasts." I affectionately smoothed her silky black fur.

Maggie let out a mild roar in approval.

"Go," Gabriella said. "Never good to ignore a hungry woman."

"How are you feeling?" I asked as Maggie followed me to the truck. In response, she gracefully jumped to the top of the cab and started cleaning her front paw. I opened one of the bags where I'd stashed a large roast. "Inside or out?" I asked, holding it up to her. She lay down on the cab and I took that as my cue. Pulling the meat from its packaging, I set it in the truck's bed and watched as Maggie jumped down, sniffed it and then worked on it in earnest.

I returned to the kitchen with the remainder of the packages to find that Gabriella had already started mixing eggs. "What's on deck for today?" she asked. I found I had difficulty taking my eyes from her.

"Insurance, bank and Andy. Probably not in that order. If it rains, we'll ruin a lot of the structure. I could cover the new hole with plastic, but who knows what those witches did to the roof," I said.

"I haven't looked. Is the front of the house that bad?"

"Bad enough," I said. "I'm guessing at least a hundred thousand dollars in damage."

"I'll work with the bank, if you like. I'm sure this will fit the 'emergency' provision of the trust," she said. "The only issue is whether insurance will cover it."

"Do you think insurance companies have a rider for castles under siege?"

"It will be interesting to see what they make of the damage, but it's not flood damage." She opened cupboards and drawers, not finding what she was looking for. "Do you really not have any cutting boards or a decent knife?"

I'd finished putting the groceries away and slid around her, running my hand along her waist. I was having some difficulty ignoring our previous contact. She smelled wonderful and I pecked her on the cheek as I took an old-fashioned cutting board out from under the counter. "That work?" I pulled my knife from my belt and opened it up. "And, this is what I generally use."

She sighed. "If you weren't so darn cute, you'd be annoying. And, we're going shopping someday soon. Nobody could cook in this kitchen the way it's set up." She chopped carrots and onions into the eggs.

"Once I have access to the full trust, you can redesign it for me." I watched as she continued cooking and dreamed of the life we might have together.

"Ready for eggs?" She finally pulled scrambled eggs laced with veggies from the pan and loaded two plates, setting them on the rustic kitchen table.

"No bacon?" I asked.

"Sorry, I care too much about you to make that," she said.

I shook my head. Some sacrifices would need to be made.

"What will happen to the witches who joined the Order of the Left Hand now that Liise and Felicia are out of the picture?"

"Most of them came from Illuminaire, Camille's coven. It's a tricky situation, they should be excommunicated. I'm glad that's Camille's problem."

"What about Whyte Wood coven? Won't you have a seat at the Witches' Council table?"

"I suppose… I'd have to start recruiting."

"How many do you need?"

"If Kelli stays, I'd need two more at a minimum, but really we'd need more like four more to make it work. I do know of several emerging witches in our territory that Victoria wouldn't talk to," she said.

"What was that about?"

"Most of them were from rough families or were runaways. All tough, with poor attitudes and very colorful mouths. Victoria wouldn't have anything to do with them," she said.

"I was one of those kids," I said. "I wouldn't have made it without Judy."

"It would be worthwhile for several reasons to help those types. Untrained witches cause a lot of damage to the people around them and without an outlet, they often die young. There's this one girl, Misty, but kids call her Miss-fit... a real hard case. Something about her..."

But that's another story entirely.

ABOUT THE AUTHOR

Jamie McFarlane is happily married, the father of three and lives in Lincoln, Nebraska. He spends his days engaged in a hi-tech career and his nights and weekends writing works of fiction. He's also the author of:

Privateer Tales
1.Rookie Privateer
2.Fool Me Once
3.Parley
4.Big Pete
5.Smuggler's Dilemma
6.Cutpurse
7.Out of the Tank
8.Buccaneers
9.A Matter of Honor
10.Give No Quarter (Spring 2016)

Guardians of Gaeland
1.Lesser Prince

Word-of-mouth is crucial for any author to succeed. If you enjoyed this book, please consider leaving a review at Amazon, even if it's only a line or two. It would make all the difference and would be very much appreciated.

If you want to get an automatic email when Jamie's next book is available, sign up on his website. Your email address will never be shared and you can unsubscribe at any time.

CONTACT JAMIE

Blog and Website: fickledragon.com
Facebook: facebook.com/jamiemcfarlaneauthor
Twitter: twitter.com/mcfarlaneauthor